THE
SOUTHERN
CRIMINAL

PETER O'MAHONEY

For Ash. Rest in peace.

The Southern Criminal: An Epic Legal Thriller
Joe Hennessy Legal Thrillers Book 2

Peter O'Mahoney

ALSO BY PETER O'MAHONEY

In the Joe Hennessy Legal Thriller series:

THE SOUTHERN LAWYER

*****

In the Tex Hunter Legal Thriller series:

POWER AND JUSTICE
FAITH AND JUSTICE
CORRUPT JUSTICE
DEADLY JUSTICE
SAVING JUSTICE
NATURAL JUSTICE
FREEDOM AND JUSTICE
LOSING JUSTICE

THE SOUTHERN CRIMINAL

JOE HENNESSY LEGAL THRILLER BOOK 2

PETER O'MAHONEY

CHAPTER 1

"I OWE him a favor, Wendy," Joe Hennessy said into the speakerphone of his cell as he drove under the alleyway of live oak trees draped in Spanish moss. "And I've never gone back on my word."

"Joe, you know how corrupt this family is. The McGoverns have ruined hundreds of lives for the sake of money. That's all they care about—money, money, money." Wendy's familiar loud exhale on the other end of the line expressed her frustration more than any words could. "And you said you would avoid any more dangerous cases, remember? You said that you were going to steer clear of any drama. You've only been back as a criminal defense lawyer for six months, and you've already had enough danger to fill a lifetime. Working for the McGoverns is asking for more trouble, and I'm worried about you."

Hennessy eased his foot off the accelerator, taking in the sights as he drove along Bohicket Road, returning from an early morning walk along the beach. Many trees in the South Carolina Lowcountry were draped in Spanish moss, and the sight of the beautiful layers of the gray-bearded plant evoked memories of his childhood—running free under the summer heat, chasing his cousins, spending countless hours perfecting his baseball pitch. The Spanish moss was always there, a stunning backdrop to his childhood memories.

"Is that what this is about?" He lowered his tone. "You don't think I can handle myself?"

"You're getting older. Slower. You're mid-fifties now. You should be mature enough to know that you can't run around pretending you're twenty-five."

"You know, with age comes wisdom, and I've discovered that the secret to success is sincerity." Hennessy smiled. "Once you can fake that, you've got it made."

"This isn't the time for jokes, and this isn't something you need to take on," she groaned. "There are plenty of other opportunities for a man with your talents. You're a very intelligent man, and you're a talented lawyer, and people are lining up for you to take on their cases."

Compliments, he thought. It was Wendy's way of guiding him gently toward what she believed was the right course of action.

He looked to the road again, beyond the tarmac laid out before him. There was no traffic. His attention focused more on what lay beyond, flanking the road in the way memories popped up while trying to think of something else entirely.

As he remembered his own childhood, his thoughts inevitably turned to the memories of his son. Luca, beautiful Luca, forever ten and forever young. This was the way he and Wendy had driven a very excited Luca during a weekend devoted entirely to the kid's eighth birthday. They went to the beach, then stopped for boiled peanuts before arriving at a family fun-center just off the Maybank Highway, the perfect place to hold an exhilarated eight-year-old's birthday party. The roller skating had been a huge draw for the birthday boy and his friends, although it wasn't the main draw. No, that had been the laser tag and the bumper cars, all the things young boys loved.

"Joe? You still with me?"

He smiled, doing his best to push the memory aside once more and focus on the here and now before his wife really did give up on reaching him.

"Sorry. Was running your words through my mind." It was a small lie. "What I do know is that if I do this, there's a good paycheck at the end of it."

"Now you're motivated by money? Really?"

"That's the only reason I'm back in Charleston. That's the only reason I'm working as a lawyer again. I can't let the banks take the vineyard." He paused, then swallowed. "The bank called again yesterday. They need us to increase the payments. They said interest rates are about to go up."

"Did you speak to Tom?"

"I did."

"And even Tom said we need to raise the loan repayments?"

"He did."

Wendy was silent for a few moments before she asked, "Can we afford to do that?"

"We're going to have to. I'm not letting the bank take Luca's Vineyard. It's our vineyard, and they can't have it. I know we've had some poor seasons, but we can get back on track this year." He gripped the steering wheel tighter. "And listen, if it helps ease your nerves, I won't be the lead counsel on this case. I'll be the second chair, so I'll avoid most of the danger. John Kirkland has that honor."

"But do you trust any of them?" Her voice

lowered again and he understood why. The point she was trying to make, the one she wanted to bring up more than anything, was the rumors and whispers about the corruption surrounding the McGovern family.

Elliot McGovern, a thirty-five-year-old corporate lawyer, was part of a dynasty within their part of the world. The McGovern and Brady Law Offices were an institution in the city of Charleston and the outlying areas, the first choice for the region's wealthier businesses in corporate and tax law. Deals were done on golf courses and in whiskey bars with judges, politicians, businessmen, and anyone with money.

Charging top dollar, the law firm performed well under rumors of corruption, bribes, connections with illegal entities, as well as the manipulation of cases. When Elliot McGovern was arrested for the murder of his wife two days earlier, it had run as the headline story in every news source in the state. Katherine McGovern was found murdered on their kitchen floor, a single bag of cocaine next to her. The police investigated the case for five days before they put the handcuffs on the husband.

"The rumors, Joe. The whispers. You know as well as I do, they haven't changed in all this time. People have been saying the same things about McGovern and his family for more than fifty years."

She was right. Of course, she was. In South Carolina, everyone was connected somehow, in some way, by a small degree of separation. Everyone knew each other's business. Everyone knew each other's problems. And everyone heard the rumors.

Not wanting to push the issue further, she

changed course. "How about Zach Miller? Think he'll deliver the right song in court?"

"Did you just make a joke about my client, Mrs. Hennessey?"

"Let's face it. A folk singer charged with drug trafficking is bound to get a few one-liners thrown at him. I even heard that the late-night show hosts were laughing at his expense."

"Well, it depends on how much of his ex-manager's testimony holds up."

Zach Miller, a folk singer with one major hit under his belt, had been charged with drug trafficking, something he swore had been a set-up courtesy of his disgruntled former manager.

"Ok then. I can tell your thoughts are elsewhere. I'll leave you alone to think," Wendy said, then finished with, "I'll see you soon. Love you."

"Love you, too."

She hung up, leaving him in silence.

As he drove on, his mind drifted away from the cases before him, with Luca's face dominating his thoughts. Driving past the landmarks had stirred up old memories that still affected him. Despite the twenty years that had passed since the tragedy of his murder, at that moment, it felt as if none of the grief had subsided.

Hennessy didn't see the blue BMW until the last second.

It swerved onto his side of the road. He slammed on the brakes, pulling his steering wheel to the right. He skidded off the road, hitting the dirt on the shoulder.

On instinct, Hennessy whipped the door open, jumping out to prepare for a confrontation. As he stood beside the open door, he watched as the last traces of the BMW disappeared around the bend, leaving him with nothing but a racing heart to contend with. Standing alone on the side of the road, he knew it wasn't an accident. He knew it wasn't a mistake. The driver had seen him.

With the cases he had on the books, he knew danger was coming his way.

And Joe Hennessy expected nothing less.

CHAPTER 2

FOR JOE Hennessy, South Carolina was the most beautiful place in the world. It was a seductive mistress, a place so captivating that it made his eyes ache with pleasure. The Palmetto State was mesmerizing, from the dramatic edge of the Atlantic Ocean to the Lowcountry marshes, to the rivers, to the lakes, to the devastatingly beautiful mountains upstate.

And the city of Charleston was the state's masterpiece.

The streets of Charleston were saturated with history, its people charming and welcoming, and the smells of the pluff mud and summer storms seeped into a person's soul. The city was a part of Joe Hennessy, the playground of his youth, the streets where he met the love of his life, the place where he etched out a career in law. His heart lived for the city. Deep inside, he could feel the rhythmic beat of the tides against the High Battery seawall. He knew the timing of the church bells. He could sense a summer storm long before it arrived. He loved the colors of the azaleas when they bloomed, he loved the smells of the jasmine and wisteria, and he loved the shade from the palmetto trees. This was his city. His home.

But like any great city, like any place with hundreds of years of history, Charleston had a criminal underbelly, and Joe Hennessy often found himself in the middle of it.

He parked his 1996 red Ford pickup truck in the lot next to the Kirkland Law Firm, located toward the eastern end of the historic Broad St., downtown Charleston. The law firm was in the heart of the action. It was walking distance to the most expensive lunch spots, and a stone's throw from some of the most exclusive bars, perfect for one of the wealthiest criminal law firms in the state. Hennessy parked his truck between a Maserati and a large Mercedes SUV, careful not to get too close to them as he pulled in.

With briefcase in hand, he entered the foyer of the Kirkland Law Firm, taking a moment to look over his surroundings. The excess of wealth was obvious—large abstract paintings on the walls, new armchairs in the waiting room, and a small gold-plated statue of Lady Justice by the reception desk. A beautiful young woman stood from behind the desk and welcomed him. They were expecting him. She led him through the spacious foyer and up the stairs to the second-level boardroom.

The boardroom was large and open, a long wooden table in the center surrounded by leather chairs. The windows facing the street let in the natural light, and all the other office essentials were there—a potted plant in the corner, a tall bookshelf to the left, and a notable painting of Charleston hanging on the right. The smell was musty, mostly thanks to the old, ducted air-conditioning that ran through the historic building.

"Ah, Joe. Welcome." John Kirkland stood up from the head of the long wooden boardroom table and walked down to greet him. Hennessy towered over the man as they shook hands.

John Kirkland was a compact man in his sixties. He dressed well in a fitted suit, he smelled of Old Spice, and the remaining hair he had left was dyed jet black. He'd been a leader his whole life, a man who came from old money, and his confident demeanor spoke louder than his words.

"Thanks for coming. Glad you could accept the job." Elliot McGovern stood at the far side of the room, blowing the steam off his mug of coffee. Tall and thin, McGovern was dressed in black trousers and a white button-up. His sleeves were rolled up, showing off his Cartier watch, and his sunglasses were hooked in the middle of his shirt. "I know you're here because I helped save the vineyard from an IRS error five years ago. You said you owed me a favor after that, so I've called it in."

When Hennessy offered to help McGovern, he expected the favor to be repaid in bottles of wine, not a legal defense. But still, he was a man of his word.

Once each man had taken their seat, Kirkland called out for his assistant. The same woman returned, took their coffee orders, and disappeared back out the door.

Right from the start, Hennessy couldn't help but notice just how at peace Elliot McGovern appeared. Considering the man had a murder charge hanging over his head, for killing his wife no less, he looked remarkably laid back. Almost content.

"How's Wendy and your daughters?" Kirkland began.

Kirkland had obviously been well briefed. Hennessy hadn't seen or interacted with Kirkland for more than a decade, and yet, he said his wife's name like they'd only talked last week.

"She's well," Hennessy replied, and not wanting to be drawn into prolonged small talk about his life, he shifted the focus away from himself. "And how's your family?"

"They're good. Kids have all grown up now. My girl met a boy and is working for a law firm in Columbia, and she even went to a Gamecocks game. I call her a traitor every time I see her now." Kirkland smiled broadly. "But that's life. You teach your kids how to support the Tigers, and yet, as soon as a boy comes along, she switches her alliance."

"That's worse than changing your religion," McGovern grunted. "But enough small talk. I've got a murder charge that needs to be thrown out before the trial."

Not that he had to be proven innocent, Hennessy noted.

McGovern had made bail, thanks to his family's connections to the area. Kirkland had convinced the court that McGovern was no risk to the public, and that the prosecution's case was circumstantial, at best. The judge was lenient, allowing McGovern to await his trial without any restrictions on his movements in South Carolina, as long as he was monitored by a GPS tracker, at the cost of $150 a week from his own pocket. His privilege and wealth were already showing in the justice system—a poorer defendant had no hope of putting up that money and would be sent to jail while they awaited trial.

"I'm sure you know why we called you and asked you to come onboard, Joe," McGovern stated as he leaned against the far wall.

"For my skills."

"Of course," McGovern sipped his coffee. "But also to manage the media and appeal to the public. You're their darling at the moment. You're tall, handsome, and a distinguished southern gentleman. If I'm going to protect the reputation of my corporate law firm, then I need someone with the type of southern charm that wins over the public in our press conferences."

"Your father's law firm," Kirkland stated and eyed McGovern. "McGovern and Brady. Your father built that into the biggest and best corporate law firm in the state."

"And the old man is almost gone. He's almost retired. I'm a partner there now. It's my law firm, and I have to protect its reputation."

"Don't let Elliot's bluntness put you off. Corporate lawyers are all like that." Kirkland smiled and turned back to Hennessy. "I need your skills. It's not just about your looks and how we present this case to the media. You're here because you're a talented lawyer who can help get this case thrown out. This is a complex case, and if it makes it to trial, we'll need all the help we can get."

"I've read the file." Hennessy reached down, opened his briefcase, and placed the files on the table. He looked at McGovern, studying his reaction. "You claim that last week you were out to dinner, and when you came home to your place on Seabrook Island, you found your wife shot to death with a bag of cocaine by her side."

"An unfortunate event." McGovern looked away from Hennessy's stare. "That's all it was."

"But the police claim you shot and killed your wife. She was found with a bag of cocaine next to her, but the police believe this was an amateurish attempt to make it look like a drug deal gone wrong."

"What can I say? I didn't do it. I didn't shoot her. I was in the restaurant the whole time. There was video surveillance in the parking lot of the restaurant, and I'm on the video arriving at 7:30pm, and I'm on the video leaving at just after 10pm. And according to the coroner, her time of death was 9pm. I have an alibi. I don't even understand why I was arrested."

"He called the cops at 10.15pm," Kirkland explained further. "And the paramedics arrived in fifteen minutes. They put the time of death at least one hour earlier, due to temperature testing of the body and that rigor mortis had begun. The coroner later confirmed that the time of death was likely around 8.55pm."

Hennessy looked at a page in front of him. "However, a witness came forward last night who states that you weren't in the restaurant for that entire time. They claim there was a gap of forty-five minutes when no one could place you there. That doesn't look good."

"This is the first I've heard of that." McGovern paused and looked at Kirkland. "Who is it?"

"Roger Steinberg."

McGovern grunted and started pacing the floor. "Roger Steinberg. Really? The guy hates me. I took on a contract case against him once and destroyed him. Absolutely destroyed him. Probably ruined his career. He's never forgiven me for that. He'd say anything to destroy me."

"He stated he was also at the restaurant and was going to go to the bathroom but saw that you stood up first. In order to avoid you, he was waiting for you to return." Hennessy read the notes. "And you didn't return for forty-five minutes."

McGovern shrugged. "I had stomach problems."

"For forty-five minutes?"

"I didn't realize my toilet habits were on trial."

"The prosecution claims that you left the restaurant during that time." Kirkland leaned forward on the table. "They're saying that you snuck out of the restaurant and went home, shot your wife, and then planted the drugs to look like a deal gone wrong before returning to the restaurant forty-five minutes later."

McGovern stopped by the window, shaking his head. He looked out at the people passing on the street below, a tourist group stopping to take photos of a nearby building. "This is ridiculous."

"Was Katherine known to take drugs?"

"She'd been to rehab once for cocaine addiction in the past. She'd do a few lines of coke before any big social event. I don't know where she got it from, or who she got it from, but it has to be the guy who shot her. This is a drug deal gone wrong. Why can't they see that?"

"Your fingerprints are on the bag of cocaine," Kirkland said. "And your DNA is all over the place."

"Of course, they're on the bag of cocaine. I picked it up. I didn't know what it was. And my DNA? It's my house. Of course, my DNA is all over the house. This is ludicrous."

"If you want sympathy from the public," Kirkland stopped and thought for a moment before he continued, "we could say you were addicted to drugs, but not cocaine. We could say pain killers. Nobody has sympathy for rich cocaine addicts, but opioids, well, the message there is the drug is bad, and the public should feel sorry for you."

"Ok, I can make some arrangements to set up that story," McGovern said. "What else do they have?"

"They'll have more," Hennessy said. "This is just enough to get you indicted with the Grand Jury. There'll be more evidence coming, but the prosecution will want to hold off on presenting it. I suspect it's got to be some sort of surveillance footage."

"I agree," Kirkland added. "There's more coming. They've got something else that will clinch it because they wouldn't take it to trial on this alone."

There was a knock on the door, and the assistant entered the room. The men paused their conversation while she placed three new mugs of coffee on the table, nodded to Kirkland, and then left the room, closing the door behind her. The men sat in silence for another moment before Hennessy continued.

"Motive?" he questioned.

"We were going through a divorce." McGovern came back to the table and sat down. He stared at the brown table for a few long moments before continuing. "We'd hit a brick wall in the divorce proceedings. Katherine had come from the poor side of town, but she'd grown used to the lavish lifestyle, courtesy of my money. If they had continued, the divorce proceedings would have meant a lengthy court case, and she was seeking a significant chunk of my wealth in her settlement."

"I know it's been a while since you studied any criminal law, Elliot," Kirkland continued. "So let me describe the situation for you. The South Carolina Code of Laws does not define degrees of murder, such as 'First Degree Murder,' or 'Second Degree Murder.' Rather, all murder charges in South Carolina are defined as the killing of a person with malice aforethought, either express or implied. Under South Carolina law, 'malice' is a willful or intentional doing of a wrongful act, without just cause or excuse. And 'aforethought' refers to the time when the evil intent is conceived. If you intentionally kill another person with the premeditated evil intent to do so, you will be charged with murder."

"But can they prove premeditation? I might not have practiced criminal law, but I know that murder has to be premeditated."

"A common misconception is that premeditation needs to be days or weeks in the planning. Under the laws of South Carolina, premeditation can happen in an instant." Kirkland snapped his fingers before he reached across the table and pulled a file from the middle. He opened it and read over the first line. "At this point, our best option here is to push for Manslaughter, under Section 16-3-50 of the South Carolina Code of Laws."

"Sentence?"

"The lowest they can go is two years," Hennessy stated. "And the maximum is thirty."

"We can get you two years," Kirkland added. "I know a few people, and they love the almighty dollar. If all goes well, we can get you into a nice wing of a nice prison where you'll never be threatened or bothered by the local inmate population."

Hennessy shook his head. There was no equality when it came to prison—the poorest inmates, those without the resources to support themselves, were the worst hit, thrown into the lion's den and told to survive. Those with money, which was sometimes illegally gained, could buy their way into comfort behind bars. When Kirkland continued talking, he pushed those thoughts aside.

For the next hour, the three men talked about legal strategies, from third-party culpability to how to push for the charges to be downgraded to manslaughter. McGovern paced the floor the entire time, barely saying another word, just grunting when he was required to answer. After they'd covered the groundwork, Hennessy wished the men well, and then shook both men's hands solidly, before the assistant returned to walk him out to the exit.

After he exited the building, sitting back in his slightly rusted pickup truck, he loosened his tie and unbuttoned his collar. He threw his head back, looked up at the ceiling, and took a moment to calm himself.

With the evidence he'd already seen, with what he knew about the McGoverns and the Circuit Solicitor's Office, there would be months of trouble ahead.

CHAPTER 3

ELLIOT MCGOVERN walked out to the deck of his Seabrook Island mansion.

Part of a gated community, his property was a five-minute walk to the beach, two minutes to the golf course, and fifteen minutes to the club. Behind the private gates of Seabrook Island, there were two championship golf courses, an equestrian center, a fitness complex, long unspoiled private beaches, along with the island's private club that had a bar and restaurant. McGovern's two-story, multi-million-dollar home was situated with ocean and golf course views, complete with a swimming pool and a spa. The infinity edge pool looked out over the golf course with far-reaching views of several golf holes and the nearby lagoon, while the interior of the mansion was overwhelmingly white and cream-colored. The sea breeze, blowing in from the Atlantic, was blowing strong, causing a ripple through his pool.

His maid, a workhorse named Dorothy Sparks, had been on the family's payroll for nearly fifteen years and knew the ins and outs of the role. She had been crying a lot since Katherine's death. McGovern had little time to comfort her. He gave her two days off after the murder, and then demanded she come back to work to clean his home.

Shortly after finishing the last of the clean-up, she

went out the front door and left him alone. McGovern listened for the familiar sound of her Corolla starting up, before the sound of the engine faded out into the nothingness of the day.

Sinking into a sun lounge next to the swimming pool, he crossed his arms across his chest and let the heat from the afternoon sun soak in. Yes, he had a murder charge hanging over his head, but he also had the finest legal team he could muster up. John Kirkland was a master in the courtroom, and Joe Hennessy's name was synonymous with positive results since his return to the law.

Hennessy was also the current public darling. McGovern knew that if he wanted to continue his career after beating the murder charges, he needed someone as likable as Hennessy to convince the residents of South Carolina of his innocence.

McGovern reached for his Old Fashioned cocktail, but his cellphone, sitting on the table beside him, beeped with one of its obnoxious notifications. He took a sip of his drink and then reached for the phone.

The pit in his stomach twisted a little as his father's name stared back at him from the screen, the four words flat and demanding, just the way the senior McGovern liked to conduct himself.

'*I need to talk.*'

It meant one thing and one thing only—he wanted to lecture him on the case.

McGovern considered his father an antique, a man caught up in the past in both character and belief. He almost considered ignoring the message, simply locking the cellphone and setting it back down on the table, but he also knew the consequences of such actions. If he didn't answer within a reasonable amount of time, his father would decide for him and simply come over himself, turn up on the doorstep, and force his hand.

McGovern took another sip of his Old Fashioned, holding it in his mouth for a long time while staring up into the emptiness of the sky. His father was old, stuck in his ways, but he still held the controlling share of their law firm, which meant he had no choice but to continue following the old man's demands.

Feeling the anger rise within him, McGovern swallowed the rest of his drink, gripped the glass tightly, and launched it over the swimming pool. It fell short, hitting the edge of the pool instead and dropping into the clear water with an audible pop.

"Just my luck," he muttered, kicking the sun lounge as he went to get changed.

Five minutes later, he fired up the Maserati and pulled out of the driveway. If he was going to see his father, then he would make sure he drove a vehicle that he knew irritated the man. As a confirmed Scrooge, nothing irritated the senior McGovern up more than wasting money, and sports cars had always been viewed as one of the biggest ways to do that. The younger McGovern grinned widely as he navigated the streets, already anticipating the familiar look of disdain when he rolled into the driveway.

By the time he turned into his father's home, the cockiness was gone, replaced by a sullen look of contempt. He didn't want to be there, looking at the interruption to his day as an insult. This had been his day, his moment to kick back and forget about the drama which had consumed his existence.

His father lived on a sprawling estate on the

nearby Kiawah Island, along with his much younger Japanese mistress. The estate was on a two-acre oceanfront lot, complete with a saline pool, a separate pool house, and a manicured back lawn with a bridged walkway to the beach. The house, a six-bedroom two-story mansion, was impressive, but for Elliot, it held nothing but terrible memories of his lonely childhood.

A small man of Scottish descent, Harold McGovern's jaw seemed to be constantly clamped. He had little hair left, and his beady eyes glared at everything. As he stood at the entrance to his home, dressed in slacks and a polo shirt, his fists were clenched.

"How nice of you to join me," Harold McGovern's tone was flat as he stood by the door watching his son exit the sports car.

"Did I have a choice?" Elliot's voice sounded exasperated.

"Everyone has a choice. It's the consequences that people have an issue with."

"Thanks for the life advice." Elliot rolled his eyes like a spoiled teenager.

Harold led his son through the foyer of the mansion and into his private office, where he proceeded to sit behind his large oak desk and indicated to his son that he should sit in front of it, like it was nothing more than a business meeting. The room smelled of whiskey, but most things around his father smelled the same way.

As Elliot dropped into the leather armchair, he felt a lecture coming on, and not one he had any desire to sit through. Once his father got going, it was hard to shut him down. The man had an opinion about everything and seemed to get fired up the most when it meant talking down to his son. All Elliot could do was sit in the dimly lit room and take it.

"Tell me how the murder charge is going."

"It's fine," Elliot said, knowing his father wasn't looking for an answer. What he wanted was to start off slow, to open the floor with a question before he really got going. "I had a meeting with the legal team yesterday—" was as far as he got before the senior of the two took over, cutting his son off mid-sentence.

"You need to plan what you're going to do if you go down. You need to have an escape plan. Costa Rica, the Bahamas, Brazil, wherever. You need to start thinking about how you will disappear out of the country. I can help you fake your death. I have connections to make sure nobody ever comes looking for you." He leaned forward, resting his elbows on the desk. "Guilty men sometimes fall. Not all of us can beat the wrap a hundred percent of the time."

"Guilty?" The question felt almost invasive as Elliot dropped it into the conversation, the word itself not one he was prepared to pick up. "You think I'm guilty?"

"You're telling me you're not?"

The two men stared at each other across the desk. The first man to speak lost. It was something McGovern senior had taught his son from an early age, and the junior wasn't surprised to see his father's refusal to yield.

"That's exactly what I'm telling you," Elliot said, feeling as if he'd folded with a full house. "Why? You don't believe me?"

He expected his father to give in, to say the words a son should've been entitled to. But Harold

McGovern would never give in so easily.

"No, I don't believe you. I think you killed her. I think she wanted to take you for as much as possible through the divorce, and you couldn't live with the idea of her beating you. You've always been a terrible man, you've always been evil, and you've always been weak. I think you killed her because she couldn't have your children, but we all know it's your fault that you couldn't have a child. You're not much of a man."

Elliot felt his cheeks warm up, the heat burning into him like the anger building from within. He wanted to lash out, to scream his innocence directly into his father's face. Harold gazed at his son, seeing the color rise, and smiled, only further infuriating Elliot. Elliot's fingers squeezed into the chair's armrests.

"And I know it wasn't your first time," Harold continued.

"What are you talking about?" he squinted.

"Deny it."

When Elliot didn't respond, Harold continued. "I don't know how stupid a person has to be not to understand what this kind of incident does to a family's name, but you are destroying everything I've worked decades to achieve."

"The family name? That's what concerns you?"

"The family name! My business!" Harold slammed his fist into the desk, droplets of saliva jetting from his lips across the desk. "That's what concerns me!"

"How about your son? Does that matter to you? Does what happens to me matter to the family?"

"You think this is about you? We don't have the—"

"And how about your secrets?" Elliot snapped

back, pointing a finger at his father. Harold's lips slammed shut as Elliot interrupted him, his teeth clicking together with an audible snap. "Imagine if word got out about your secrets, huh?" The pair stared off in silence for the second time before Elliot found the strength to continue. "What goes around comes around, Father."

Elliot stood, feeling his father's eyes burning through him. He didn't bother waiting for a response, walking toward the door before he stopped and turned back.

"If you tell the world my secrets," he said, "then I'll tell them yours."

CHAPTER 4

A TROPICAL storm had arrived.

The October rain belted down on the street as the darkness descended over the city. There was a wind swirling, swaying the trees, dancing in the morning as the dark clouds moved over Charleston. A strong, heavy sheet of rain blew through with the wind, drowning out Hennessy's thoughts as he walked.

Hennessy loved the intensity of the October rain. He loved the refreshing smell of the approaching storm—the feeling of electricity in the air, that distinctive smell of a late-season storm, the anticipation brought on by menacing clouds as they blew over the wide southern skies. He stopped for a moment at the entrance to his building, under the shelter of an awning, and watched as the rain pounded down.

He smiled, then shook his umbrella off and climbed the stairs up to the second level of his office building, feeling the possibilities of the week ahead in the air.

Located on Church St. in Downtown Charleston, his office was on the second floor of a plain red brick building. His floor had been empty for years before he rented it for cheap from an old associate.

"G'day, Boss," Barry Lockett said as Hennessy reached the top of the stairs and pushed through the door into the office. The big Australian investigator sat on one of the waiting area couches, a takeaway Starbucks cup held in one hand, a cellphone in the other.

Jacinta Templeton sat behind her desk, her own coffee sitting beside the keyboard, which she was already rattling awake. She looked up as Hennessy entered, shot him a smile, and said, "He wanted to get to you early."

Her sweet smile brightened his morning. With a five-year-old at home and a husband who worked in finance, Hennessy couldn't fathom how his cheery assistant beat him to the office each day, and the fact that she always managed to do it with a smile was even more surprising.

"Good morning, Mr. Lockett. Good morning, Jacinta," Hennessy said, greeting them together, and then nodded over his shoulder back to the entrance. "It's blowin' up a storm out there."

"Too right." Lockett stood and shook hands with Hennessy. "I hear the meteorologists have predicted a few more on the way for the rest of October as well. Something about the warmth of the Atlantic. Should be an interesting end to the storm season."

Hennessy led Lockett into his office. He dropped his briefcase beside the desk and went to the window, opening the blinds. The rain pelted hard against the window, blowing through in sheets of wind. There'd be flooding this time, all over the city. On the roads that lead to the Battery, on the highways, and on the low-lying streets. There was no escaping the flooding in Charleston when the rains arrived.

As Hennessy watched the rain dance down the window, he remembered the shop owner in

Charleston telling him that morning, "It's not the storm that scares me; it's being without the air-conditioner!" Hennessy smiled, before he turned back to his desk.

Lockett had already claimed one of the seats facing it, with Jacinta coming in carrying her writing pad for any necessary notes. Lockett's muscular frame filled out most of the chair. He'd maintained his strength as he entered his mid-forties, his thick arms covered in tattoos, slightly visible from under his short-sleeve button-up.

"Elliot McGovern's case," Lockett said as he rocked slightly on the chair. "That's a colossal task."

"I take it from your tone that you know a lot about the McGoverns."

"Charleston's a small city, only 150,000 people. Everybody knows everybody's business here. And if you're an investigator like me, then it's my job to know everybody's business. I know the McGoverns. I know their law firm, and I know their family. And let's just say, I wouldn't invite them over for a cookout."

"Corruption or just nasty people?"

"When it comes to the McGovern family, the rumors, which have been circulating for decades, have far too much in common with the truth to be ignored. The family connections alone are enough to raise eyebrows. Add to that the history of the family, and the amount of power they hold in this city?" He shuffled in his seat a little. "Well, I'm surprised they charged the man at all."

"The current Ninth Circuit Solicitor is known to have a problem with the behavior of the rich and powerful in South Carolina. She was elected on the premise that she would clean up the corruption in the corporate world, and Elliot McGovern is the perfect place to start."

"And you want to be part of that case?"

"I'm not the first chair, so I'm not taking most of the heat. Plus, this is about the money. A lot of it," Hennessy said. "And Harold McGovern isn't in the best of health, and from what I know, he's the one holding the majority of the power in that family. Elliot is small fry compared to his father."

"I wouldn't say he's exactly small fry."

"You're right, maybe a bad choice of words. But there are plenty of other powerhouses in the area who sense an opportunity here. With McGovern Senior knocking on death's door, a lot of these heavy hitters smell victory and want to push their own narratives." Hennessy noticed Jacinta looking at her watch for the second time since she sat down. "I'm there as the second chair, which means we're responsible for ensuring that everything runs smoothly during any pre-trial motions, depositions, or any possible trial. We'll need to keep track of everything that needs to happen behind the scenes, including exhibits, witnesses, briefs, jury instructions, and notes, with an eye toward a record for appeal. But I think I'm mostly there to be the face of the case, and make a good impression to the public. Kirkland is a brilliant lawyer, but the media, along with the public, don't like him. They think he's too arrogant. And since the last case, the media has given me positive press. That's what McGovern needs to protect the reputation of his corporate law firm."

"Sounds like fun."

"It will be when they pay me. It's a good contract,

but they have a history of avoiding paying other people. Both Kirkland and McGovern are known to avoid contract payouts." Hennessy drew a long breath. "What have you got for me?"

"Alright, so since you called me yesterday, I did some preliminary digging. Surface level stuff." Lockett reached into his satchel, removed a file, and placed it on the table. "And it doesn't look good."

Hennessy sighed. "How bad?"

"Elliot McGovern threatened to kill his wife in open court." Lockett sat forward as if to highlight the point. "It's on the record. Happened during a divorce hearing. Exactly one week before she wound up dead. He threatened to kill her, to put a bullet in her skull, and save himself the hassle of paying her out. She went to the police to file a report, and her statement was recorded, but no further action was taken. After talking to the police, she decided not to take it further, not to take out a restraining order, but a week later, she's dead."

Hennessy rubbed the sides of his head, the thumb working deep into his temple. Despite the AC doing its job, he could sense the humidity of the day picking up, a headache slowly letting him know it was on its way. The fall heat did that to him.

Knowing how water had a way of keeping the headaches at bay for him, Jacinta went to the small fridge she kept stocked in his office and grabbed him a bottle. He thanked her, popped the cap, and drank deeply. As he lowered his eyes again and set the bottle down, he saw Jacinta look at her watch a third time.

"Everything ok?"

She looked across at him, a hint of guilt on her face. "Sorry, yes. It's just that you have Zach Miller due any minute. I penciled him in for 9am, but he called to say he might arrive a bit early. I'm sorry to be a spoilsport. I know Elliot McGovern is a friend and all, but maybe your focus should be on Miller."

As if sensing her tone might have been a little too over the top, she threw in a quiet apology.

"I hear you," Hennessy said to her. "But just so we're clear—McGovern isn't a friend. He's a client, and that's how I'd like to keep it. I owed him a favor from years ago, but that's it."

"Noted," Jacinta said, offered him a smile, and rose to her feet.

Lockett took the cue and also got out of the chair. "There's more in the file. Have a look over it, and we'll catch up soon."

Hennessy nodded, putting one file away and replacing it with another.

There was always more than one case, always more than one place to shift his focus.

And based on the evidence he had, he didn't think he could win either of them.

CHAPTER 5

THE SECOND Zach Miller stepped into his office, Hennessy felt his nervous energy.

He was a slight man, early thirties, with thin blonde hair hanging down to his jawline. He'd worn a blue suit for the meeting, although he moved uncomfortably in it. He pulled at the collar, trying to loosen it, and his shoulders looked restricted. Hennessy had watched some of his music videos online—on stage in a leather jacket, Miller was confident, charming, and had a smooth voice that women swooned over. Off stage, he seemed slightly uncomfortable, awkward, and apprehensive.

"Mr. Miller," Hennessy began, getting to his feet and holding a hand out. "Thank you for coming in."

Miller didn't respond as he shook Hennessy's hand, just nodding his greeting.

Jacinta followed the singer in, pulled out the chair for him, then sat down while Hennessy opened a file on his desk.

As he sat down, Zach Miller looked around the office suspiciously.

Born and bred in South Carolina, Miller had made it big with a hit folk song, topping several charts worldwide. His face was recognizable, as was his smooth voice. After his success on a national tour, he returned to the stage for a five-concert tour back in his hometown of Charleston, his way of giving back after making it big.

A month after the case had started, the pressure was starting to get to him. After making bail with Hennessy's assistance, Miller had spent weeks avoiding the press, repeating the line 'No comment,' over and over again whenever someone approached him.

"I hope this is over with quickly," Miller sighed. "Lawyers aren't cheap, especially not good ones like you."

"What you have to remember is that, right now, you have a police officer who wants to convict you, a solicitor who's paid to do it, and a judge who's demanding to know what you're going to do. And cheap lawyers generate income through volume. Your case would get lost in a whirlwind of activity. All they want is numbers."

"I spoke to a cheap lawyer, and he stunk of alcohol. Not the type of guy I wanted to represent me in court." Miller drew a breath, filling his chest, before releasing it loudly. "And I read about you online. I read that you're a vineyard owner who returned to law after a twenty-year absence."

"That's right. After a personal tragedy, I retired from the prosecutor's office, and bought a vineyard Upstate. Unfortunately, the last few seasons on the vineyard have been plagued by drought, and then large storms, and we fell behind on the bank loans. It's no secret that I'm back here, working as a defense lawyer, to earn enough money to keep it." Hennessy turned a page on the file. "But Mr. Miller, we should—"

"Zach, please." He turned to Jacinta and

whispered, "Mr. Miller sounds like my father."

"Ok, Zach. We're now a month into the case. What we have is a classic case of drug possession which has been classified as trafficking due to the amount of cocaine that was found."

"I've been thinking about that. It's absurd." His expression changed to one of disgust, throwing his hands up in the air. "I don't even do drugs anymore. I told you—after I went to rehab last year, I haven't touched the stuff. I'm as clean as a whistle." His tone turned serious; his voice quiet as he again looked at Jacinta. "I had a friend die from an overdose two years ago. It hit me hard. Hit all of us hard." He looked up at Hennessy again. "Stuff like that has a way of staying with a person for life. I couldn't touch the stuff now."

"I understand, but the police found a black backpack in your dressing room with a lot of cocaine. They found the backpack stuffed under a chair, and you were the only one with a key to the room."

"The DA has that wrong. They have it wrong."

"We don't have a District Attorney at the state level," Hennessy said. "We have a Circuit Solicitor, which is comparable to that of a District Attorney in other jurisdictions. The position of Solicitor was created by the South Carolina General Assembly in 1791, and the Solicitor is elected for a four-year term. I suggest that when you talk to the media, or the court, that you get the term correct. We don't want to sound ignorant, and we don't want to make the wrong people angry."

"Right. No DA."

"The Circuit Solicitor has charged you under Section 44-53-375, which is the possession, manufacture, and trafficking of methamphetamine and cocaine base. Cocaine trafficking is considered a violent offense in South Carolina, even if no actual violence took place when you were charged. Mandatory minimum sentencing also comes into play, with no suspension or probation, and if convicted, you're looking at a long stint in prison. With the amount that you were caught with, more than 28 grams, it's a felony, and has a mandatory minimum sentence of 7 years, all the way up to 25 years and a $50,000.00 fine."

"Seven years? I can't do that. I wouldn't survive seven days."

"There are different levels of drug charges in South Carolina, with trafficking being the highest. Beneath this is Possession with the Intent to Distribute, or PWID, and the lowest level of charges is possession." Hennessy moved a file across his desk. "In South Carolina, all the higher drug charges include the lesser charges. If they can't prove that you intended to sell the drugs, the jury is still given the option to find you guilty of the lesser charges. If they want to pursue the trafficking charges, there are three things that they have to prove here—one, that you acted knowingly or intentionally with the drugs, two, that the drugs were in fact cocaine, and three, you were actually in possession of the controlled substance."

"That's the thing, Mr. Hennessy. I wasn't in possession of the drugs. What they found was a backpack which I hadn't seen before. I wasn't even holding the bag when they came in."

"This is what's known as constructive possession. While the law covers physical possession, it also covers the term 'constructive possession.' The State must prove you had the power to control the disposition or use of the drugs, and they must prove you had knowledge of the drugs and the intent to control or use them. And they need to do this beyond a reasonable doubt, which, based on the evidence they have at the moment, looks like a fifty/fifty call. If this case had come up a year ago, then I doubt it would've made it this far. But right now, the Circuit Solicitor has made it her mission to make it clear that money won't get a person out of prison. She has an eye for the rich and famous."

Miller stood and paced the room. "So it all comes down to timing?"

Hennessy gave him a few moments to work through his feelings.

"If we can get it down to possession, then we're looking at a misdemeanor. If we can do that, you might not have to do any time at all," Hennessy noted. "A recent amendment to Section 24-13-40 of the Code of Laws means that time served with a GPS monitor can qualify for time served in prison. It means if you're sentenced to five months in prison, we can include the time you were wearing the ankle monitor."

"Really? That doesn't sound right," Miller said.

"I don't make the laws." Hennessy raised his hands in the air. "What I do is find the right path for my client through the mess. The decision will be up to the sitting judge, but we'll be able to argue for time served, as you haven't been allowed to leave South Carolina, which restricts your ability to tour."

"But I didn't have any tours planned."

"Doesn't matter. We can argue that you were

restricted from promoting yourself further. Time served would mean that by the time this gets to trial, you'll walk out a free man."

"You're a clever man, Mr. Hennessy," Miller smiled and waved his finger in the air. "I knew you'd be a great lawyer. So, how do we do that?"

"With a long fight in court. With the media attention on the case, the prosecution isn't going to go easy on this one, so we'll be making numerous trips to court to fight it out. If they don't offer a better deal, then we'll have to go to trial in around five weeks, and it's there that we can try to convince a jury that the drugs weren't yours."

"I'm ready to fight all the way." Miller nodded his head adamantly. "Hand on my heart, I swear it wasn't me. They weren't my drugs."

"Then do you have any idea who would have placed it in your dressing room? Perhaps there was a member of the crew that was a user?"

The question had barely left Hennessy's lips before Miller reacted, his head nodding furiously, his face scrunching up as he brought forth the name.

"I certainly do." He locked eyes with Hennessy, forcing the name through his teeth. "And I've had a month to think about it now, and I know exactly who it was. It was Preston Wheeler."

Hennessy took another look at the paperwork sitting before him, finding the name amongst the statement he had been reading.

"Your former manager." He tilted his head a little as he continued reading before looking up. "But as far as this statement says, Preston Wheeler was never at the event."

Miller screwed his face up again, the frustration

written across it like a neon sign. "No, he wasn't." He pointed a finger at Hennessy. "But I'm telling you, this was him. One hundred percent, this was him. He set me up to get back at me."

"How can you be so sure?"

"Because he told me he would do it."

"Preston Wheeler told you he was going to set you up with drugs?"

"Not exactly, but close." He closed his eyes and rubbed them vigorously. When he looked up at Hennessy again, his eyes were red. "Look, I know how this looks. Successful folk singer, needs a few hits before getting up on stage, knows a lot of people in the industry, and has an opportunity to make some extra money by selling some gear. But this isn't me. Preston and I had a falling out a month ago. He knew my contract was coming up for renewal and when I told him I intended to split, he got fired up."

"Fired up how?"

"Fired up in the way a manager would get angry when one of their biggest earners threatens to jump ship. There's no way he would let me go without a fight," Miller said, his voice lowering as he recalled the interaction. "He was so angry. At first, he told me I'd never make it without him in my corner. Told me I'd be washed up before year's end. When I still refused to renew the contract, he took things to the next level. He told me that it was he who had opened up the doors for me. He said I would still be an unknown singer in Backwater, USA if it weren't for him. He thought he owned me, like some sort of possession. Like my talents were for him to use."

"But that still doesn't explain how the drugs got into your dressing room."

Miller took a moment, rubbed his eyes again, and sighed. He looked down at his feet for a few seconds before refocusing his attention on Hennessy. "Have you ever heard of a man named James Balter?"

While he didn't immediately recognize it, Hennessy felt something nudge him in the back of his head. Miller saw the reaction and nodded.

"Yeah, you have. James Balter. Known in our circles as a man with some questionable connections. He's the kind of guy people turn to when they want to, you know, buy something on tour in Charleston. He has the phone number of a contact, and every singer that tours through here calls him. Lots of other singers on tour use him. They say what sort of drugs they need, and he gets it for them."

"James Balter," Hennessy said. "And you think he's the one who planted the drugs?"

"I'm positive. It all makes sense. Preston Wheeler buys a backpack for whatever reason, and then, after things turn frosty between us, hands it to James Balter, who turns it into a pharmacy."

"Ever used his services?"

"No, but I know a lot of people who have. That's how I recognized him at the concert. And then, when the cops busted me for the stash, I just knew he had something to do with it. Why else would he have been there, right? He doesn't seem like the type of guy that would go to a folk concert."

"Maybe he was there for a good time?"

"Thanks for the compliment, but something tells me otherwise." He shook his head again. "He was there to do me in, and Preston is sitting pretty in his office laughing while I get arrested and have to face court."

Hennessy looked down at the notes, glanced back at the statement, and returned to Miller. "The next step in the process is that we'll head to court next week to file a number of pre-trial motions to have the evidence dismissed. They're not likely to win, but we're signaling our intention to the prosecution that they're in for a fight. That may force them to present a better deal. The idea of these motions is to apply the pressure to them."

For the next hour, they discussed the case. Jacinta took notes, jotting down the main points said between them. After the hour was up, Miller left the office feeling confident he could beat the charges.

The problem was, Hennessy didn't share that confidence.

With what he'd seen in the evidence, Zach Miller was looking at a long stretch in prison.

CHAPTER 6

HENNESSY DRAFTED another motion for the Miller case on a piece of paper, scribbling in handwriting so messy it could pass for a code. Before he had a chance to forget, he called out to Jacinta. "Can you please check to see if I have anything planned for tomorrow lunch?"

It took his assistant a few moments to gather herself, but rather than call back, she walked into his office, leaning against the door. "Actually, no you don't, but I was about to pencil in a sweet old lady who just called and asked for a meeting with you. I told her tomorrow at one would be fine. Need me to reschedule her?"

"Who's the lady?"

"Helen McGovern."

"Helen McGovern, as in Elliot McGovern's mother?"

Jacinta nodded.

"Can you call her back and see if she's available this afternoon?"

"Sure. Give me a sec."

Jacinta left the room and returned five minutes later, carrying a small post-it note and a smile of accomplishment. After sticking the note in the middle of his desk, she said, "Booked her in for five, and she jumped at the chance for the earlier appointment. She wants to meet at her place."

"You're a star, Jacinta," Hennessy said, looking down at the note to see the woman lived on nearby Ladson St. He looked out the window, checked the weather, and then turned back to Jacinta. "It's only fifteen minutes away, and the rain has stopped. I'll walk."

At just after 4:45pm, after a day of reviewing file after file, editing motion after motion, he was out the door, stepping out into the jungle-like humidity that seemed to drench everything in a layer of wetness. He could smell another storm. It was somewhere in the distance. He loosened his collar, took off his coat, and began the fifteen-minute walk to his appointment.

Storm season in Charleston was a setting that drew a person into its intimacy. It was the seductive sights of massive clouds, the fervent smells, the thick humid air that wrapped its arms around a visitor, encouraging them to fall into the gentility of the Southern way of life. Once tasted, it was hard to forget the sensual, semi-tropical pull of the Peninsula.

As he wandered slowly through the streets of the lower end of Downtown Charleston, he looked over the historical townhouses with gallery porches turned to the side. He loved those buildings. So much history. So much charm. They were like works of art, standing proud and strong through hundreds of years of history. Over the brick fences, Hennessy glanced in, eyeing elegant gardens and admiring the intricate designs of the exteriors.

He turned onto Ladson St., full of stately townhouses and walled gardens. Ladson Street was a beautiful part of a beautiful city. By the time he walked up to the front of the modest home, it was

5:05pm, and he hated nothing more than to be late for appointments.

"Mrs. McGovern, I'm so sorry for the late arrival," he began as she welcomed him with an open door. It was a small, skinny, and quaint two-story with a well-managed front yard and the unmistakable display of a resident green thumb.

"That's quite all right, Mr. Hennessy," she smiled. "It's been years since I've needed to live by the clock. The only thing I need to be around for is *Jeopardy!* at 7:30pm."

Despite being eighty-plus years old, Hennessy couldn't get past how much younger she looked, and she moved with the grace of a woman still enjoying her fifties. She was fit, and wore a floral dress, and judging by the look of her garden, he wasn't surprised by how incredibly well maintained it looked.

"You have a lovely home," he said. "And it's a lovely garden. They say you really appreciate gardens once you mature, and I have to agree. I own a vineyard Upstate, and when you watch the gardens, when you watch how they transform and change and grow, every year seems like a miracle. Gardens have an eternal optimism, a new growth after a dark winter, a kind of love and pleasure in every season."

"That's beautifully said, Mr. Hennessy. And I agree, this garden fills me with so much joy." She indicated to the sofa on the deck at the side of the front door. "Why don't you take a seat?"

Hennessy nodded and placed his coat over the edge of the sofa, waiting for her to sit before he did the same.

The front yard and the lawn were kept in a near manicured state. Not a single blade of grass looked out of place, with each garden bed perfectly displaying all manner of colors. Hanging baskets adorned the outside of the decking, swaying in the gentle breeze with more displays of bright greens, reds, and blues.

It also appeared as if she'd already prepared for their meeting, with a pitcher of homemade sweet tea sitting beside two glasses, each half-filled with fresh ice cubes. Hennessy noted that the ice hadn't had a chance to melt and wondered if she had dropped them into the glasses when she saw him walk up the street.

"Please, sit down," she offered, dropping down into a rocking chair next to the sofa. "I prefer sitting out here, if that's ok. I don't feel as lonely when sitting out on the porch and watching people pass on the street. Some of them are even nice enough to say hello and tell me about their days."

Rather than ask, she leaned forward and poured the sweet tea, then held out a glass to him. Not one to pass up an opportunity for a cold drink, Joe thanked her, and when he sipped the drink, he felt a tingle of satisfaction run down his spine as the tartness from the lemons hit him. The sweet tea was delicious—not too fragrant, not too sweet, and just the right punch of cool flavor. The ice clinked at the side of the glass as he held it up.

"This is perfect."

"Thank you. I always like to keep a jug of it on-hand for drop-ins." She pointed to the pitcher. "It was my grandmother's, and she never used it for anything other than sweet tea. It adds to the flavor, I'm sure."

"It's beautiful, and this garden is equally amazing.

It must take some work keeping it looking so beautiful."

Her smile told him it was a compliment she had hoped for, looking pleased that he noticed. If she had told him that it was her pride and joy, her one and only escape from an otherwise dull existence, it wouldn't have surprised him.

"Oh, it keeps me entertained at times," she said before taking another sip of her drink.

"May I ask you a personal question?" Just as he always did, Hennessy cut to the chase and dove right in.

"Yes, of course."

"You live out here, away from your family. I don't mean to pry. I've just always had an issue with curiosity."

"Curiosity may have killed the cat, Mr. Hennessy, but it also discovered penicillin." She smiled and then shook her head. "I could never divorce Harold." Hennessy noticed how she dropped her eyes when she mentioned her husband's name, a trait he was more than familiar with. "To be honest, if I had initiated such proceedings, I don't doubt for a second that he'd retaliate."

"You think he would have hurt you?"

"Hurt me? No. He would have done much worse. If we'd divorced, I'd be dead. In a heartbeat." She nodded at that, and he noticed her grip on the glass of sweet tea became tighter. She took another sip, set the glass down on the table, and looked up at him. "Divorce has never been an option for me. There's the family name to uphold, there's the church to consider, and then there's the money. Oh, Harold is very protective of his money. This way, he gets to save his fortune as long as he continues looking after me. And as you can see, I have everything I need to keep myself comfortable."

"Sorry to hear that."

"Don't be," she waved his concerns away. "But I guess you also want to know why I contacted your office." She drew a long breath before she continued. "It's about my son, Elliot. I need to tell someone what I know. I heard you were defending him, and I'd seen you on television before. And I can't talk to Mr. Kirkland. The man is as arrogant as Harold. But you," she looked at him and smiled, "you seem like a gentleman."

"I'm flattered." He smiled.

She smiled in return, and again Hennessy noticed her tense a little, as if fearing the man himself might hear her speak about him. She pursed her lips as her eyes drifted down, staring through the table and into the past.

"Elliot was not a nice boy. He was an only child, and he was terrible. Even growing up, I could see so much of Harold in him. The anger, the short fuse, the insecurities. The cunning nastiness. The narcissism." Looking up again, she tried to force another smile, but it didn't appear to catch hold. "I want to be honest with you, Mr. Hennessy. Honest in a way perhaps only a mother can be." Lowering her voice, she leaned forward. "There's a reason why I've always feared for the safety of his wife. Sometimes, bullied people have a tendency to try and pass on the pain they themselves experienced, and Elliot didn't have it easy growing up. He not only faced the constant wrath of Harold, but I think others caught on and followed suit. He faced bullying wherever he went, and as a mother, it saddens me to this day that I failed him."

She picked up the glass again, and as she sipped, Hennessy noticed her lip quiver just enough to tell him she was close to tears. This wasn't an easy subject for her, and he didn't interfere.

"What I'm trying to tell you is that Elliot isn't exactly a nice man. He's harsh and can turn on a person with his words, as well as his hands."

"Did you ever see him strike his wife?"

"Many times. It was as if it was his way of regaining control whenever she tried to get the upper hand." She paused, the silence hanging heavy between them before she looked up at him again. "There's no other way to say this, but part of me believes the charge against my son to be true. I think he killed her."

Hennessy nodded. "I have a job to do, Mrs. McGovern, and that job is to defend your son against the system that's trying to convict him. If there's enough evidence, he'll be found guilty. If not, then that's up to the police and the prosecution to follow through."

"I know," she whispered. "But I need you to know the type of man you're defending. If he's offered a deal, I'd like you to encourage him to take it. I know you can't force him, but I'd like you to strongly encourage him to take a deal."

"That'll be his decision to make."

She didn't respond, looking out to the garden as a tear rolled down her cheek.

They sat in silence for another five minutes, watching the world pass by, before Hennessy finished his sweet tea, thanked Mrs. McGovern for her time, and moved on.

As he walked away from her home, he wondered just how much she knew about the incident, and he wondered just how guilty Elliot McGovern was.

CHAPTER 7

HENNESSY SPENT the early morning walking the streets of Charleston before the city came to life.

Walking the streets brought back so many memories, from the seemingly unimportant to the unforgettable. He remembered throwing the football with his father under the flowing Spanish moss in the city's many parks. He remembered cooking with his mother, her kitchen always full of love, laughter, and passion. He remembered his roommates during the early years, the drinking beers on the porch, the partying late at night in bars. He remembered the early morning swims, sunrises over the Atlantic, the rare South Carolinian snowstorm, the cold darkness of the winter mornings, regattas, the flashes of lightning on the horizon, herons on the marshes, the smells of the pluff mud, his younger brother, camellias blooming, the long summer nights, and the love of his city.

He remembered Hurricane Hugo in '89, tearing the streets apart with such ferocity and torment. He remembered the storms that tore at the walls of his home, the flooding, the wind roaring through the broken windows louder than any concert he'd ever been to.

And he remembered meeting Wendy, the love of his life, falling for her harder than anything he'd ever known. She taught him how to love, how to open up and become vulnerable. He remembered the years when he would wake Wendy at 5am, drive out to the coast, and watch the colors dazzle the horizon. Nothing beat a sunrise over Folly Beach, the tinges of oranges, reds, and blues painting the vast southern sky.

Knowing he would see Wendy later in the day always had a way of adding an extra glint to the morning sunshine, and after the previous day of revelations he had endured, he looked forward to a nice change of pace.

He'd spent the previous evening alone in his apartment, a glass of bourbon and a pizza for company. He spoke with Wendy just after nine, wishing her a good night and promising to see her the next day. But the second he hung up, the thoughts of work descended over him.

McGovern's case seemed to have eclipsed everything else in his life, having taken center stage as he grappled with the idea of the man's guilt. Before meeting with his client's mother, the prospect of his guilt had been something only vaguely possible, but after hearing the man's own mother also raise the possibility of him killing his wife, the idea refused to let go. This wasn't just about representing a man he owed a favor to. This was about representing a man who might have murdered his wife in cold blood.

Most of the morning in the office whizzed by in a haze of documents and meetings. He was there physically, but mentally, he was somewhere else entirely. Was McGovern guilty? The thought played over and over in his mind. It was Jacinta who finally managed to bring him back to earth, reminding him of the time as he sat staring out through his office window.

"Don't you have a lunch date with Wendy?"

He checked his watch, saw it was five minutes from midday, and jumped up.

"Oh," he hissed, picked up his cellphone, and hurried for the door.

Out on the street, the heat of the day hit him square on, beads of sweat instantly populating his brow as he jumped into the pickup. Wendy's message to say she had arrived at the waterfront café came through as he fired up the engine and he sent his own ETA through to her, just five minutes away.

The Fleet Landing Restaurant not only offered waterfront views, but also the added benefit of watching ships come and go from the nearby pier. At the end of a hurricane-proof reinforced pier, the restaurant hovered over the marshes on the east side of the Charleston peninsula. Built in 1942 by the US Navy as a debarkation point for sailors, the building was now known for its stunning Southern seafood dishes, along with an unobstructed view of the Charleston harbor.

Wendy loved the big ships, and the outside table she normally sat at had become something of a regular meeting point in recent months. Wendy's family had a long history in the state. She had come from a great South Carolina family, with their history dating back to when her forefathers first arrived in 1795, with their descendants still scattered all over the Palmetto State. She was proud of her history, proud of her state, and never considered living anywhere else.

She was already sitting at the table by the time Joe

arrived, a couple of cold glasses of Lemon, Lime, and Bitters waiting for them. He leaned down and kissed her, then sat opposite her as someone nearby called for a waiter.

"Busy today," Hennessy said as he set his phone down beside the glass. The drink felt cold in his hand and even colder as he took a taste. The chill ran down into the pit of his stomach as he drank. "How was the drive down?"

"Certainly a great day for it," Wendy smiled, closing her eyes and letting the fresh breeze blow over her from the nearby river. "Not too much traffic."

"And Kerry?"

Kerry Jackson had not only been Wendy's maid of honor at their wedding, but had also been one of her closest friends since the pair met during the first year of elementary school. Kerry was the reason Wendy had made the trip to Charleston, her friend asking for help with a private matter. Hennessy knew better than to ask for specifics.

"Doing it tough. Roger's refusing to come to the party on Doug and Buster, and Kerry's not about to let them go without a fight."

This brought a grin to Hennessy's face, imagining his wife's best friend gloving up as she prepared to enter the ring against her husband for the sake of a couple of Pomeranians. The pair had been through a tough time since Roger's infidelities surfaced the previous Christmas, and their subsequent divorce proceedings weren't moving as fast as anyone had hoped.

The couple had tried for years to fall pregnant, but due to reasons no doctor could figure out, found themselves childless a decade after tying the knot. It was one of those situations where nobody could be blamed, and yet the reality of it had sent the relationship into uncharted territory. Wendy believed Roger's cheating was partly due to their inability to fall pregnant.

It wasn't long before the conversation turned closer to home, with Wendy bringing up a subject she didn't often voluntarily touch on, especially when so close to reality. "I don't know why, but for some reason, I felt so close to Luca driving to see Kerry this morning."

Hennessy thought back to his own drive out of the city the previous week and how he had completely zoned out on the interstate. "On the Maybank Highway?"

"You too?"

"Yeah, me too. Driving along that road reminded me of his eighth birthday. Remember the place we took him and his friends?"

"How can I forget? I got to run around with a wild gang of armed eight-year-olds wielding laser rifles." She grinned, and he watched the memory stir something deeper, beyond the happy recollections.

Since his death, Luca's memories always came flanked by something darker, his parents no longer able to enjoy memories, with a deep sense of loss accompanying them. It was as if there was a price to pay for the memories themselves, now each demanding payment in grief.

Hennessy reached out and held his wife's hand, feeling the warmth from her infiltrate his own. She looked up at him, met his gaze, and forced a smile, one they both understood.

"The vineyard is doing well," she finally said,

changing the subject. "Managed to snag another wedding on the way in this morning. You remember Matthew Connelly and Jane Owen?" Hennessy nodded. "Well, they've finally phoned through with their deposit."

"Does that mean August and September are now completely booked out?"

"Sure is," Wendy nodded, a grin of accomplishment adorning her face. It gave her an extra glow he appreciated. "It also means that with the money you bring in with these two cases, it might be enough to finally keep the bank off our backs for a few months."

Hennessy smiled, picked up his glass, and held it high, the words music to his ears. "Now that is cause for celebration," he said before taking another drink.

Just as he was about to raise her hand and kiss the back of it, she reached out and touched his face, gave his cheek a bit of a rub, and looked at him sideways.

"Have you been loading up on pizzas?"

The question caught him off guard, and he sat back in shock. "Did you just call me fat, lady?"

She grinned at that, her cheeks coloring with a tinge of red. "Well, if the shoe fits, mister. Maybe it's time to sign up to that gym you keep talking about."

He burst out laughing, a sound Wendy wished she could hear more of. It had been far too long since the last time and, if given a choice, would tell him jokes all day long if it meant hearing the sound.

They enjoyed the scenery during their lunch, with the atmosphere almost brimming with a distinct vacation feel.

Their lunch arrived, and they both smiled broadly—hers a she-crab soup with blue crab roe and sherry, and his stuffed hush puppies filled with shrimp and lobster. While eating the delicious food and sipping their drinks, they chatted about their weeks. Wendy chatted about the vineyard, the workers, and the rains that had passed through. Joe chatted about the winds, the humidity, and how the storm season was predicted to be a long one. They chatted about their daughters, one almost finished high school and the other studying law in New York, and about their varying personalities. They chatted about Charleston, how the flooding streets never seemed to be fixed. They chatted about the road to Columbia, and how the traffic was getting thicker every year. They chatted about everything and nothing, all at once, smiling in the fresh breeze.

But all the time they talked, all the time they laughed, smiled, and grinned, there was one day still hanging over them like a wet blanket. Luca's birthday was fast approaching, and for both of them, it was the worst day of the year.

Even after twenty years, that day never got easier.

CHAPTER 8

HENNESSY COULDN'T sleep.

It was another night of tossing and turning under the constant heat and humidity. The AC in his small apartment had broken, the ceiling fan wasn't much use, and there was little breeze coming through the windows.

He lay in bed staring at the cracks in the ceiling as the time ticked past 6am, and he thought back to what Wendy had told him during lunch the previous day. The moment had caused such a reaction in him, he tried to suppress a new urge to laugh. The message from her had been loud and clear, and knowing he wasn't getting any younger, he wondered whether he needed to take action. He rose out of bed, pulled on his sweatpants, jogging shoes and a t-shirt, and headed for the door.

By the time he reached the sidewalk, the first rays of light had begun to pierce the morning clouds. The day was beginning, the dawn casting a gentle orange glow on the city. After days of wind, there was a quiet stillness to the morning, as if the earth was holding its breath, waiting for the sun to touch the horizon.

The distinct smell of the pluff mud was strong that morning along Church St. It was a mixture of tangy, oystery, marshy goodness that hung on the humid air. Hennessy drew a breath, smiled, and continued walking, meeting other distinct smells, which seemed to awaken the senses. The aroma of coffee, the delicate fragrance of freshly cut flowers, the smell of fresh baking bread; each scent intermingled with the last to form a playground for the senses.

Hennessy headed up Meeting Street, crossed over Ann, then took a turn at Mary. When he reached King and made a right, the strong aroma of coffee from a nearby Starbucks remained with him until he passed by a diner, which smelled like it was in the middle of a bacon cooking marathon. A little further along, the smell of another bakery filled the air, enveloping him for almost an entire block before more coffee took over.

He was about to turn down Columbus when he heard someone calling his name.

"Mr. Hennessy. Sorry to interrupt your morning."

He turned, unsure of who she was, and she must have caught on almost immediately, as she held out a hand.

"Sorry, Mrs. Jennifer Brady. I work at McGovern and Brady."

"A Brady?" Hennessy smiled. "Pleased to meet you."

"Michael Brady is my grandfather. He started the firm before the McGoverns joined a few years later. My father is Gerald Brady, and I work there with my sister as well. Our side of the firm looks after the tax law, and it's quite the family affair." She looked down the street he was about to walk down and smiled. "Mind if I join you for a bit?"

"Not at all," he said. "Just don't expect me to break any records. I'm not much of an athlete any more, and walking pace is about where I get up to these days."

"That's alright. I've already finished my daily five miles. Was just heading home."

"You walk five miles every morning?"

Another grin, flanked by a hint of embarrassment. "I run five miles. Normally aim for a couple of marathons a year. One in the spring and another in the fall." And then, as if to break the ice a little, she asked, "Have you ever tried?"

"Running a marathon? That would be a decisive no."

"Well, you're never too old to try. I mean, you're very tall. I'm sure those long legs could swallow a mile very quickly." She looked up at his towering figure. "And there's a guy I know who ran his first at seventy-five."

He grinned as he pictured Wendy listening in on the conversation, finding amusement in the way this woman subconsciously mocked his age.

Wanting to deflect her attention away to another subject, Hennessy asked, "Was there something I could help you with, Mrs. Brady?"

"I needed to talk to you about Elliot." She tried to smile but failed. She lowered her voice, drawing Hennessy in a little closer so he could hear. "I could probably get into a lot of trouble for saying this, but there's something I need you to know. And if you ever repeat what I'm about to tell you, I'll deny I said it. Understand?"

"Understood," Hennessy nodded his agreement. "Go on."

"I think he's guilty."

The comment took Hennessy by surprise. He stopped walking. "You think Elliot McGovern murdered his wife?"

The woman stopped as well, before she turned back to him and nodded, her eyes darting up and down the street to ensure their conversation was still private. "I do."

"I'm hearing a lot of that," Hennessy sighed and began walking again. "But why would you say that? Has he told you anything?"

For a brief second, he wondered whether this woman had perhaps been somehow romantically involved with McGovern, or somehow just had a brief fling. But when he saw the look of disgust in her eyes, he knew the possibility of such a notion was practically zero.

"No, but I've heard him speaking to his wife on the phone. I walked in on him talking to her a couple of times as well."

"And what did you hear?"

"Enough to tell me their relationship was anything but amicable. If I had to guess, I'd say their marriage had been in trouble for a very long time. My first marriage was violent, and I know how that feels. I know what it looks like—hiding the bruises, missing social appointments because of the anxiety, the fear of your partner snapping at any second. And I could see that with their relationship. I always felt that Elliot would beat her. There were all the same signs in their relationship that I had with my first husband."

"Did you ever see Elliot lay a hand on his wife?"

"I never saw it, but a person doesn't need to see the physical act to know it's happening. Perhaps the generation before mine would've turned a blind eye to it, but this whole 'Me Too' movement has given us women a lot more confidence when it comes to reporting violence. I met Katherine a few times in passing at functions, and I always wanted to say something, but I never did. I feel horrible for this now. It breaks my heart that I let her down."

"You didn't let her down," Hennessy tried to comfort her. "But I'm confused about why you're telling me this? My job is to keep Elliot McGovern out of prison."

"I know. You've got a job to do, and you have to defend him." She shook her head, her blonde hair falling to the side. "But I thought you should know. I thought you should know about the type of man that you're dealing with. I wouldn't be the only person who feels this way, and you can be guaranteed that the prosecution is finding people to say exactly what I just said to you. I'm giving you a heads up before the trial starts, so that you know what you're facing."

"If the prosecution approached you, would you be willing to confirm what you just told me?"

"Not a chance." She didn't hesitate with her response. "To say something like that against a family like the McGoverns? It'd be suicide, or at the very least, career suicide, at least in these parts. I'd never work in South Carolina again." Just before she took off into the day, she leaned in a little closer again, looked past him, and whispered. "Maybe I'm not really sure why I wanted to tell you what I did, Mr. Hennessy, but I know this. The McGoverns aren't a family you want to be messing with. Watch your back."

Hennessy paused again, watching her closely. "And the Brady side of the law firm would wield a lot more power if another McGovern was to leave."

She avoided eye contact, brushing a strand of

loose hair over her ear. "I'm not going to lie—I'd be happy to get rid of the McGoverns. Harold is just about gone, and Elliot is the only thing stopping us from taking their name off the door."

She turned back to him, glared, and then walked away without another word.

The murder case had many moving parts, and with every day that passed, it seemed to become more complicated.

CHAPTER 9

"THIS IS where it all happens?" Zach Miller said, approaching his lawyer on the sidewalk in front of the Charleston County Judicial Center. "This is where I get to prove my innocence?"

"That's right," Hennessy responded, shaking his hand solidly. He wiped his brow with the back of his hand. The humidity was only getting thicker. "This is where all the action happens."

"What are we doing here today?" Miller had his jacket off, holding it in his left arm, and the top button of his collar was undone. "Is this where I tell the judge I'm innocent?"

"Not yet. Today is an evidentiary hearing on a motion to suppress."

"And what's that?"

"The suppression hearing is a short proceeding limited to the issues raised in the motion. We're lodging two pre-trial motions today. One is to suppress the evidence based on the lack of specific information in the tip-off, and the second motion is to have the drugs dismissed from evidence due to a gap in the chain of evidence. In general, the prosecution has the burden of showing that the evidence sought to be used was lawfully obtained."

"Are they likely to get approved?"

"It's a fifty-fifty call on both motions." Hennessy

turned and led Miller into the courthouse. "But what we're really doing is showing the prosecution that this won't be an easy fight. They should expect us to fight these charges on every front, and they should know that we're going to challenge everything. If they get an indication from the judge that we have a strong argument, then they'll present a better deal."

"No deals. I'm innocent, remember?" Miller said as they stepped inside the front doors and approached the security checkpoint.

"I hear you," Hennessy nodded to the guard as he stepped through the metal detector. "My job is to get the best outcome, and given what we know about the case, we have to leave our options open."

They entered the foyer of the courthouse. It was quiet and subdued inside, with a few people mingling around. The discussions between lawyers and clients were hushed, and the tones were low. There were several people standing around looking lost, waiting for their turn in the separate courtrooms.

Miller excused himself and turned for the bathrooms. As Miller stepped away, a well-dressed man approached Hennessy.

"Mr. Hennessy?" When Hennessy nodded his response, the man offered his hand. "Jamal Lincoln."

Hennessy shook the man's hand. Of African-American descent, Lincoln had a broad smile, and short cropped black hair. His frame was big enough to be a linebacker, standing tall and proud, and he smelled of a woody cologne.

"I'm leading the case against Mr. Miller," Lincoln stated in a hushed tone. "I hear that he's going to take this all the way, and I just wanted to let you know that the Circuit Solicitor's Office is ready to fight this one on all fronts. There's a lot of media attention for this one, and we're going to show the public that the rich and famous are accountable to the law as much as everyone else."

"And they're allowed to be innocent as much as everyone else as well."

"Not today," Lincoln smiled, nodded, and when he saw Miller returning, he stepped back. He greeted Miller briefly and then moved away. Hennessy kept his stare on Lincoln for a few moments before he turned back to Miller and explained the process in more detail. He then led them into the courtroom.

Once inside the almost empty courtroom, Hennessy paused for a moment, taking in his surroundings. Without a jury or an audience, the courtroom felt lifeless. A cleaner sprayed cleaning products over the defense table, wiping it down, before smiling at Hennessy. Hennessy greeted her and thanked her for her work. Cleaning protocols had changed, the woman explained, and she had to wipe it down after each session.

Hennessy sat down at the defense table and opened the file. Miller sat next to him. At 10.55am, Lincoln entered the room, followed by two junior assistants. Five minutes later, the clerk at the front of the room read the case number, and then asked the room to rise for Judge Andrew Fedder.

Judge Fedder was a younger judge, only in his mid-forties, and had a sharp wit to match. His understanding of the law was revered in Charleston, and he had a reputation for being fair but firm. The stocky judge adjusted his thick-rimmed glasses, cleared his throat, and brushed his hand over his thinning brown hair.

Once he was settled, Judge Fedder looked up to Hennessy. "I see you've entered a motion to suppress evidence?"

"Yes, Your Honor." Hennessy stood at the defense table. "We've lodged a motion to suppress evidence, pursuant to South Carolina Code of Laws, section 17-30-110, supported by an affidavit, because we believe there are gaps in the chain of evidence based on the fact the tip came from an anonymous source and as such, it violates Mr. Miller's 6th Amendment right to be confronted with the witnesses against him. He has a constitutional right to confront his accuser, and the prosecution has provided no such witness. We cannot allow shadowy figures to run our courtrooms, as maintaining a secret identity makes it easy to lie. Tips provided by confidential informants are knowingly and purposely made to accuse someone of a crime. The very fact that the informant is confidential heightens the dangers involved in allowing a declarant to bear testimony without confrontation. The allowance of anonymous accusations of crime without any opportunity for cross-examination would make a mockery of the Confrontation Clause."

"Noted, Mr. Hennessy," Judge Fedder looked over the affidavit. "Can you please explain where the tip-off was lodged?"

"It was lodged with the Crime Stoppers of Lowcounty, which is a non-government funded organization." Hennessy moved a file and picked up a piece of paper. "There is precedent for this, Your Honor. In the State v. Sweets, 2007, an unknown confidential informant led to the defendant being charged with purchasing drugs at a motel. The

Supreme Court overturned the conviction, ruling that the State couldn't prove the chain of custody required to admit the drugs into evidence. The Supreme Court ruled that the chain of custody was defective because no witnesses testified how they knew the drugs would be purchased. Without testimony from the informant, the State couldn't prove the identity of each person who provided the evidence, and as such, failed in the chain of evidence."

Hennessy moved another piece of paper and then continued. "And in the State v. Greene, the South Carolina Court of Appeals overturned a drug conviction based on an anonymous tip. In that case, the Court ruled the anonymous caller gave no predictive information. The investigating officer had no reason to suspect criminal activity aside from the tip. In declaring the evidence unreliable, the Court stated that: 'The only information available to the officer was the statement of an unknown, unaccountable informant who neither explained how he knew about the money and narcotics, nor supplied any basis for the officer to believe he had inside information about the accused. Since the telephone call was anonymous, the caller did not place his credibility at risk and could lie with impunity. Therefore, we cannot judge the credibility of the caller, and the risk of fabrication becomes unacceptable.'"

"Interesting arguments, Mr. Hennessy," Judge Fedder nodded his approval. "Do you have a response to that, Mr. Lincoln?"

"Yes, we do, Your Honor." Lincoln stood and buttoned his black jacket. "While the tip-off is the basis of the case, the starting point, so to speak, we believe that there is enough evidence to continue with the charges. What Mr. Hennessy is attempting to do here is obvious to all involved. Without the tip-off, there isn't a case. This is just an attempt to have the case thrown out."

"Your Honor, I'm glad Mr. Lincoln has mentioned the starting point of this case. We can't establish if the defendant's 4th Amendment rights were violated because we can't confirm the probable cause," Hennessy argued. "The constitution states there has to be a reasonable basis for the area to be searched. How can we question this reasonable basis if we can't question the caller?"

"This is ludicrous, Your Honor," Lincoln replied. "The recording of the tip-off was in the discovery material, and once the call has been listened to, it's clear that a reasonable basis for the search was established. These are nothing but tactical maneuvers by the defense to distract from the crime that has occurred."

"I'm here to make a ruling on the law, Mr. Lincoln, not on the actions of Mr. Hennessy," Judge Fedder stated. "I'll ask you again—do you have a response to Mr. Hennessy's argument?"

"Sorry, Your Honor. Yes, we do." Lincoln looked down at his files, opened a page, and continued. "We have precedent for this. In State v. Davey, 2017, the South Carolina Court of Appeals, a police drug informant didn't testify at trial. The Court of Appeals agreed the testimony was inadmissible hearsay and violated Davey's 6th Amendment constitutional right to cross-examine his accusers. However, the Court later ruled that admitting the testimony was a 'harmless error.' The Court reasoned that the testimony had little importance in the State's case against Davey for conspiracy to traffic a controlled substance."

"This is not a harmless error, Your Honor. This tip-off is what the entire prosecution case is based on. Without this tip-off, the prosecution cannot prove the chain of evidence," Hennessy argued. "If this evidence is admitted, then it is a clear violation of the defendant's constitutional rights."

Judge Fedder nodded and looked over the files in front of him. "I understand your arguments, Mr. Hennessy." He paused for a long moment, staring at the files, before he continued. "And I will consider these arguments and reserve my decision for a later time."

"Thank you, Your Honor," Hennessy replied and looked across to the prosecutor's desk.

Lincoln turned to look at his assistants, nervously chatting about the motion. After Judge Fedder adjourned the hearing and left the room, Lincoln turned to glare at Hennessy.

His glare said one thing—this case would be a fight every step of the way.

CHAPTER 10

THE AIR was thick with humidity again.

Another tropical storm was brewing in the Atlantic, waiting to burst through the heat. On the horizon, perhaps fifty miles in the distance, the clouds had become dark and ominous, threatening the ocean beneath it.

Hennessy flapped his shirt, wiped his brow, and wound down the window in his pickup as he drove through the streets of Charleston. The hot interior of the pickup didn't help and while the lowered window reduced the temperature a little, what it needed was a decent blast from the AC. As if sensing his urgency for a cooler breeze, the fan briefly kicked into gear, sent a brief burst of air through the cab, then sounded like a wrench dropped into a garbage disposal.

"Oh, come on." Hennessy tapped the dashboard with an open palm, then turned the switch off, waiting a few minutes and then repeating the process in the hope that something miraculous had changed. It didn't, and the same metallic crunching sound came screaming through the vents.

With little choice, he kept the fan off and hung one elbow over the rim of the window, hoping for the speed of the air itself to make a difference. When the temperature still didn't drop after a mile or so, Hennessy slammed his fist into the steering wheel.

The humidity was drenching.

Enough people questioned him about his current choice of vehicle, considering most lawyers normally kept something slick, modern, and German in their garage. A few people had even made jokes at his expense, asking if he needed a little retraining in order to land the big bucks. He ignored the jokes as best he could. He never had much interest in what others called fine European engineering. He'd never seen the point of needing a vehicle to uphold a certain image in his clients' minds.

And a luxury European sedan had no place in a vineyard.

But the more he thought about it, the more he knew the truth to be much deeper than that. As he pulled up at a red light, he knew the main reason he hadn't upgraded his truck was because of what it meant to him, the memories it had held from a decade before, but he would never admit that to anyone.

He looked sideways, stealing a glance at the passenger seat where an eight-year-old Casey had spilled an ice cream cone; a seat where a ten-year-old Ellie had teased her younger sister through the headrest while they waited for their mother to return from a doctor's appointment.

The truth was, losing the truck frightened him. He had lost a son and a lot of the items which held valuable memories of him. If anything happened to one of his girls, could he also risk losing the memories the truck had brought them in all the years they spent in it?

A car honked at him from behind, and he realized he'd missed the change of lights.

"Sorry," he called out the window, holding an apologetic hand up. He watched the cab driver behind him wave the apology away, snapping a few curse words into the safety of his closed-off car interior. Hennessy ignored him, focused on the road and the meeting ahead at Brittlebank Park.

Brittlebank Park was a 10-acre park on the edge of the Ashley River, popular with local families, fishermen, and dog-walkers. The park had a long, narrow stretch of marshlands that featured trails, paved pathways, playgrounds, picnic tables, a fishing pier, and a boat dock.

Barry Lockett was standing in the parking lot, leaning against his larger, and much newer, truck as Hennessy pulled his vehicle in. After a brief handshake, the pair went to grab their morning caffeine kick from the nearby café, then took their cups down to the foreshore.

"Interesting place to meet," Hennessy said as they walked along the foreshore. "I haven't been to this park in a while."

"I used to fish off the bank up here," Lockett pointed up the river, "until I realized it was a fruitless exercise. But nowadays, I look at fishing the same way I do golf—the result of neither activity is really important, it's just good to be outdoors."

"So true." Hennessy looked to the darkening skies as a few drops of rain fell.

"Need me to look further into the McGoverns?"

"Not yet. Kirkland has his own investigators, and they'll be gathering all the preliminary information about Elliot and his case. Once we have an overview and Kirkland has decided on the approach, I'll call you to follow up on a few things, but right now, I need you to focus on the Miller case." Hennessy smiled as a dog-walker passed them, giving the Labrador an even bigger smile. "So, what have you got on the Miller case?"

"It seems Miller was right about James Balter," Lockett said. "As it turns out, the man has quite a reputation."

"I'm taking it you mean not an overly friendly one?"

"People are scared of him. Just the mere mention of his name gets reactions."

"That bad?"

"That bad. And not just in Charleston, either. When I made a few phone calls, I found references to this guy across all of the east coast. This guy gets around. If you're a touring singer and you need something, anything at all, then Balter is the man people call."

"He's got the experience, then. And the connections to score a large bag of drugs."

"One of my contacts owns a small theater in Myrtle Beach, and he told me Balter is almost a legend among the staff. I'm talking anything these guys need, and he makes it happen." He lowered his voice a little as a jogger passed by. "And a man who can deliver that sort of service is a dangerous man."

"Did you manage to find out anything about the manager?"

"Preston Wheeler." He shook his head. "Nothing worthwhile. I did track down an old client who claimed his ex-manager still owed him money for several gigs he was never paid for, but other than that, nothing worth mentioning. Zach Miller was the only star in Preston Wheeler's books. Everyone else was a small-time musician. Miller would've made up most of his income, so I can see why Wheeler was upset that Miller was leaving."

"Miller claims that Wheeler set him up because of bad blood between them. If we're going to use that defense, then I'm going to need more information on him. Anything at all that I can use in court would be good. Any past behaviors that indicate he might do this sort of thing."

"There's just not much out there."

"Find out how they communicate. I'd love to find some evidence that could show he set this up. If we're going for a third-party culpability play, I need something to link them together."

"I'll see what I can find," Lockett said. "But there is one thing I needed to tell you this morning."

"Go on."

"The dressing room at the club? The one used by Miller?"

"What about it?"

"Turns out all the cameras in and around it weren't just down. They were damaged, as in broken. When I spoke with the club manager, he mentioned they appeared to have been damaged the night before Miller took the stage. He assumed it was just some punk kids, but given what we know happened the following night, I'd say the two things might be related."

"That's good, Barry," Hennessy agreed. "Keep following that line of inquiry. It might just lead us to evidence we can present in court. If we can prove Wheeler or Balter broke the cameras, we're closer to winning this thing."

"I'll see what I can find." Lockett stopped and

looked out at the slow-moving river. "And what are you going to do next?"

"Sometimes, the best action is to go straight to the source."

CHAPTER 11

PRESTON WHEELER.

A disgruntled manager who felt he was wronged. An angry man who had lost his star client. A sleaze who would do anything to win. He was the key. He had motive, the ability to set up Miller, and the attitude to follow it through.

After weeks of trying, Hennessy finally managed to nail down Wheeler for a discussion.

He walked out to the parking lot behind his office building and stared at the car parked in his space. The rental Jacinta had organized for him while the truck was having its AC serviced wasn't exactly a 'paddock basher,' as Barry Lockett had once referred to a rust bucket they had passed, but it did lack the character of his pickup.

He had a feeling his assistant was trying to show him the finer side of driving by organizing a mid-sized Mercedes Benz for the week. And while he appreciated the overall look of the car, there was just something about it that he couldn't get used to. The interior felt too clean for him, the plain trim lacking any of the worn character of the pickup he'd grown to love. And the way the car sat so low to the ground, it felt like he sat mere inches from the road itself. From the moment he sat in the Benz, he knew he would never own one. The feel was too city-ish, lacking the laid-back comfort of country driving. Jacinta had joined him for his first drive around the block and knew immediately she had made a mistake.

"I can exchange it," she said when they pulled up in front of the office building, but Hennessy declined.

"It's just a car," he said with a grin, hoping he didn't sound annoyed. "And it's only for a few days."

He sat inside the Mercedes and was impressed by the power of the air-conditioner. It cooled the interior down in seconds. He shrugged, and concluded that he'd much rather have his arm out the window anyway. In his rental, with the window down, he drove out to the neighborhood of Hampton Park Terrace and parked outside the hip new bar, The White Cocktail.

The White Cocktail was the latest joint to appeal to the rich and powerful, a place where they could congratulate each other on the lottery of their birth. Few of the people were self-made inside the doors, including Preston Wheeler. From what Miller had explained, Wheeler had come from a wealthy family, owners of a large cattle farm near the North Carolina border. He was eighteen when his parents passed away in an unfortunate car accident. Within a year of their death, he had sold the farm, pocketed the cash, and never returned.

Managing music stars had been his way to feel powerful, his way into the cool crowd, although his early years weren't successful, turning his rather large fortune into a much smaller one. It was only once Zach Miller recorded a hit song that Wheeler made any money from his chosen career.

Hennessy entered the bar, the soft, fragrant smell of wisteria in the air. Everything in the bar seemed to be white, along with gold trim seemingly on every surface. The walls were white, the chairs were white, and the tablecloths were white. The gold trims laced the bar, and the selection of drinks on the shelves must've been worth a small fortune. As the time ticked into the afternoon, several people around the bar were mingling, talking, and laughing with fake sincerity.

One quick look around and he found his target, the immediately recognizable head of hair facing away from the door near the back. Preston Wheler had his cellphone pressed against his ear, the other hand swinging in an animated performance.

Wheeler was tall, tanned, and traditionally good-looking. He was never seen without a suit, although he rarely wore a tie. His thick black hair was slicked back, and as Hennessy passed, he caught a waft of a strong woody cologne.

Hennessy ordered a Laphroaig whisky and watched Wheeler continue his conversation in the mirrored wall. Once the bartender set his order down, Hennessy picked up his glass, turned around, and took a deep breath as he stepped in the direction of the booth Wheeler sat in.

"I don't care if he's been charged, Balter. I'll pay you when—" Wheeler stopped talking, sensing someone nearby. He turned and looked over his shoulder, but by then, Hennessy was moving to sit in the seat on the other side of the booth.

"Can I help you?"

"I was waiting for you to finish your phone call, Mr. Wheeler."

"Ah. Joe Hennessy, right? Miller's lawyer." Wheeler looked at his watch. "You're early."

"I like to be punctual."

Wheeler stared at Hennessy for a long moment, and then abruptly told the person on the phone he would call him back.

"Was that James Balter you were talking to?"

The reaction was instant, the mood between the pair sinking to a low as Wheeler's eyes narrowed. After a few seconds of trying to figure out his response, he said, "So you were listening? I thought as much. So, what did you hear?"

"Enough to know you owe him money."

"I owe a lot of people money. My father always said not to pay people until they absolutely demand it. You'd be surprised by the number of people who just give up chasing it because it's too hard." He shook his head. "So, you're trying to get him off, huh? You know, if I were you, I'd convince your client to take a deal. I've heard he's been offered fifteen months behind bars, with the rest of the sentence suspended. He might be able to write some new material in there, instead of just relying on his old stuff." Leaning in a bit closer and lowering his voice, he added, "It's about the best he'll get."

Not wanting to give him too much of a head start when it came to confidence, Hennessy smiled himself, took a swig, and pointed at Wheeler. "You were upset by Miller not renewing his contract with you."

"Of course I was upset." Wheeler spat out, the anger on his face clear. "I made him. Without me, he was nothing. Nothing. I landed him the gigs. I landed him the television spots. And I made the deal to make his song go viral on social media. I made him."

"His talents have nothing to do with it?"

"Talents?" Wheeler scoffed. "I could walk down

the street tomorrow and find five guys just as talented as he is. No. The music industry isn't about talent—it's about popularity. If you can become popular, you can sing about anything and people will still come to the show. That's the approach I've always taken with my clients."

"Did you set him up?"

Wheeler scoffed again. He turned back to Hennessy with a smile on his face. "Really? You just come out and ask me that?"

Hennessy didn't respond, keeping his glare on Wheeler.

"You're straight to the point, eh? I like that. No beating around the bush. That's a good way to approach life."

"You didn't answer my question."

"I wasn't even there."

"Who did you pay to do it?"

"Ha!" Wheeler laughed, waving his index finger at Hennessy. "You really are a direct man. But I'll answer the question—I didn't set him up. I didn't have to. He has a problem with drugs. That's well documented. He was physically beaten as a kid by his drug-addicted father, and I guess you can only keep that stuff down for a certain amount of time. Miller just fell off the wagon again."

"That's not what Miller says. He says he was set up. And if you're involved, I'll prove it in court."

Wheeler's grip on his glass tightened. Hennessy wasn't sure whether Wheeler would smash the glass into his face or throw a punch, but Hennessy was ready either way. His years of junior boxing had helped him more times than he cared to count.

As they faced off, the air hung heavy between the

two men, the tension almost fever pitch as the rest of the bar grew silent. Wheeler looked up toward the bar, saw the eyes watching them, and grinned.

"Yeah, well," Wheeler began as he got to his feet. "If that's the best you got, then good luck to you. But I'll tell you this—stay out of my way. That's the only warning you'll receive. Stay out of my way, or you'll find out just how dangerous I can be."

Wheeler didn't bother waiting for a response. He drank the last of his whiskey and slapped it down on the table in front of Hennessy. He held his glare for a moment, then turned and walked off in a huff. Hennessy waited a few minutes to let his anger subside, then followed Wheeler's lead back to the parking lot. By the time he reached his car, Wheeler had split.

Although he denied involvement, one thing was clear—Hennessy wasn't done with Wheeler yet.

CHAPTER 12

IN HIS struggle to earn enough money to keep the vineyard out of the bank's grasp, Hennessy took on more work than he could handle.

Every morning started with a meeting with Jacinta, deciding where his focus should be at each hour of the day. He had a DUI to handle, a minor assault charge to defend, and a restraining order to refile. Each day, there was always more than one case, always more than one place to focus. With the assistance of Jacinta, Hennessy juggled the cases, switching between files and ideas with regularity. He had two major cases that held most of his focus— Miller and McGovern. He spent most of his week on the Miller case, searching through police files for the smallest of mistakes to have evidence thrown out, but he found nothing. As Thursday ticked past, he received a message from Kirkland.

'*The prosecution wants to meet and discuss a deal. This afternoon. 5pm. Meet at my office at 4pm and they'll meet us here.*'

The message was brief and straight to the point. Hennessy liked it that way. He called out to Jacinta, and she cleared his calendar.

At 3:55pm, Hennessy arrived at Kirkland's office, briefcase in hand, ready to discuss the case.

The pair spoke for an hour, readying themselves

for the prosecutor's arrival, drafting notes and files. A paralegal sat in on the meeting, quietly taking notes and organizing files, while both men exhausted every possible angle that the prosecution could bring.

Kirkland had an abrasive personality, firm and not fair, and it was easy to see why McGovern needed Hennessy on board. The media, nor a jury, would warm to Kirkland. He was tenacious, intelligent and cunning, but certainly not likable.

At five minutes past five, the assistant knocked on the door and advised that Nadine Robinson and her team had arrived. Kirkland told her to keep them waiting for ten minutes, and then send them through. Exactly ten minutes later, prosecutor Nadine Robinson and two assistants walked through the door of the conference room in the Kirkland Law Firm. Hennessy stood to greet them. Kirkland stayed seated.

Nadine Robinson was a confident woman, a young prosecutor with a bright future in law. She shook Hennessy's hand firmly, and then introduced her team. Around Robinson was the soft scent of sandalwood, a seductive perfume for a well-dressed professional woman in her early thirties. She stood confidently, telling her assistants where to sit, and then sat at the end of the table. The paralegal remained at the side of the room, sitting quietly, ready to take notes and assist at a moment's notice.

"Y'all ready to get down to business?" Kirkland's tone sounded almost condescending, and when Hennessy took a quick look to his side, he saw a sly grin on the man's face that he wasn't expecting.

Nadine Robinson was used to it. She didn't even flinch. Her professionalism was clear, and she ignored the undertones of Kirkland's comment, folded her hands neatly in front of her, and spoke with the clarity of a priest delivering a Sunday morning sermon.

"This may not be what you gentlemen hoped to hear today, but I don't want to waste your time. As far as the Circuit Solicitor's Office is concerned, the McGovern family has used up this city's precious resources for long enough. Elliot McGovern is the ultimate symbol of entitled privilege and, as such, it's time. Time to end this needless display of power and wealth accumulated off the misery of the people of Charleston. Time to end this reign of endless disregard for what this city stands for. And most importantly, it's time to bring down a spoiled rich kid who thinks it's ok to do whatever he pleases, including murdering his own wife. It's time to bring this man to justice. And if we have to do it through a trial, we will. Our offer, and our only offer, is thirty years for an early guilty plea."

As she let the final word roll from her tongue, it hung suspended in the air between them for what felt like an eternity. Hennessy sat stoically, waiting for Kirkland to respond.

Unfortunately, words weren't the first thing to leave Kirkland's mouth, the volume of his laughter conveying the arrogance behind it. He chuckled long and hard, pretending to wipe the tears away as he took a quick look at Hennessy for support. Hennessy didn't smile.

It took Kirkland twenty-five seconds to get himself back under control. All the while, the prosecutor watched him blank-faced. She displayed no emotion, as cool and calm as the finest poker players.

Kirkland looked across to Hennessy. "Can you believe this? This young'un wants to be a superhero."

To Kirkland's disappointment, Hennessy didn't return a laugh. Kirkland grunted, straightened himself up, and turned back to Robinson.

"You and I both know that's never going to happen," Kirkland leaned forward on the table. "For one thing, my client has built a vast network of contacts over many years, and as you already know, the connections reside on both sides of the law. And secondly, again as you already know, some of those people also hold secrets, secrets nobody wants to see raised in court. So, if you really think this case will reach the inside of the courtroom, then maybe you haven't been around long enough to know how this system works." The smug look he displayed could have come straight out of a Hollywood movie, the acting behind it almost supreme. As if needing to add a little extra boot to his attempted kicking, he added, "I'm surprised it's already made it this far."

"You're suggesting that his connections are going to get him off?"

"I'm suggesting that you present a very good deal because one way or another, this won't make it to court. This will be embarrassing for the Circuit Solicitor's Office, and I'm sure nobody wants that level of disappointment. We're willing to accept a deal under Section 16-3-50. Manslaughter."

"Manslaughter? He shot his wife in the head. No chance."

"You haven't got a case. I'm surprised this made it through the Grand Jury," Hennessy stated. "And Elliot McGovern has an alibi."

"A weak alibi, and one that will be proven to be false if you take this to court," she said. "This is a well-planned, meticulous murder, and if you take this to trial, then he's looking at life. Take the deal for thirty years. It's the best he can hope for."

"Your entire case is built around Roger Steinberg, and the guy hates McGovern. The jury is going to laugh you out of court. He's not a reliable witness," Kirkland said. "Like I said, we're willing to discuss manslaughter charges."

"If this makes it before a jury, Elliot McGovern's toast," Robinson's tone was firm. "The McGovern family is the ultimate symbol of entitled privilege, and it's time to bring the dynasty down. The family can't just do whatever they like and keep getting away with it."

Kirkland laughed again. "The McGoverns are connected to all sides of the law, and there are some secrets that people don't want to come out in court. Elliot says he'll be surprised if those people allowed the case to make it to trial."

Nadine Robinson clenched her hands, and Hennessy noted it was the only sign she gave that Kirkland was getting under her skin. "I'm not wasting any more time on this. If you think this is going to simply disappear because your client wishes it to, then I suggest you go ahead and file whatever motions you see fit. You can take the deal to your client—thirty years for an early guilty plea. And since I can see that we won't come to any agreement today, I'm ending this meeting now."

She didn't wait for his response. The woman closed the file before her, stood, and walked to the door. "Good day, gentleman."

Hennessy and Kirkland were quiet as Robinson and her assistants exited the office. They didn't say another word until they were sure she and her team were gone from the building.

"I'll call McGovern," Kirkland said. "But he's not going to like it. He's going to want to take this to trial."

Hennessy nodded.

The fight was on.

CHAPTER 13

ELLIOT MCGOVERN threw his cell across the room the second Kirkland ended the call.

He'd grown up in a world where money solved any problem, no matter how complex or dangerous. Yet when John Kirkland called after the meeting with the prosecutor and told him their offer was thirty years for an early guilty plea, he began to taste the first signs of what might happen to him.

He didn't like it—not the taste, the feelings, or the consequences.

By the time Kirkland finished relaying the details of the meeting, Elliot's voice had gone AWOL, the man unable to find the words to acknowledge the details.

McGovern slumped into the sunchair next to the pool, staring out into the fading remnants of the day. His mind worked overtime to try and assimilate the news with the emotions he felt.

This wasn't how things were supposed to work, not for him. Not for someone with his wealth.

He wasn't a wealthy introvert. He loved money and all the freedoms and benefits which came with it. What he loved most was to let the rest of the world know just how much he had. The prosecution knew how much he had, they knew how much his family could donate to their elections, and yet, they still pursued the murder charge.

Joe Hennessy was the key. He was the one that could level the playing field. He was the one that could turn on the southern charm and sweet talk them into a better deal.

His cell pinged from inside the home, not the usual buzzing ringtone he used for the masses but a discreet triple-chime he'd assigned to George Lewis, one of the many associates he liked to keep in his back pocket. Lewis owned a reputable accountancy firm, having inherited the business after his father had joined the great house in the sky. It was people like George Lewis who ensured the McGovern family would continue to reign supreme.

McGovern grunted, stood, and retrieved his cell from the floor. He checked the wall and noticed a small break in the drywall. He'd have to get that fixed.

The message from Lewis was brief and to the point, asking Elliot if he felt like an evening drink. Lewis lived on nearby Kiawah Island, and the pair's usual meet-ups took place at one of the many golf clubs, a sport Harold McGovern called the sport of champions.

Elliot hated golf, loathed the whole concept behind it, and only liked to drink at their clubs because of the networking associated with them. Plus, it had been a way for the son to get under the skin of his father, a devoted golfer since the dawn of time.

He responded to the text the way he usually did, by telling George how long he'd take to get there. With a quick change of clothes, and a few minutes to make himself a little more presentable, he'd see him in around twenty. As it was, he stepped out of his car in front of the Seabrook Island Club fifteen minutes later.

"Elliot," George Lewis called out, half running to meet him. "Hey, that was quick, but you're always quick. That's why I like you so much. You're such a legend."

Elliot grinned, enjoying the butt-kissing style of his so-called friend. Elliot didn't think much of the accountant, a weak soul with a weak heart.

The pair slowly made their way inside, headed straight for the member's lounge, and ordered two Old Fashioneds. McGovern didn't care for the conversation. What he craved was a way to forget the day, to forget the news Kirkland had brought him. He wanted to focus on something else, and George Lewis just happened to be the first option available to him.

Once they were settled at the seats near the windows offering a nighttime ocean view, George took the reins of the conversation, launching into a spiel about housing prices. Elliot found himself unable to follow. He grunted occasionally, nodded his head when appropriate, but for the most part, found himself unable to escape the thoughts running through his head. George barely noticed; the man was capable of talking nonstop with a mouth full of marbles while submerged under water.

Occasionally, random people walked past their seats, both men offering a wave to acknowledge each of them. A local judge stopped by to shake McGovern's hand and give his condolences over the man's recent loss. He'd heard about the murder charge and said he was sure that McGovern would beat it. McGovern assured him that he would.

Elliot switched off at one point, turning his attention to the windows and the ocean beyond. That was where the endless possibilities lived, the notion that it went on forever and a man could run away from whatever problems he had in his world. There were islands out there—Bermuda, Cuba, the Bahamas. Many better places than prison.

"I've got to go." McGovern stood, cutting Lewis off mid-sentence. The accountant's mouth remained open halfway through a word, and, rather than snapping shut, it appeared to drop even lower.

Elliot couldn't handle it anymore, listening to a weak man so caught up in his own story, he hadn't noticed that his audience hadn't responded in almost ten minutes of mindless chatter. McGovern didn't respond to Lewis's question of whether he'd said the wrong thing. What he needed was fresh air, craving a lungful before he suffocated from frustration.

Pushing through the front doors, Elliot stepped into the night and sucked in a lungful of cooling air. He followed the path toward the parking lot, greeted a couple he vaguely recognized as living a few houses up from his own, and headed for his car.

Just before he reached the Maserati, he stopped and looked up into the sky, the moon hanging high above the horizon. It was close to full, with just a small sliver missing from the right side. Staring at it, he wondered about the men who managed to walk on its surface, and whether they ever stopped to look back at their home and wonder how they could make all of their problems disappear.

He didn't miss his wife. Not one bit. He didn't miss her nagging. He didn't miss her tantrums. And he didn't miss the way she spent his money. But he did miss having someone to have his arm around at events. She would've been the ultimate trophy wife if she had kept her mouth shut, he thought.

McGovern drove home and saw the old car parked by his driveway. The car was dented at the back, with a busted taillight and scratches down the side of the blue paint.

McGovern pulled up beside it, and when he stepped out of his car, the overpowering smell of gasoline was clear. He wondered if the car had a leak.

He was about to call out, but a hand grabbed his shoulder and whipped him around. His legs tangled beneath him and, rather than spin on the spot, he fell back, his shoulder blades crashing into the upper edge of his car.

"You lowlife piece of trash," a voice hissed into his face, and he felt a hand grab him by the throat.

It took him a bit to react, the attack catching him completely off guard, but once he understood what was happening, McGovern didn't hesitate to retaliate. After deflecting another attempt to grab him, he pushed the attacker back hard, stepped away from the car, and prepared to launch himself. But that was when he saw the face staring back at him, an angry, twisted mass of hatred and tears.

"You did this," his brother-in-law hissed through clenched teeth. Paul Dillion's eyes were full of murderous intent, staring back with a hatred McGovern wasn't completely unaccustomed to. "You killed her."

"No, I didn't," Elliot said, taking a step back. He grabbed the collar of his shirt and pulled it forward in an attempt to straighten it. Standing tall, he looked the man in the face, resisting the urge to hit him. "I didn't kill her, Paul. I promise you."

"Promise? Who are you to make promises? You

made her life miserable." He'd been drinking. The smell of liquor was clear. "If the courts don't get you, I will. I promise you that. If you walk away from this, you'll have to be scared of every shadow."

Dillion swung hard at McGovern, but McGovern easily stepped out of the way, and Dillion fell to the ground. McGovern laughed.

"You can't even defend your sister's honor," McGovern scoffed, stepping toward his front door. "If you're still here in five minutes, I'm calling the cops. Get out of here, loser."

McGovern didn't look back, leaving the grieving brother behind.

CHAPTER 14

HENNESSY SPENT much of the time in his office thinking.

He spent hours staring out a window, letting his thoughts come and go as they pleased. It was in this free thought state that he often found the answers. Sometimes, he didn't even know the question, but still, the answers came to him when he let his mind relax.

McGovern had dominated much of his thoughts throughout the week. He didn't care to think about whether the man was guilty or not, instead he spent his time thinking about how the man found himself in that situation.

Despite all his money, despite all his financial success, McGovern clearly wasn't happy. Could he ever be happy? Hennessy didn't know the answer. He didn't know if happiness was genetic, some hidden gene that had yet to be discovered, or whether happiness was merely a mental outlook, a view of the world that could be changed on a whim. All he knew was that McGovern had no smile lines on his face. If only McGovern had been taught to help others, Hennessy thought, remembering the words of his dear late mother, 'The quickest path to happiness is to find someone to help.'

He smiled as he remembered his mother, a woman

who lived her life as a happy person filled with warmth and love. Even on her deathbed, as the cancer ate away her strength, she still tried to help others in her hospital ward, smiling all the way through her pain.

"The quickest path to happiness is to find someone to help," he repeated under his breath.

Late on Friday afternoon, Hennessy stared out the office window, losing track of time. It was the streets which had again consumed his self-awareness, distracting him with the fusion of shadows and lights which partially illuminated it against the darkening sky.

It wasn't until Jacinta popped her head through the door to ask if he needed anything else that he returned to the moment.

"Oh, hey, you still here?" He said as he spun back around from the window to face her. "I thought you'd already left."

"Just finishing up some reports so I can close them and file them away," she said.

It was one of her many qualities which he valued most. The woman hated leaving anything unfinished, and in an environment as hectic as a lawyer's office, it made things so much easier when dealing with multiple cases.

"Want a coke?" She held out a can, and she knew he would accept. As well as her incredible job-related skills, Jacinta also seemed to have a maternal version of ESP, she was always aware of when someone needed a shoulder to lean on, or a caring ear to listen.

She handed him a drink, and he cracked the can. She grabbed her own coke and came into the office, dropping into the seat before him, and popped the top.

"Cheers," she said, raised the can, and drank deeply. When she was done, Jacinta leaned back, held the can on her leg, and stared at the ceiling. "Much happening with McGovern?"

"Apart from him being an arrogant pain? No. The longer this goes on, the angrier he becomes. It makes him furious that he can't just buy his way out of this mess. His whole life, he's been able to solve his problems with money, but he hasn't been able to bribe his way out of this one."

"Never ceases to amaze me how people with money assume it's the answer to everything. I wonder what it'd be like to have that much money?"

"Money is worth nothing if you have too much, but it's worth everything if you don't have enough. Which leaves the question—how much is enough?"

"Just a few million, thanks." Jacinta smiled. "Just enough to own my home, travel the world, drink good wine, and afford a good education for my son. That would be enough."

"Cheers to that." Hennessy drank again, held the can steady, then finished the rest. He squeezed the sides of it and tossed it into the trash before he leaned all the way back in his chair, its protesting screech filling the air. "Still, you can't really blame Elliot."

"What do you mean?"

"He was born into it. He didn't really have much of a say in the matter. It's the only world he's ever known."

"But common decency isn't something which needs to be educated through school. Morals don't need to be taught."

"If you knew Harold McGovern, you might

change your opinion."

"That bad, huh?"

"That bad. He was a ferocious lawyer, focused on corporate law, and when I was a prosecutor twenty years ago, we met each other in the courtroom several times. He was a rude man with an appetite for conflict. If he could argue it, he would." Hennessy shifted uncomfortably in his chair as the flood of memories returned. He paused, caught the pain before it broke free, and pushed it back down as deep as it would go. "I don't trust the guy, not one bit, but I have to do my job."

"You're doing what you have to do to save the vineyard. There's honor in that."

Hennessy nodded, although unconvinced by her words. "I think it's time we called it a day."

As he went to stand, there was a knock at the door. He looked at his watch and raised his eyebrows. 6:25pm.

Jacinta shrugged, acknowledging she had no idea who was at the door before she went to answer it. She returned a few moments later.

"There's a Senator Richard Longhouse here to see you," Jacinta said. "And he says he has a deal for you."

CHAPTER 15

RICHARD LONGHOUSE. Trouble always followed the name.

Longhouse stepped through the door to Hennessy's office and greeted him with an uneasy smile. In his fifties, Longhouse's olive skin was deeply tanned by the southern sun. He was tall, thin, and well-groomed, with a thick mustache. He spoke with a smooth accent that said he was a South Carolina man through and through.

"Joe Hennessy," Longhouse offered his hand as he neared. "It's good to see you again. I was hoping that I could catch you before you went home for the week."

Hennessy didn't respond. He didn't stand up, and he didn't shake his hand.

"Sure. I understand," Longhouse withdrew his hand. He paused in front of Hennessy's desk and looked over the table. "You're working the McGovern case, aren't you?"

Again, Hennessy didn't respond.

Longhouse sat down without invitation, crossing one leg over the other. "It must be hard for Elliot McGovern—having his face splashed all over the papers like that. The poor man has just lost his wife, and now he has to deal with the media scrutiny. That must be heartbreaking for the poor man. I've reached out and told him that he has my support as he goes through this. His father and I used to be quite close."

Hennessy kept his stare on his former colleague. "I'm intrigued to know why you're here, Richard. You and I aren't friends."

"Aren't we?" Longhouse scoffed. "I would like to change that, Joe. I'm a Senator now, and I'd like to be friends with everyone. I know you've been Upstate for the past two decades, but I'm sure you haven't forgotten how a place like Charleston works. Everyone knows everyone. Everyone is in everyone's business. We're all connected. That's why it's important to make peace with people you may have wronged in the past. And I'm here to try and smooth over any issues we might have."

Hennessy kept his stare on Longhouse.

"I need to make peace with the past," Longhouse continued. "That's why I'm here. I want to help you, and I want you to help me. I know you need money to keep the banks off your back with the vineyard, so I'd like to help. As a sign of goodwill, I'm willing to put an offer on the table for $10,000."

"In exchange for what?"

"For your signature."

"Get to the point."

"Ok." Longhouse drew a breath. "When you and I were working in the Circuit Solicitor's Office all those years ago, you may have seen some things, perhaps even researched some things that didn't make me look good."

"I know you took bribes from people to drop their criminal cases."

"Now, now. Nothing was ever proven."

Hennessy glared at Longhouse, feeling his

temperature rise.

"Listen, Joe, even though they were sealed records and never made it to court, I know it was you who lodged the complaint against me while we were working together. I know it was you that was the suppressed witness. Even though the case against me never made it to court, I know it was you who started it."

"I've never denied it. I didn't even ask for my name to be suppressed. I wanted it all out in the open, but the Office insisted everything was suppressed. I wasn't scared of you then, and I'm not scared of you now."

"They were all lies, Joe. I never took a bribe."

"And I never believed a single word that came out of your mouth."

Longhouse nodded and then removed a folded sheet of paper from the inside of his jacket. He placed it on Hennessy's desk. "This is the offer."

"For what?"

"It's a non-disclosure agreement."

"An NDA?" Hennessy stared at the piece of paper but didn't touch it. "Of course. You're making a run for Governor, and you need to clean up all the loose ends. You want to pay me off and keep me quiet."

"You've got nothing, Joe. Nothing was ever proven, and nothing was ever taken further. If you say anything publicly, I'll sue you for defamation. Just sign the document, take the 10K, and put it toward the vineyard."

"No."

"No?" Longhouse scoffed. "Really? Just like that? Why would you even say no? It's free money, and you need it."

"I'm not going to compromise my morals for someone like you."

Longhouse looked around the room and nodded. "$15,000. All you have to do is sign it. Just a scribble at the bottom of the page."

"I know what you're doing, and you must be spending a lot of money cleaning up your past. How many of these have you had others sign? 15? 50? 500? That's a lot of money."

"$25,000, Joe." Longhouse's voice was firm.

Hennessy sat back a little.

"Ah, there it is. There's the price. Even a man of honor has a price. Money breaks most men, you just have to find the right point." Longhouse smiled and then stood. "I'll give you a week to sign a deal. Come to my office, and I'll adjust the contract to reflect the new amount. All you need to do is sign on the dotted line, agreeing to never discuss anything about the past, either in private or in public, and then we have a deal."

Longhouse offered Hennessy the pen. Hennessy shook his head.

"Think it over. It's $25,000. It'd keep the bank off your back. Let you keep the vineyard in your son's name," Longhouse said. He placed the pen on the table. "After you sign it, give me a call. The contract is good. It's solid."

Hennessy watched the man leave and then stared at the piece of paper for a long time.

CHAPTER 16

THE ANGER was still burning through Hennessy as he sat on a stool at the Blind Tiger Pub in Downtown Charleston.

He hated himself for wanting to take the money from Longhouse. Were his morals for sale? Or was it just a sensible and logical decision? He was never going to have an opportunity to expose Longhouse's past. He had no evidence. When he lodged the complaint more than twenty years ago, he was still working for the Circuit Solicitor's Office, alongside Longhouse. Both had long since moved on from that job. When Luca was murdered, he forgot about the complaint, only to receive a letter two years later that stated there wasn't enough evidence to prosecute. He didn't have the energy to fight on after that.

And he needed the money to save Luca's Vineyard. It was easy money, an easy win, but he felt so dirty for even contemplating taking it.

When Barry Lockett arrived a little after seven, Hennessy was already three beers into his night. Lockett patted Hennessy on the shoulder and ordered a pale ale.

"Tough day?" Lockett could see the look of pain and confusion on Hennessy's face.

"Yeah," Hennessy stared into his beer before he raised his eyes to look at Lockett. "An old colleague offered me a good sum of money to stay quiet about things that happened in our past."

"That sounds like a great day to me." Lockett nodded to the bartender when his beer was placed in front of him. "I wish some people from my past would do that."

"It was Richard Longhouse," Hennessy said the name quietly. "He wanted me to sign an NDA about the complaints that I lodged against him when we were working as prosecutors. 25K to stay silent about things that happened over twenty years ago."

"Whoa." Lockett whistled. "Sounds like you know something important."

"I knew he was taking bribes from certain people to make cases disappear. Longhouse was in charge of prosecuting drug cases. One was a drug dealer who was importing cocaine from Columbia. The drug dealer was looking at life in prison, and Longhouse dropped all charges the day after he played golf with the defense lawyer. I saw the money in his car that afternoon. One great big envelope stuffed full of cash. I couldn't believe it, so I confronted him about it. He admitted everything. Said he'd been doing it for years. Then he offered me a slice of the action."

"I take it you declined?"

"There was no chance I was getting caught up in drug money coming from South America. I punched him in the stomach, told him he was dirty, and filed an official complaint."

"What happened then?"

"The complaint was going to take years to process, but everyone knew Longhouse was guilty. I was busy dealing with other cases, but Longhouse kept doing his thing. A year later…" Hennessy drew a breath. "A year later, I left the job and moved upstate."

Lockett nodded slowly before he reached out and placed a consoling hand on Hennessy's shoulder. He left it there for a minute before he turned back to his pint and took a long drink.

"I need you to do something for me," Hennessy turned to him. "Find out who else Longhouse is asking to sign these NDAs. See if you can get any information about it. He's making a run for Governor and tying up all the loose ends from his past. I'm sure there are a few others."

"On it, boss."

Hennessy nodded his thanks and then turned to look around the dimly lit bar. The Blind Tiger was an alehouse dating back to the early 1800s, only a block from Hennessy's office. It featured a brick-walled courtyard at the rear, simple décor inside, and a large assortment of ales. The atmosphere was subdued, the smell of beer and liquor filled the air, and the temperature was cool. It was the perfect escape from the humidity outside its door.

"So, I've got something on James Balter." Lockett kept his voice low. "I tracked down a few people willing to talk about him, and what they told me isn't nice. They said that most people are scared of him. Whatever he's done to the people that cross him, he's done it good and made sure nobody does it again. Wouldn't surprise me if he's beaten a lot of people up. Whatever it is, nobody's talking. If you need something on him, we're gonna have to find a different way."

"How many people does he deal to?"

"The rumor is that he gets his supply of drugs directly from a large-scale dealer in Miami, no middleman, no risk of being sold out in a buyers' deal. He then deals to touring musicians and their crews, and get this, wealthy housewives."

"Wealthy housewives?"

"Yep. Along with some wealthy husbands. Not bad work if you can get it. Dealing to rich people is a very low-risk strategy."

Hennessy nodded, a thought starting to build. He took a sip of his Palmetto Brewing Company IPA, and then stared at it. It was strong, both in flavor and alcohol content. Just what he needed.

"I met with Wheeler. If it was a set-up, then Wheeler has to be involved. I need to know how Wheeler and Balter contact each other, and then I need to know what they say to each other. If you can get your hands, legitimately, on phone records, do it. If you can get computer records, do it. If they use a carrier pigeon to communicate, I need you to put a trace on the bird. I need to know what they say to each other."

"I'll look through Balter's trash this week and next and see what I can find."

"What about video feeds around the concert that night?" Hennessy asked. "We need to find some. There has to be footage of Balter backstage. I don't think Miller does drugs, and I don't think he needs the money, or the risk, to deal them. He's at the height of his career—why would he need to do this?"

"I'll see what I can find. I'll check social media to see if they're any links. I take it that you're going to use Balter as the third-party culpability play?"

Hennessy nodded.

"Are you sure it's a good idea?"

"We'll try and downgrade the charges to

possession, and after that, yes, we'll go for a third-party culpability play and blame James Balter. He was there, and he had the connections to get backstage and into the dressing room. He's the dealer that put the drugs there for the crew."

"Ok. I'll see what I can find, but men like Balter don't like surprises, especially not in the courtroom."

"And I won't pressure him in the courtroom. I'll approach him tomorrow. Let him know what's happening."

"Are you sure that's a wise move?"

"No, it's definitely a dangerous idea," Hennessy agreed. "But that's not going to stop me."

CHAPTER 17

"ARE YOU right there, Pal?"

Hennessy stepped through the doors of The Two Bob's Barbershop on Remount Road in North Charleston. Hennessy looked down at the barber and nodded to the short and skinny man appearing to be nearing retirement age.

Walking into the shop, he saw that two of the three stations were busy, both barbers working their way through their latest cuts. The middle station sat empty and, ignoring the waiting area completely, Hennessy sat in the unused chair.

"Just come to have a chat with my friend here," Hennessy nodded. "James Balter."

James Balter turned to look at him, gave him a quick up and down, and turned back to face the mirror.

"What do you want?" His voice was gravelly as if belonging to a two-pack-a-day smoker.

Balter's skin was weathered beyond his fifty years, a scar down his right cheek. He wore gold rings on his hands, and his graying hair was being trimmed short, the job almost completed. He nodded to the barber. The barber stepped back, giving the men a little space.

"I just wanted a chat." Hennessy raised his hands.

Balter took another look at him and grinned.

"Why would Zach Miller's lawyer track me down all the way to a barbershop? Hoping to catch a break?"

"What makes you think I'm here about Zach Miller?"

"You represent him, don't you?"

"I do."

"Why else would you come here? Your client's going to prison for carrying enough coke to fuel a two-day rave festival."

Hennessy didn't respond for a few moments before he said, "Tell me, how does a housewife like Katherine McGovern pay for her supply of cocaine?"

It was Balter's turn to grow silent, taking a long pause to consider the new arrival's surprising line of questioning. His eyes narrowed a second time. "What makes you think I had anything to do with her?"

"You know the McGoverns. You've delivered there in the past."

Balter turned back to the mirror. "I've worked for many people. Doesn't mean I had anything to do with either of their problems."

"But you're the problem solver, aren't you?"

Hennessy noted a change in facial expression, the man losing his cool for the briefest moment.

"Do you know what I think?" Hennessy continued. "I think Wheeler paid you to set Miller up, to fill his backpack with drugs, plant it in the dressing room, and then make the anonymous tip-off to the cops. And I think you're also the one that supplied the McGoverns with their cocaine."

"Is that what you think?" Balter scoffed. "You've got nothing. Otherwise, it'd be the cops here, and not you."

"I might have nothing at the moment, but I'll find

something that links you and Wheeler together. And then I'll expose it in court."

"So you are here about Miller." Balter shook his head. "You won't find out how Wheeler and I communicate. I can guarantee it." He chuckled slightly. "You're not smart enough to find that out."

Balter didn't bother looking at Hennessy again, waving for the barber to come back and continue. The arrogance the man held inside oozed out through controlled releases, just enough to show the world how confident he was.

"I might not have it yet," Hennessey said. "But I'll find the evidence I need."

"Careful who you play with, lawyer. I'm not the man you want to cross."

"Is that a threat?"

"A threat?" he laughed. "All I know is that the roads are dangerous out there."

Hennessy could sense the apprehension in the man, despite his best effort to continue his macho charade. Balter pointed two fingers at him, then brought the thumb down on top as if firing a pistol.

Hennessy stood and walked out of the barbershop without another word. The meeting served its purpose. He confirmed Balter was involved.

But he wasn't sure if Balter was involved in the Miller or McGovern case—or both.

CHAPTER 18

ELLIOT MCGOVERN couldn't get his brother-in-law out of his mind. The confrontation rattled him, and his inability to get to sleep was getting worse. Each night, he tried to settle his nerves with tequila, and when that didn't work, followed it up with shots of bourbon until he passed out.

Five nights after the confrontation, he sat out on the deck, glass in one hand, open bottle in the other, staring up into the night sky as he tried to relax on a chaise lounge. After two shots, his hands began to calm, and he could feel the rapid beating in his chest subsiding.

Paul Dillion had never been a fan of his, not when McGovern began dating his sister, and certainly not when they married. He attended the wedding but left the reception soon after it began, not staying for any of the ceremonial things like the speeches or cake. Nobody seemed to miss him.

During each of their relationship milestones—engagement, marriage, anniversary dinners—there was a distinct lack of Paul showing up, or even an acknowledgment of their marriage at all. It was as if the man had effectively cut himself off from his sister's family, something McGovern felt neither here nor there about. He wasn't in the business of family politics, and it wasn't as if Paul had anything significant to offer him.

Paul Dillion was a loner, and not a very bright one. Last McGovern heard, the man worked construction in Georgia. He'd heard Savannah mentioned once, but couldn't be sure that was where the man had settled himself. The truth was, he didn't care.

He sank a couple more shots in rapid succession, considered a fifth, but changed his mind. The last one didn't feel like it hit the right spot, and he set the open bottle on the table. His eyes had begun to feel heavy, and he knew unless he went upstairs right then, he would most likely fall asleep right there on the deck.

Forcing himself up, McGovern managed to pull himself back up to his feet, but dropped the glass in the process. It shattered on impact, the explosion sending shards across the deck. He swore under his breath, stepped over the mess, and headed back inside.

Sleep didn't come quickly, nor easily, despite the fatigue plaguing his brain. He tossed and turned for hours, repeatedly bouncing across the precipice of sleep without falling beneath it. It was as if each time he had relaxed enough to drop off, something inside pushed him back up to consciousness, refusing him entry into the kingdom of rest.

By the time sleep finally allowed him into its depths, the clock read a little before five. He didn't move again until he stirred almost five hours later, waking to the sounds of someone talking to him.

Opening his eyes, the face staring back at him was a mystery at first. He jumped, pushed himself back, and hit his head on the timber bed frame.

"Ah," he snapped, his hand grabbing the top of his head and feeling for blood.

"You always were a deep sleeper when you wanted to be," Helen McGovern said as she sat on the edge of the bed. She wore no expression, her face blank and lacking any sign of affection.

"Mom? What are you doing here?"

He pushed himself up into a sitting position, wiped his eyes, and grimaced at the throbbing in his head. If the previous night's alcohol consumption didn't leave him with a headache, his mother's surprise visit had ensured he had one anyway.

"I've come to see what my son is up to now that he's a single man again. I'm surprised this room isn't filled with women every hour of the night."

He looked at her through squinting eyes, trying to bring her into focus so he could ascertain the mood she was in. He'd always been able to tell how a conversation would go based on her expression. When he managed to see her clearly, he knew this wasn't going to be a good one.

"Single man? What are you talking about? I'm a widower." Elliot climbed out of bed, adjusted his pajamas, but paused to look at his mother. "What do you want?"

"I've come to ask you why."

"Why what?"

She was still sitting on the edge of the bed, looking at him with little emotion. "Why you killed her."

As if firing on nothing but instinct, McGovern took a step forward and swung his hand without thinking. The sound of the slap fired across the room like a gunshot, his mother's head twisting sideways as he connected flush with her cheek.

He expected her to reach for her face, to cup her cheek. He expected her to cry out in pain, in shock, to let him know he gave her something to think about. He expected her to at least react.

None of that happened.

When his mother simply turned and looked back at him, a thin trickle of blood weeping from her lip, the face staring back resembled a brick. She sat stone-faced, not a shred of emotion from the slap. It rattled him the way she looked back at him, and he almost took a step back. As if to save face, he leaned down a little.

"You repeat that accusation to anybody else, and I'll make sure your life becomes a living hell." When she still didn't respond again, he added. "Now get out of my house, you cranky old cow."

He wanted to feel bad, and in a way he did as he watched her silently get up from the bed and walk toward the door.

He expected her to turn back, to tell him she was sorry, but she never did. Elliot stood his ground as he watched her disappear through the door, listened as she walked down the stairs, and left his home as the front door slammed shut.

Whatever had just happened between them, he knew that this was something she would never forget.

CHAPTER 19

HENNESSY FIRED up his truck and checked the air-conditioner. It was working, thankfully. Another storm was brewing over the Atlantic, and the humidity wasn't easing.

Judge Fedder had decided on the pre-trial motions in the Miller case. He rejected the motion on the argument that the tip-off was specific and ruled that the tip-off wasn't essential to the case. Judge Fedder made his decision on the 'totality of the circumstances,' and no rights violation had been made. Hennessy disagreed, and while it didn't help them now, it did give them grounds for appeal if they lost.

After his morning confrontation with Balter, he'd spent the day in the office, drafting a motion in limine for the Miller case, in an attempt to squash potentially prejudicial testimony against his client. As the time ticked past 9pm, he struggled to keep his eyes open.

He was sure that if his cell didn't ring at that very moment, there was a possibility he might have fallen asleep right then in the truck. Grappling with the phone, he almost dropped it, but he snagged it between two fingers and flung it onto his lap. Wendy's number stared back at him, and he answered it with a slide of his thumb.

"Hey, honey."

"Just thought I'd check in with you. Everything ok?" Wendy asked.

"Everything's A-OK down here. Just tired, that's all. Any news on Ellie?"

"You mean about her work experience at Mitchell and Turner?"

Ellie had hit Hennessy up for several recommendations about where she could spend some of her spare time while continuing her law degree. She was already interning for a law firm, but just like her father, she could never focus on just one direction at a time. She needed more, and after making a few phone calls on her behalf, he managed to track down a position with one of his old college friends.

"Just curious, that's all," he said as he pulled out of the parking lot and onto the street.

"She said they're nice people but hard workers. Each night the work day ends after 9pm, and they're expected back at 9am in the morning," Wendy commented. "You know, I found a hundred dollars on the ground when I went into town earlier today."

"A hundred dollars? It must've been a lucky day."

"Yeah, and I was wondering what I should do with it, and I thought, 'What would Jesus do?' So I turned it into wine."

He grinned, then, realizing it wasn't such a bad joke, slowly chuckled. "Ok, I'll remember that one. That was good."

"And yesterday I was watching a nature documentary about a chameleon that couldn't change colors. Yep, the poor guy had a-reptile disfunction."

Hennessy burst out laughing at the punchline.

"You like that one? I've got more, you know. Just say the word."

"Haha, no, please. I'll take a pass for now. Straight home, a hot shower, and bed for me."

"Ok, sleep well. I'll see you over the weekend."

Wendy ended the call. Although it was short, it lifted his spirits. Wendy had always known when he needed cheering up, almost as if she had some sort of telepathic connection to him. Either that, or she was just an in-tune wife.

He smiled as he passed through a green light.

The truck coming from the other direction didn't brake, running the red light as if taking direct aim at him. Hennessy had time to look at the driver grinning through the windshield as he hit the brakes of his own pickup and felt the tires lock up under him.

Gripping the wheel tight, he veered off to the right, but when the wheels locked up, he had no chance.

The other truck never veered off its target, maintaining its line without ever slowing. The vehicles clipped each other.

Hennessy's truck came to a sudden halt as it hit the back corner of the red-light runner, while the other pickup jolted violently to one side, but continued on. By the time Hennessy climbed out of the truck, the offender was gone.

He was about to climb back in as the rest of the traffic began to move, but he caught sight of a blue BMW out of the corner of his eye, the sedan's chrome mirrors catching the streetlight above.

He'd seen it before, and, as he took a closer look, he saw James Balter staring at him from the driver's side window.

Ignoring the honking of cars, he walked toward the BMW.

This was an attempt at intimidation, something he knew Balter specialized in, and he wouldn't become a victim like so many others.

Balter's BMW slowly rolled forward as Hennessy walked toward him.

Balter took a drag on a cigarette, then flicked it out the window toward the oncoming lawyer, before he accelerated away.

Hennessy froze for a moment and watched him vanish into traffic. He kept staring for a few moments, oblivious to the chaos his parked truck was causing.

By trying to intimidate him, all Balter had done was confirm Hennessy's suspicions.

CHAPTER 20

THERE WAS an ominous grayness about the city as Hennessy walked the streets the following morning. Something was brewing in the Atlantic, something big, and everyone was preparing. Supermarket shelves were empty. Shops were being boarded up. People hurried with a frantic buzz around them.

In a season full of storms, this was a big one, the news said. Flooding was to be expected in Downtown Charleston, as the arrival of the storm coincided with a king tide, but flooding was nothing new. It'd been happening for longer than anyone could remember.

Hennessy arrived at the office earlier than normal. He didn't sleep well. The weeks of investigation had taken their toll. So much information had poured in for both cases, but there was also his own involvement in a lot of it.

"You ok, Boss?" Jacinta was sitting behind her desk, looking up at him with concern. "You look like death warmed over."

"I'm fine," he managed and held out a tray with two takeaway coffees and waited for her to select her usual. "Slept terribly."

"You and me both. It's this weather. I'm just waiting for it to break. So let me warn you—today I have three speeds: on, off, and don't push your luck," she said, taking the coffee. She took a long sip and sighed with delight as she closed her eyes. "Oh, that's amazing. Thank you."

He set the briefcase down and dropped into the chair opposite her desk. As usual, it creaked under the strain.

They sat and chatted for a few minutes while drinking their coffees, before the conversation turned to work.

"Mrs. Edith Gilliam wants to meet with you today." Jacinta read the notes off her pad. "She said she's been approached by the prosecution in the McGovern case, but would like to speak with you first."

"Edith Gilliam. I haven't heard that name in a long time." Hennessy looked to the ceiling, trying to remember her face. "Where does she want to meet?"

"A café in Mount Pleasant. I've penciled it in for 11am."

Hennessy looked at his watch, nodded, and then proceeded to his separate office. He switched on his computer, replied to several emails, and reviewed the files for another case that had just come on the books. At 10:30, he left the office, catching a cab across the river toward the agreeable suburb of Mount Pleasant.

The cab pulled up to the café twenty minutes later. Hennessy thanked the driver, tipped him well, and went inside, searching for the woman he hadn't seen in almost two decades.

The Vintage Coffee Café was in a cute 1930s cottage under a large oak tree, with indoor seating for twenty-five and outdoor seating for fifty more. The interior was southern styled with narrow plank wood floors and shiplap walls, but most importantly, the café served some of the best coffee in the state. The powerful aroma of the roasted coffee beans was enough to get a caffeine hit the second a person walked in the doors.

Edith Gilliam stood and waved to Hennessy. He smiled and walked over to greet her with a hug.

"Mrs. Gilliam. It's been a long time," Hennessy said. "You look lovely."

"Oh, bless your heart, Joe Hennessy," she smiled. "I know I haven't aged well, but you always were a charmer."

Gilliam was far from the middle-aged suburban mother he remembered. She had lost weight, and as she passed into her mid-sixties, she looked healthier than ever. She embraced her gray hair, her red dress was flattering, and her skin looked healthy and vibrant. Hennessy ordered a cappuccino and sat down opposite Edith, who was already halfway through her latte.

"How are Wendy and the girls?"

"Good," Hennessy replied. "The vineyard up near Greenville keeps us all busy."

"That sounds like the retirement dream."

"Right up until the bank pressures you to repay the loan." He struggled to remember her husband's name and felt relief when his name zoomed from the shadows. "How's Doug?" He paused for a moment, searching for the child's name. "And Daisy?"

"Daisy's great. She's a very confident young woman," she said, smiling her appreciation for him remembering. "Doug passed away five years ago, and Daisy is up in Boston studying medicine. Life has a way of moving on, and if you don't keep rolling forward, you become stuck."

"I'm sorry to hear about Doug." He waited a moment before continuing. "You're still with McGovern and Brady?"

"I am. Still an administrative assistant there. Although these days, I'm more of what you'd call a part-timer. Not exactly in the office much, but I still help Harold when he needs to know the day-to-day stuff." She looked down into her coffee. "I had some health problems a few years ago. Cancer. Just after Doug passed. Harold was kind enough to keep me on, still paying me while I got treatment, and when I got better, he offered a part-time gig which I couldn't pass up. He might've been a horrible boss, but he was good to me when it mattered."

"Well, you look great."

"Thanks, Joe," she said. "Of course, I've heard about Elliot and how you and John Kirkland are representing him."

"You don't think he's innocent."

"Why do you say that?"

"Something I sense from you." Hennessy paused as the server placed the coffee in front of him. He thanked her, then brought the coffee close to his nose, taking a long whiff of the potent scent. He took a sip and placed the cup back down. "And let's face it, the McGovern family is not known for their kindness."

"If I'm going to be completely honest, then I should tell you that I also believe he did it. I know that's what Jennifer Brady told you."

"You spoke to Jennifer?"

"I did."

"And what makes you think he's guilty?"

She looked away. "Because he slapped me once." She took a moment to compose herself. "And on many other occasions, when he first started with the firm, he grabbed my butt and told me he was going to sleep with me. He was twenty-five and I was fifty-five. He loved older women, he said. It was almost a goal for him."

"I'm sorry to hear that."

"I pushed him away, and I was lucky that Harold liked me, or I would've been fired the next day." She drew a breath. "And if he did that to me, could you imagine what he would've done to his wife?"

"He thought he owned her."

"Exactly. And when she wanted to divorce him? That would've been a nightmare. Can you imagine what would have happened if she had won a large divorce settlement? There was no way Elliot would have been able to face his father, and from what I saw behind closed doors, Harold was pressuring his son about getting his life in order."

"Harold McGovern was pressuring Elliot? About what?"

"About controlling his wife. Harold had a feeling she would try to go for a nice chunky payout, and that was never going to happen. Not while he was still around. So, he used to pull Elliot into his office, and I'd hear them shouting at each other, sometimes for up to an hour." She shook her head. "What some people do to their own families for the sake of money is horrible. It breaks my heart."

"Why tell me this? You know we're representing Elliot."

"I know. I'm telling you because the prosecution approached me and asked me to testify against him."

"What did you say?"

"I told them no, but if they've approached me, you can be guaranteed that they've approached just about every woman who has worked with him. And there are many stories just like mine. I thought it was best if you heard it from me first. I was going to call Kirkland, but I don't really know him. But then I saw your name on the list, and I knew I had to give you the heads up."

"Thank you."

"You should know that if this case makes it to trial, this will be a complete character assassination. He stands no chance against it. I know at least ten women, all past employees, who would love to stand up there and testify against him. No jury is going to be able to ignore that. The picture they paint is going to be very clear."

Hennessy leaned back in his chair.

"Joe, this is impossible to win, and it's going to be a disaster for the McGovern and Brady Law Firm. You've got to encourage him to take a deal."

"Did Jennifer Brady tell you to say that?"

"She didn't have to. This is my job on the line as well."

Hennessy nodded.

One thing had become clear—McGovern's case looked impossible to win, and a lot of people wanted to see him go down.

CHAPTER 21

THE HEAVIEST rains had hit the coast further south.

Charleston caught the edge of the weather system, causing torrential rain and minor flooding around the Battery. The king tide was a problem on the best of days, but coupled with the storm, it was a major issue on the cross-city commute.

Hennessy jogged into the office building, shaking off his umbrella, and walked up the stairs to the second-floor office. He almost jumped when Jacinta called out to him as he entered. Barry Lockett sat next to her, a proud grin on his face.

"See? This is what happens when you persist with something," Jacinta said, gesturing for him to stand behind her so she could show him what was on her screen. "Barry was just showing me what he's found."

"Did you find something good?" He brushed the splashes of rain off the shoulders of his jacket.

"I don't think so," Lockett said, and then nodded to the screen. "But it might just break this thing wide open."

Hennessy walked around the back of the monitor, and Jacinta opened a window on the computer. Hennessy immediately recognized it as the inside of the restaurant McGovern had used as his alibi on the night of the murder. Before she hit play, Jacinta turned to him, saw that he was standing and pointed to one of the chairs.

"Grab one, drag it over." He did, and she didn't speak again until he was down on her level.

"Ok, so hear me out," Lockett said. "You said there had to be some sort of footage that was incriminating. I was going over the footage from the restaurant and decided to go back even further than before. The curious part is, the video inside was working fine right up until the day of the actual murder."

"Ok," Hennessy said, lacking the excitement he could see Jacinta and Lockett aiming for.

"So, when I went back and worked my way through the previous few days, I found something rather interesting."

Jacinta hit the play button, sat back, and turned the laptop a little more his way. "Check this out."

She moved her finger across the computer pad and brought the pointer over to the play bar. "Ok, five-hours, twenty-five-minutes, and twenty-seconds," she whispered under her breath, found the location, and clicked.

In the video, the frames jumped to the new timestamp, and as the video rolled, Hennessy watched a familiar face walk through the front door and take a seat near the back of the restaurant.

"James Balter," Hennessy said, his interest raised. "Fancy seeing him there."

"Yes, fancy that," Lockett said. "But wait, there's more."

Again, Jacinta moved her finger across the computer pad, moved the pointer to a new timestamp, and pressed the button. Just like it did before, the video jumped forward. When James Balter appeared in the footage a second time, Hennessy briefly wondered whether she had rewound it somehow. But that was when he noticed the man wearing a different shirt.

"He's back again."

"Yes, he is. On each of the two days before the murder, James Balter came to the restaurant and met with McGovern on the second occasion."

"Scoping the place out?"

"Maybe. But there's more."

"Still more?" Now he was beginning to be impressed, another reminder of why he had hired Lockett in the first place.

"Still more," Lockett confirmed.

Jacinta hit a couple of buttons and changed the feed to a different camera, this one located somewhere outside the building, which covered a section of the parking lot. Almost parked near the very limit of the camera's range, sat a distinctive Maserati, the license plate clearly proving who it belonged to.

"McGovern's car," Hennessy whispered.

"Yes, it is. And according to the timestamps, it shows him never leaving the parking lot during the supposed dinner which was happening inside but wasn't captured due to the broken camera."

"That's convenient."

"For him, yes."

Again, Jacinta tapped a couple of buttons, and the feed switched to a new angle.

"This is from a tennis center across the street on the night of the murder," Lockett noted. "They also have their surveillance set up, and part of it records the back of the restaurant."

Jacinta pointed across the street to the back of the building. From the new angle, it showed a backdoor that led to the restaurant's kitchen. "This video gives us another view of the area. Watch this."

This time, when she went to a specific timestamp, Jacinta sat back and let the magic of the video do its thing. Hennessy didn't notice anything specific for a few seconds, then held his breath as a familiar vehicle pulled into view. James Balter's blue BMW briefly stopped, then took off again.

"And now for the grand finale." Jacinta hit the player again, fast-forwarded the feed, and waited.

Balter's BMW returned a second time, but this time, they could make out a shadow climbing out of the car before disappearing back into the restaurant. While they couldn't make out the face of the person, they noted the distinctive shape, remarkably similar to one Elliot McGovern.

"My guess is that the prosecution is betting their entire case on this feed. And if I'm right, they'll share it with the rest of us sometime next week."

"The tennis center said the police already have this footage, and they were wondering why we didn't have it," Lockett said. "They said they'd given it to them the day after the murder."

"I bet," Hennessy whispered, watching the feed a second time in slow motion. "And I bet the prosecution is also saying that the identity of the person getting out of the vehicle needs to be verified first."

"Wouldn't it be verified already?"

"It's almost certainly verified. But these guys don't want to let the cat out of the bag too early. They want to cut down the time we have to scrutinize it."

"But they can't do that."

"No, but there's always a way around these kinds of things." Hennessy leaned back, rubbing his hand over his forehead. "And one thing's for sure."

"What's that?"

"With this footage, it's going to make McGovern's defense significantly harder."

CHAPTER 22

IT DIDN'T take Hennessy long after seeing the footage to decide his next move.

The clips had opened up a huge chasm of possibilities for him, but instead of making things easier, they'd only confused him even more. He needed answers.

Hennessy called Kirkland and delivered the news. Kirkland wasn't surprised. He expected additional evidence to arrive soon. Kirkland agreed he would talk to McGovern, while Hennessy would track down Balter.

Hennessy spent the morning in the office, reviewing the footage several times, and considering how they could get it thrown out. He asked Lockett to find Balter and give him an update on his whereabouts.

Jacinta spent the morning on the phone, trying to find a video technician that could throw doubt over the footage from the tennis center.

Hennessy had to talk to Balter. The best case scenario was that he might also be the only person able to offer McGovern a rock-solid alibi. That was, if he was willing to give one.

After a morning of frantic activity, he caught himself by the window, looking past the large oak tree and down to the street below.

"Superpowers are what I need," he said to himself. "I need the power to predict the future. Maybe then I can figure this mess out."

"Oh no," Jacinta said, standing at the office door. "They say that talking to yourself is the first sign of madness."

"I'm well past that." Hennessy turned and smiled.

"The second sign is growing hairs on the palm of your hand."

"Hairs on the palm of my hand?" Hennessy looked down at his palm, searching for any sign of newly growing hairs.

"The third sign, and the most important sign that you've gone mad, is actually looking for hairs on the palms of your hands."

Hennessy broke into a laugh. Jacinta smiled. Their laughter was interrupted by the ringing of his cell on his desk. He picked it up. It was Lockett.

"I've found him. He's right in the middle of lunch at Sweetwater Café on Market St."

"I know the place. Great staff, great service, and they have amazing shrimp and grits," Hennessy said. "Thank you. I owe you one."

"Yeah, yeah. I'll add it to your bill," Lockett mocked, but Hennessy knew he wasn't joking.

Hennessy looked at Jacinta, nodded, and told her that he'd be back in a little while. Knowing his propensity for spur-of-the-moment outings, she didn't object, simply waving him off.

He decided against taking the truck, figuring he'd cover half the two-block walk by the time he fired the engine up.

The rain had cleared, but he'd still worked up a sweat by the time he arrived at the café. He wiped his brow and stepped inside.

The restaurant was busier than normal, with every single table filled. The noise was vibrant, happy, and the lunch smells were delicious. The kitchen took up half the floor space, tucked away from the customers by a chest-height bar. The staff's enthusiasm for cooking local foods only added to the atmosphere. Balter sat alone near the front window, almost finished with his lunch burger. Hennessy didn't hesitate to make a beeline for the man, bypassing the server.

"Really?" Balter quipped as he wiped the side of his mouth with a napkin. "A man can't eat in peace?"

"You tried to run me off the road."

"Nothing to do with me," Balter grunted. "You were just in the wrong place at the wrong time. Seems you have a habit of doing that."

Hennessy ignored the comment and pulled out one of the dark wooden chairs, taking a seat opposite him. His tall frame struggled to fit on the small seat, and he leaned forward for effect. "I just had a special viewing of some footage."

"Zach Miller still trying to—"

"I'm not talking about Miller. I'm talking about Elliot McGovern. Turns out there's video evidence of you turning up at the restaurant on the night of his wife's murder. Not once, but twice, and you know what happened between when you picked McGovern up there and brought him back."

Balter froze for a second.

His eyes locked onto Hennessy's, his mouth hanging open as his tongue rolled around as if searching for the right thing to say.

Finally, he managed a comment to try and save

face.

"Well. Let's see what they do with it."

"From what I've seen, it looks like you met with McGovern a couple of times in the days immediately before the killing, then drove back and forth to the one place McGovern used as his alibi on the night of the murder. There's a video from the tennis center opposite the restaurant, and it shows you picking him up from the backdoor. Seems to me like you might be involved." He paused for effect. "Did you kill his wife?"

"Me?" He scoffed at the idea, looking away, but Hennessy could sense a sliver of nerves in the man. "In my line of work, it doesn't pay to get your own hands dirty. I'm in the clear. Regardless of what's on that tape."

"Did you drive McGovern home so he could kill his wife?"

Balter grunted, rubbed his hand over his short-cropped hair, and then turned back to Hennessy. "Just whose side are you on there, counselor?"

"I'm on the side of the truth. And only the truth is going to save Elliot McGovern."

"You do things your way, and I'll do them my way," Balter growled, keeping his voice low, locking eyes with Hennessy. "But let me warn you once, and only once. Do not throw me into your dirty trial. If you try to pin this on me to get Elliot off, then you're going to come face to face with a lot more trouble."

"You don't understand. The prosecution has the footage. It's only a matter of days before you're subpoenaed to appear in his trial. They don't know we have it yet, but once they present it to us, I can guarantee that they'll come and talk to you."

Hennessy pressed his finger into the table. "And if I were you, I'd start working out how you're going to explain it, or you'll be going down as an accessory to murder."

CHAPTER 23

HENNESSY MET with Kirkland the next day. Their opinions were the same—the outlook was dire. They spent the next two days strategizing, but there was no easy way out.

"We have to talk deals before the prosecution knows we've got our hands on this evidence," Hennessy said as he rubbed his brow, seated next to Kirkland's desk. "If they know we've seen it, and we go to them to negotiate a deal, they'll take us for everything. We have to try and get a deal for manslaughter, even if it's fifteen years."

"Agreed." Kirkland picked up his phone to buzz his assistant. "Mary, call Nadine Robinson and tell her that we wish to discuss a deal in further detail for the McGovern case."

Twenty-four hours later, they were walking through the door to the prosecution's office in the O.T. Wallace County Office Building, at 101 Meeting St.

They waited in the boardroom, seated and ready, at 2pm, but they expected to be kept waiting. It was a power play from the prosecution, showing the men that they were in control. The boardroom was long, spotless, and smelled of disinfectant. There was a painting of Charleston hanging on the right wall, a portable drinks tray sitting in the far corner, and a large television monitor against the left wall, for the times when the meetings had to be conducted online.

"I tried some of your wine last week, Joe," Kirkland made small talk. "Ordered a bottle to be sent down from Greenville. A Pinot Noir from a few years back. And I must say, I was impressed. A good delicate drop with a strong punchy overtone of flavor. I didn't even know you could grow Pinot grapes out here."

"It's hard to grow in the Lowcountry, just about impossible, but our place is on the right latitude for the wine."

"Well done," Kirkland congratulated him again. "It was a lot better than bottles that cost five times more. I've ordered another six for my cellar."

"Thank you," Hennessy nodded, then opened a file on the desk, refocusing on the case. "That email this morning was worrying. The prosecution has lodged a motion to add more witnesses, and this time they all seem to be character witnesses. We knew this was coming, but I didn't expect them to lodge fifty-five statements. Do you know what I think?"

"They're trying to bury something important in there."

"Exactly. It's an old play—try and cover us in a mountain of statements so that we miss the important one."

"None of this looks good, Joe," Kirkland kept his voice quiet in the large boardroom. "The tennis center footage looks like he was deliberately trying to cover his tracks, and he'll get destroyed by the character witnesses. We'll have to pull a rabbit out of the hat to get McGovern off on manslaughter."

There was a knock on the boardroom door, taking

them away from their conversation.

Nadine Robinson looked just as frank as she did the last time they met, her dark hair pulled back in a tight bun. Stone-faced, she sat down at the head of the table, the case notes sitting before her in a neat stack. Flanked by two other prosecutors, she began.

"Good to see you again, Gentlemen," Robinson said, opening a file. "I'm glad to see we're back at the negotiating table."

"Yes. Let's see if we can make this work," Kirkland began. "Y'all know how this goes—we argue and argue and argue, and try to get our points across. But truthfully, in this case, it would be best for everyone to come to an agreement earlier than later."

"Let's hope we can do that," Robinson said, agreeing with words alone. "We can begin to talk Section 16-3-20."

Kirkland sat forward, shocked by the reference. "I hope you're not talking about the death sentence?"

"It's still an option."

"Nobody has been sentenced to death since 2011," Hennessy said.

"Mostly because pharmaceutical companies refuse to supply the drugs for lethal injection," Robinson said. "But all that may change soon. The firing squad is back on the table."

"The firing squad?" Kirkland scoffed, sitting back in his chair. "What is this? The 1800s?"

"There are no aggravating factors under Title 16, Chapter 3, Article 1, Section 16-3-20 of the South Carolina Code of Laws." Hennessy looked over his notes. "You won't be able to chase a death penalty."

"We've come across new evidence that may change that," Robinson said, then she turned her laptop around. "We're about to enter this video into discovery, and it makes for very interesting viewing."

She hit play and presented the footage from outside the tennis center. The two lawyers pretended to watch it, both remaining expressionless as the grainy footage showed a figure that looked like McGovern leaving the restaurant and returning fifteen minutes later.

When the footage came close to its end, Robinson paused the video on McGovern's shadowy figure.

"This is very robust evidence that Mr. McGovern wasn't in the restaurant at the time of the murder. This makes it clear that the murder was thoughtfully planned." Robinson looked at Hennessy and then at Kirkland. "But by the look on your faces, you've already seen this footage." She smiled. "That's why you wanted to meet and discuss options for a deal, but you've already played your hand."

Kirkland didn't respond, staring at the table. Robinson waited a few moments before she continued. "The best offer you'll receive is this—we don't chase the death penalty and make it thirty years. That's the best offer your client will ever see."

CHAPTER 24

ELLIOT MCGOVERN didn't believe in family.

It was a secret he'd carried inside him for the better part of his life. He knew that if his father ever found out, it would mean the end of whatever protection the man provided him. That, as well as all the financial benefits he enjoyed. Having a share in one of the most prestigious law firms in the city meant more to Elliot McGovern than anything, even his pride, which he'd had injured on more than a few occasions in run-ins with the family's patriarch.

Kirkland had called and delivered the news about the footage from the tennis center. McGovern had no excuses left, so he kept his mouth shut. Thirty years was as low as the prosecution will go, Kirkland said, along with no parole.

As he prepared for a late afternoon jog, he remembered the run-in he had with his father that morning. His heart beat hard in his chest, and it took him more than a few minutes to calm himself. He sat on the edge of the bed, one running shoe on, the other held in his hand as he sat up and collected himself.

It wasn't so much the actual fight itself which had angered him to such an extent, but the fact his father had driven all the way out to his home just to repeat what he already knew.

"We take care of our own," Harold had said. "One way or another, we take care of them in our own way. I can get you out of this."

"Like the way you take care of Mom by keeping her on the end of your leash in some ramshackle place where you can keep an eye on her?"

Harold didn't like that, becoming enraged in a way Elliot hadn't seen in years. He began ranting and raving about how he'd worked hard to earn every dollar, how he wasn't about to give it to some freeloading gold digger, all words which Elliot refused to stand still for.

The pair clashed when Harold got into his son's face and told him he was an embarrassment to the family for bringing so much tarnished attention down on them. Elliot struck back by telling his father that he wasn't the only one who worked hard for their money, that he also worked his butt off, which brought Harold to a raspy chuckle.

Elliot never wanted to punch his father in the face more than he did at that moment. But he knew if he started, he mightn't find a way to stop himself, with years of pent-up anger rising in one massive rush.

He ended up rooted to his spot, unable to move as he watched his father continue mocking him, telling him to get his life in order. The firm had no time for bad press, and Elliot needed to make things right.

For Harold McGovern, facts never mattered as much as the publicity did. To him, it was all about the bottom line, and if he could twist things in such a way as to increase his profits, then the method used didn't matter.

Elliot couldn't push the image of his father laughing at him from his mind, the rage boiling up to the very edge of implosion. His fingers shook as he gripped his shoe, the laces jiggling back and forth in mid-air as he closed his eyes to try and suppress the anger.

"I can get you out of the country," Harold had said. "Get your life together, and start somewhere else."

Elliot told him to get out of his house. He told him he'd beat the charges. Harold responded by telling him that he had no chance of winning in court.

He reminded himself of his father's age and how each passing day, every passing hour, brought him closer to the moment when he would retire from the firm altogether. Elliot knew the day would come when he would get the phone call, which would propel him to the top of the ladder, when he would be in charge, and he could finally do things his way.

A smile formed on his face, the corners of his mouth moving ever so slightly into position as the rest of him calmed. It was a thought which he'd managed to bottle up, to only take a sip from when he truly needed to taste that moment. At seventy-five, he knew it wouldn't be long until Harold McGovern would finally hand him the keys to the kingdom and walk off into the sunset.

"Yeah, one day," he whispered, savoring the grin as he refocused his attention on the shoe and attempted to slip it on. Once the laces were tied, he stood and went to the window, ensuring his father's Mercedes was gone. Only once his breathing had returned to normal did he venture downstairs.

The late afternoon heat didn't feel too bad as he stepped outside. He walked toward the end of the drive, paused a couple of times to stretch, then slowly jogged down the road. It didn't take long for his father's face to disappear from his thoughts, moving aside to make room for something else.

Elliot had always enjoyed running along the foreshore, one of the many reasons he considered buying his home in the first place. He loved being close to the ocean, smelling the air as he jogged along the walkways that crisscrossed the area.

Twenty minutes in, he took a breather from running and slowed to catch his breath. There weren't as many people around as he would typically see, which is why the man in the black top and red baseball cap stood out to him. He wasn't completely convinced, but something told him the man was following him.

He'd noticed him earlier in the run, leaning against a bench as he passed by. The stranger looked up at him as he ran past, then immediately followed at a distance. If the path only continued one way, it mightn't have been so obvious, but with several forks in the road, and Elliot choosing his own unique way, he found it odd that the man continued to follow him.

He almost considered turning back and running at the stranger, to question him on why he was following him. But while he might have had an abundance of courage in his mind, he knew he wasn't that guy. Not considering himself quite on the cowardice level, he knew he lacked the self-confidence to do what he wished he could.

As he took another look back, he saw a second man. This one also paused a little further behind the first. This time he thought they were following, perhaps under contract to take him out. Before he knew it, wild thoughts began flooding his brain, with everything from his father taking out a hit on him to his maid.

He wasn't a fighter, never had been. It was one of the downsides to having money, with most of his threats able to be paid off before they could follow through. Elliot stole several nervous glances behind him before turning toward home.

The run back wasn't nearly as relaxing as the first half. His heart had again taken a dark interest in what his brain continued to manifest, his heartbeat rising and falling with each new imagined scenario. He continued taking quick looks back, seeing the same red baseball cap following behind each time.

When he turned for another look behind to see whether the pursuers had followed him home, his nerves got the better of him, and his feet got tangled, sending him crashing onto the pavement.

His hands felt on fire as tiny spots of blood appeared across his palms. To add to the pain, his knees had also taken a decent scrape, but the second he saw the car parked at the end of the road, none of it mattered. The heat in the wounds faded out entirely as he recognized the car, the distinctive patch of rust on the hood standing out like a neon sign.

Elliot looked wildly from one side of the street to the other, his frayed nerves giving him the appearance of an escaped mental patient. If Paul Dillion's car was parked in his street, then the men following him were more than likely paid by him, his ex-brother-in-law ready for revenge.

Fearing himself a target out in the open, Elliot broke into a run, forgetting about the small slivers of blood running down each leg. With each step, he waited for the familiar pop of a gun, a rogue bullet tearing into his back as the hitmen made good on their contract.

He didn't slow until he reached the front door of his home, bursting through the front door and slamming it behind him before securing each of the three locks. But instead of hiding behind the door, he leaned sideways and gazed out the window, carefully peering around the corner just enough to see the driveway beyond.

Only when he was sure he wasn't followed all the way home did he step back from the door, feeling like a man on the edge of a nervous breakdown. He reached for the handgun stored in the hallway cabinet.

He didn't have many options left.

CHAPTER 25

HENNESSY SPENT the morning before work wandering through upper King St, a takeout coffee in his hand.

When he came to the Charleston Music Hall, the location where Zach Miller had been found with the backpack of cocaine, he paused on the other side of the street and leaned his shoulder against a tree. He studied the beautiful building as his own memories of the place came flooding back.

Originally built as a passenger train depot before the Civil War, the building functioned as one of the most eclectic venues in the Lowcountry. It was well-loved and well-attended, with crowds swelling on the streets outside almost every night. The 19th-century Gothic Revival building was used as a venue for concerts, dance, theater & comedy shows, and with only 1000 seats, it was an intimate experience for any performer. The space combined historical elegance with modern style, and with amazing acoustics, there wasn't a bad seat in the house.

When he finished his coffee, he threw the cup in the trash and headed to his office, fifteen minutes away on Church St. As he walked, the morning sun warmed up the air, and by the time he reached his destination, a small amount of sweat had begun to build on his brow.

"Zach Miller called again," Jacinta said as he stepped inside. "He needs to meet with you today. He asked if you could drive out to his place on James Island?"

"Good. I need to talk to him about a new witness that has stepped forward. Let him know I can get out there after two," Hennessy agreed. "I could do with some time out of the office."

The drug trafficking trial date was getting closer, and the closer they came to a trial, the more nervous his client became.

Zach Miller wasn't the only thing on Hennessy's mind, though. And neither was Elliot McGovern. Something else had crept into his subconscious, slowly invading his mind a little piece at a time.

As he checked the days on the calendar, this wasn't something he could avoid, and as he began to think about it, he reminded himself that it was something he needed to face. The coming day was one of the hardest for him each year, not just for him, but also for Wendy. It was Luca's birthday. A time of the year when they returned to the one place where the three of them could be together, to reminisce, to cry, to grieve the way a parent needed to. Tomorrow was a day when he knew he would be off the grid, uncontactable, when the rest of the world ceased to exist for twenty-four hours.

Lockett had checked in.

He'd found no leads about how Balter and Wheeler communicated, but he wasn't stopping his search. He periodically checked their trash cans, looking for clues about their lives to link them together.

Hennessy pleaded with him to continue trying.

They were his key to exposing the drug set-up.

Zach Miller lived on James Island, a short ten-minute drive from Downtown Charleston and a further ten to Folly Beach. Situated near the deep blue waters of the Charleston Harbor, and near the twisting Stono and Folly Rivers, James Island had scenic marsh views, a plethora of established trees, and a laid-back culture.

Zach Miller's home on the edge of the township was welcoming. A nice garden, nice architecture, nice interior design. He had nice furniture, nice flooring, and nice paintings. Nothing offensive, nothing outstanding, and nothing out of the ordinary. He'd been married once, but that marriage broke down two years ago, and while she took a large sum of cash, Miller was left with his two-story home in his hometown. There was a recording studio at the rear of the yard, something he'd spent $150,000 building, but apart from that, the musician's home was no different from any suburban abode.

"Mr. Hennessy, hey," Miller said as he opened the door and, for once, Hennessy thought he appeared far less wound up than usual. He wondered whether the guy just had a bad case of anxiety, and that perhaps his home was the only place where he could relax. For a man who made a living up on stage in front of thousands of people, that level of anxiety must have been torture.

Miller led him through to the living room.

Seeing the man in his own environment showed Hennessy a side he hadn't considered. Dressed in board shorts and a white t-shirt, he looked the picture of Zen. He offered Hennessy a soda, and then they moved to the backyard, taking seats on the porch overlooking a small pool, a grassed area, and the recording studio, which was about the size of a double car garage.

"Before you ask me some questions," Hennessy began. "I need to inform you that a new witness has stepped forward. A man named Stefan Moore. Do you know him?"

"I don't think so."

"He's testifying that he saw you snort cocaine backstage after the show on the 5th of September."

"What?" He shook his head, a confused look washing over his face. "He's lying. I never did that. Who is he?"

"We don't know yet. The new statement has only come through this morning, but there's no need to panic. What we'll do is an investigation into who this man is. My investigator is very good at pulling apart people's backgrounds. He'll investigate everything about this man, and we'll see if he has any links to the other people in the case, including Wheeler. He'll look into Stefan Moore's work history, his family history, and residential history. He'll look at the addresses he's lived, he'll check the internet for any references to his name or nicknames, and he'll go through Moore's social media profiles with a fine-tooth comb."

"Good luck with that. Most people have their social media privacy settings on tight."

"That won't stop my investigator. He'll create a new social media profile with a photo of someone that looks around Stefan Moore's age, perhaps even female if Moore is single. He'll befriend several of Moore's friends first, and join similar groups. Once those links are established, he'll send Moore a friend request, citing their shared history, and mention a time they probably met. When people see that a new friend has mutual friends and shared interests, most people accept the request. Then, he has full access to his social media profiles."

"Wow." Miller expressed his surprise. "I wonder if that's happened to me before?"

"Only if someone wants to look at your profiles," Hennessy responded. "What is it you wanted to talk to me about?"

"There's so much hate in the case." He rubbed his hand over his brow. "I wanted to know why the prosecution hates me so much? It's like they want to eat me for breakfast."

"That's the adversarial process, and it's the system we have. It allows opposing parties to present their side of a case and attempt to sway the jury to rule in their favor. People often argue that the system is fair and less prone to abuse than the opposing approach, which is the inquisitional approach, because it allows less room for the state to be biased against the defendant."

"What's the inquisitional approach?"

"It's where the court actively investigates the case. That approach is open to fraud and corruption because the responsibility is on the court to investigate. In an adversarial system, the court acts as a referee between the prosecution and the defense. The entire process is a contest between two parties, and that's why it's so aggressive."

Miller nodded with a blank face, taking the information in.

"What did you want to let me know about?" Hennessy asked.

"I needed to let you know about a run-in I had

with Preston Wheeler about a week before the drug bust," Miller said. "I don't think I mentioned it before, but it happened in his office during a briefing on an upcoming gig."

"You mentioned one," Hennessy reminded him.

"Yes, but not this one. I had actually forgotten about it entirely, because at the time, I was too caught up with the whole decision not to sign the new contract."

"Why does this one stand out?"

"Because it's not about the actual meeting I had with him, but what happened after. The clash we had that day wasn't the first when it came to me signing on with him again. It was like the third. Each time, he tried to pressure me into signing on the dotted line, using different sweeteners to try and seal the deal. But that day, I think he realized that no matter what he offered me, I was gone. He may as well have kissed me goodbye that day."

"So, why does that help?"

"Because it was the next day that I saw him talking to James Balter."

"You saw him speaking with Balter?"

"I did, in a diner not far from his office."

"That's going to help." Hennessy tapped his finger on the side of the can. "The best way to persuade an audience, and in this case our jury is the audience, of the truth is not through legal jargon, but rather through compelling storytelling. By combining credibility, logic, and emotion, we can create a compelling narrative that convinces the jury of our truth. And every great story needs a villain. Balter and Wheeler are our villains."

"Is that what we're going to say? That they set me

up?"

"That's our best option," Hennessy said. "We go to trial in a couple of weeks, and we've got to find something that links them to the case. I have my investigator on it, and he's searching for that one piece of evidence that will be compelling enough to get the prosecution to throw this thing out."

"And clear my name," Miller added. "That's what this is about."

Hennessy nodded. "And to clear your name."

CHAPTER 26

JOE HENNESSY sat in silence, the engine switched off, with rain pattering on the roof of the pickup. The soft tinkling added to the grief-stricken ambiance, the windows slowly beginning to fog as the moisture in the cabin built up.

He stared out toward the front yard where his son had taken his first steps. The tree where he first learned to climb still stood in the very center, the branch he used to pull himself up hanging much lower to the ground than the grieving father remembered. The window, which had sat open most days, still held the American flag sticker his son had put up one Fourth of July.

The memories flooded him like a raging torrent, each tiny sliver of the house offering yet another memory of a boy long gone. The pain he felt in his chest rose and fell with each heartbreaking sob, the pain radiating through his clamped fingers that were tightly gripping the steering wheel.

Joe didn't fight the grief, letting the pain course over him like a summer storm. This had been the reason he had made the trip, something he secretly did when the memories became too intense. This was his way of dealing with the loss of a child, to revisit the very heart of the memories and let Luca himself fill him once more.

Hennessy ended up starting the truck again a little after 6am. Wiping away the tears felt just as painful as turning the pickup back toward the main road, taking him away from the only place where he truly felt his son's presence.

As he drove, the skies cleared, and by the time he hit the city's outer limits, an incredible sunrise lit up the eastern horizon. Hennessy pulled the truck over at one point, climbed out, and stood on the edge of the road as he watched Luca put on a light show for him. Silently watching it, the heaviness of the day rose with that dawn, and as he climbed back inside, he wondered whether he would have the strength to get through its entirety.

Wendy was driving down from the vineyard. Despite her objections, Hennessy had convinced Wendy that he would pick her up from Columbia, an hour and forty-five minute drive away. There was something about them driving to Charleston as a couple that felt right to him.

He drove to the state capital in silence, staring at the road and yet barely seeing it. Inside, it was a never-ending battle to keep his emotions in check, long enough to get to the place where he could finally grieve in private. He only stopped for boiled peanuts.

When he pulled up to the truck stop, he found Wendy already waiting.

"Hey," he called. The smile she returned told him exactly what he already knew, her struggle with the day mirroring his own.

"Hey there, yourself," she said, locked her car, and came to the truck. Beautiful, sweet Wendy, the woman who had loved and cared about him for the better part of three decades.

Wendy climbed in and reached across the seat, kissing him on the lips. But like the pain in her eyes, the kiss felt flat, almost lifeless. He didn't say anything, only smiled and put the truck into gear. Once they were out on the road, he reached over and held her hand as he drove, feeling her warmth as he fought back the coldness inside.

They drove mostly in silence, the radio remaining off for the trip. The small conversations they had felt as flat as the kiss, each knowing the other's struggles. The one good thing was that the silence didn't feel uncomfortable. In twenty years, they had grown accustomed to how the day affected the other and understood how to accept it.

As he drove through the outskirts of Charleston, Joe remembered Margaret Taylor, a grief counselor one of his old colleagues had put him in touch with a few months after Luca's funeral. It was the one secret he had never shared with Wendy, feeling as if it was something he needed to do on his own.

The woman had opened his eyes, not only on the grief and how to deal with it, but also what it meant. There was so much more to it than just plain old pain and torment. But it was one piece of advice he remembered above all else, her voice returning as he drove.

"The intensity of grief never changes," she had said. "Some people think so, but that's not it. What changes is your body's ability to accept it. Once it learns how to deal with it, it becomes easier."

One of Hennessy's biggest fears in the months and years after Luca had died, was that by letting the grief diminish, he was losing his son all over again, the connection between them vanishing into nothingness.

He couldn't bear to imagine life without him, and the idea that, in time, his grief would wither away completely just about killed him. Hennessy had always believed that Margaret Taylor's advice was what had saved him.

By the time they reached their destination, both felt the intensity build up as the moment of the day caught up with them.

"I know you've never forgiven yourself, Joe, but it's time. Forgiveness strips you of anger and resentment, and it allows for growth in God. Forgiveness allows growth in life," Wendy said. "Holding onto that pain, all that grief, only suffocates you."

"The pain is all I have left of him," Joe whispered. "If I let go of that, I let go of him."

Wendy held his hand tight as he turned the truck into the parking lot. He found a space near the front, pulled into it, then killed the engine. As if telepathically linked, both of them hesitated to climb out, both sitting in silence as they stared out toward the front gates of the cemetery.

"We should do this," Wendy finally said, and Joe gave her a faint nod.

They walked through the gates hand-in-hand, both wearing sunglasses, not to shield themselves from the sun, but to hide their grief from the world. Hennessy took a quick glance to his side and saw Wendy's lip quivering, the pain as raw as it had been the first time they walked the same path. He gave her hand a squeeze, pulled Wendy closer, and swallowed hard.

When they reached the place where so many tears had already fallen, they stood before the gravestone, reading the inscription both of them had taken days to agree on. Wendy placed a photo of their son at the foot of the gravestone, his innocent eyes smiling back at them from better days. Seeing his face was the last push both of them needed for their grief to finally flow.

When they couldn't stand anymore, they sat down. They each took turns to talk to their child, sharing the details of what events had taken place since the last time they visited. Wendy had brought a small toy with her, a transformer.

As his wife chatted to their son, Joe remembered the eulogy he gave, barely able to get the words out between bouts of crying. At first, he was embarrassed to cry so much, the stoic man unable to hold back his emotions, but time had taught him that it didn't matter. He remembered the photos that were displayed at the funerals and the wake. Much of the day was a blur, but he still had the hand-written eulogy. He took it out occasionally, and read over it. The pages were stained with tears, the words slightly smudged, but he would never throw it out.

He ended the eulogy with the words, "Love means there's no end. Not today, not tomorrow, and not a single breath I take, will be without love for you. In the stars, in the oceans, and in the woods, you will find my love. I've had the opportunity to love you, to feel deeply, and there is no end to that love. To my beautiful Luca, I will love you always. Rest in peace."

For three hours, Wendy and Joe sat by Luca's grave, singing him happy birthday, talking to him as if he was sitting beside them, and sharing their life with him. When the tears fell, they fell hard, the crying punctuated by the sobbing of grieving parents. They laughed, sharing family stories. The emotional rollercoaster took them from the highest highs to the lowest lows.

When they finally managed to say their goodbyes again, Wendy and Joe were exhausted, emotionally and physically drained. They returned to the truck supporting each other, climbed back into the cabin, and dropped into the seat. While the initial plan had been to drive back to Columbia that afternoon, they both knew it wasn't going to happen.

"Casey is staying at Emma's tonight," Wendy whispered to him, and Joe looked at her, tried to force a smile, and simply nodded. If nothing else, it meant he could spend the night in the arms of his wife, and it was exactly what she wanted as well.

CHAPTER 27

"HOW WAS it?" Jacinta asked as Hennessy walked through the office door. "Was it a good weekend with Wendy?"

"It was lovely," Hennessy replied. After Luca's birthday, he returned to the vineyard and spent the weekend readying the land for the months ahead. He'd spent the time with his wife and his sixteen-year-old daughter, Casey, laughing, cooking, and doing repairs around the vineyard. He loved working on the land. Rolling up his sleeves, getting dirty, working hard to produce something that others could enjoy. The vineyard had captured his Lowcountry heart, as did the fresh air and rolling mountains of Upstate South Carolina. "I only wish it'd been longer."

"I can imagine. I'm almost sorry you had to drag yourself back here."

"Almost?"

"Well, you have to pay me, and I am a momma, so you know. Plus, red wine isn't cheap, and there are some days I need it more than others."

He laughed, asked her to join him in his office, and led the way.

He opened the blinds and slid one of the windows open. After the fresh air of the vineyard, he didn't want to face the prospect of recycled building air, the musty stench of chemicals and moisture robbing him of nature itself. Sitting on the second floor and facing away from the main road meant the toxic fumes from traffic weren't quite as bad, and if that was the extent of fresh air in the city, then that's what he got.

Jacinta took him through the week ahead—Jamal Lincoln, the prosecutor in the Miller case, was due that morning, he had meetings with Kirkland and McGovern lined up, and he had to attend court on Friday to represent a client on his DUI charges. The Miller case was due for pre-trial motions the following week, before it went to trial in the days after that. They talked about managing the workload and filing the cases, and Jacinta suggested he should hire another lawyer. He shook his head. He couldn't afford that. Not yet.

After spending the morning planning their week, there was a knock at the door. He looked at his watch.

"11:05am, Monday morning." Jacinta stood, walked out to the reception area, and greeted the arrival. She returned to Hennessy's office and noted, "Jamal Lincoln is here to see you."

"Send him through."

Hennessy waited by his desk as Jacinta went and got his first appointment of the day.

"Mr. Lincoln." Hennessy stood and offered his hand as the prosecutor entered. "It's good to see another young prosecutor. It's great to know that the future of the Circuit Solicitor's Office is in good hands."

"True Southern charm," Lincoln smiled. Lincoln's handshake was firm, solid, the type that a man could respect. "Despite being down here fifteen years, I'm not quite used to it yet."

"Please, take a seat." Hennessy opened his hand and pointed to the chair in front of his desk. "I hear you're from Harlem originally?"

"I grew up there. Good spot, great people. I've still got family up there. But I had the opportunity to attend the University of South Carolina, and then I got a job with the Circuit Solicitor's Office." Lincoln placed his briefcase next to him and sat down. "I love it down here now. It feels like home."

"Usually, there's an arrogance to big city folk who move here—like they think they're a notch above us small city locals, but you seem quite relaxed."

"You won't hear any arrogance from me."

"I hope not, but I'm also surprised you scored the job. South Carolinians love South Carolinians, and we tend to have an inherent distrust for northerners."

"Hey, I promise I'm not a Yankee," Lincoln raised his hands in the air and smiled. "I support the Mets."

Hennessy laughed, and Lincoln laughed with him, breaking any tension. Lincoln had a wide smile, his set of pearly whites almost glowing as he talked. He smoothed his blue tie down the center of his shirt and adjusted his sleeves, exposing his shiny pair of cufflinks. He crossed one leg over the other, brushing a small piece of dust off his polished brown shoes.

"This is a big case for a young man like you," Hennessy said. "A star like Zach Miller will demand media attention, and you'll have to hold a press conference with the news crews at some point."

"That's why they wheeled out this pretty smile." He smiled again, this time a little forced. "But I'm not the only one who seems to love big cases. I see that you're doing a lot of the media for the McGovern case. That was a smart move by the McGoverns. Kirkland is a brilliant lawyer, but he comes off as very arrogant. Putting you in front of the media makes the whole family almost likable. So how's that case going?"

"I don't talk about my other cases."

"Come on now. We're all talking in the office. I see Kirkland filed another motion at the last hearing, so that'll hit the courts in five weeks? What are you going for—that he didn't do it, and you've got evidence that someone else did? Or are you saying the one-arm man did it?"

Hennessy shook his head.

"Alright, I get it. You don't talk about your other cases." Lincoln held his hands up. "So why don't we talk about Mr. Miller and the backpack full of drugs that were found in his dressing room?"

"That's a good idea."

"Now, I love the attention, but I also know this isn't the best type of publicity for your client. So why don't we settle it here and now?"

"Another offer for Miller?"

"Down to drug possession. Five years in prison, with one year suspended. Bonus for time already served with the ankle monitor, and he's only looking at four and a half years."

"Four and a half years?" Hennessy raised his eyebrows. "He doesn't want to do four and a half days."

"It's not about what he wants. It's about the law, and it's about justice. Just because he's rich and famous doesn't mean he gets to avoid the consequences of his actions." Lincoln picked up his briefcase, reached into it, and removed two files. "The first file is the new offer, signed and ready to be accepted. And the second file is the discovery information. We've added new witnesses and their statements, and I'm sure you'll find it interesting reading."

Hennessy took the files from his hands. He ignored the first file but opened the second, looking over the file and scanning the lines of information. He read the first few pages before he arrived at the extended witness list. "I see you've finally added Preston Wheeler to the prosecution witness list."

"We have."

"And I trust that his testimony is also in this file?"

"It is."

"But I don't see James Balter on the list anywhere?"

"James Balter," Lincoln nodded slowly. "He's not on the witness list because we're not calling him."

"But you know who he is."

"Of course. And we also know that you're planning to use him as a diversion from the facts. We can see it coming, Mr. Hennessy, and you can be assured that unless you make it clear in your opening statement, we'll be objecting to any indication that Mr. Balter planted the drugs."

"You're suggesting that he did?"

"Now, now, that's not what I said. So, do you think your client will take the deal?"

"I'll take it to him." Hennessy closed the file on his desk. "But I don't think he's going to accept it."

"Then I'll see you in court, Mr. Hennessy," Lincoln stood. "And I'll make sure that Mr. Miller gets what's coming to him."

Hennessy walked Lincoln to the foyer, shook his

hand, and wished him well. Once he was sure that Lincoln was gone, he turned to Jacinta. "It's time to issue a trial subpoena for James Balter."

CHAPTER 28

KIRKLAND CALLED again. "Elliot McGovern took out a restraining order on his brother-in-law."

"Paul Dillion? About time. Surprised it took him this long."

"I think you should chat with him. He could've made a statement to the prosecution, and I'd like to know what he told them."

"Then you should call him."

"Come on, Joe," Kirkland scoffed on the phone. "A man like Paul Dillion isn't going to talk to a man like me. He wouldn't even give me the time of day. But you're a farmer at heart. You're a man of the land. He'd respect that. You'll connect with Dillion better than me or my investigators."

Hennessy hated to admit it, but he was right. He agreed with Kirkland and ended the call, jumping straight on the phone to Lockett. By the afternoon, the Australian had information on Dillion's routine.

"He's been working on a construction site in Savannah," Lockett stated. "His daily routine is to work until four, then head to a bar named The Broken Knuckle until midnight."

Hennessy thanked him, looked at his watch, and then decided to make the two-hour drive south.

He loved Savannah. The enchanting Southern city was an escape where art, architecture, trendy boutiques, great food, and ghost stories were all set under a veil of Spanish moss.

He loved it even though it outlawed lawyers when founded in 1733, with the original founders writing that the city should be 'free from that pest and scourge of mankind called lawyers.'

He smiled as he drove south, soulful blues playing on the radio, weaving between traffic on the Coastal Highway, Route 17. After the easy two-hour drive, Hennessy pulled into the parking lot opposite the bar.

In a residential area, the stand-alone building had seen better days. The dark brown outside lacked any signage. The door looked like it had been broken and replaced more times than one could count, and the sidewalk outside had trash blowing along it. It was opposite a small Baptist church, a takeout restaurant specializing in wings, and small stand-alone homes.

As he watched the entrance from his car, Hennessy searched online for information about The Broken Knuckle. According to the reviews, when Randy Mason, the owner, had first purchased the place twenty years ago, he'd taken offense to a couple of bikers conducting their business in his bar and had taken care of them personally. During the scuffle, he had broken every knuckle on both hands, thereby christening his premises with a new name.

The bar was mentioned in several news articles for being the location of a dozen drug busts, and numerous brutal assaults. Fights seemed as common as hookups.

Hennessy took a deep breath and headed inside. The bartender gave him a cursory glance, huffed, and returned his attention to wiping a glass.

The small bar was dark, and the stench rocked his

senses as soon as he stepped through the door. A thick slurry of urine and stale beer filled his nostrils, mixed with an unhealthy dose of cigarette smoke, the aroma almost strong enough to taste. The lack of lighting did little to help improve the setting, although it did manage to cast a shadow dark enough to hide the floor.

Paul Dillion was hugging a Budweiser, the glass gripped tightly between both hands. Despite people standing on either side of him, he spoke to nobody, keeping to himself. He looked lost but felt comfortable surrounded by strangers. He didn't want attention but needed people around him. It was as if he needed a direct contradiction to every emotion he was feeling.

Dillion wore a dirty gray sweater, which covered his Hi-vis top. His hands were stained with grease and oil, and he hid his receding hairline under an old cap.

"Paul Dillion?" Hennessy approached, and the bartender eyed him cautiously. The men around Dillion stopped talking, staring at Hennessy.

Dillion turned to look at Hennessy, whose white shirt and black trousers looked out of place in the worker's bar. "You a cop?"

"Not a cop."

"Detective?"

"Not a detective. Not even with the police force."

That seemed to relax everyone in the bar, who then returned to their conversations. The man next to Dillion gave up his stool and moved to the other end of the bar, where a game of darts was taking place. Hennessy sat down on the vacated stool.

"Who are you then, and what'da ya want?"

"My name is Joe Hennessy. I'm a lawyer."

"And what are ya doing here?"

"I'm here to talk to you. I need to know what you know about Elliot McGovern."

Dillion gripped his beer tighter. Hennessy was surprised it didn't break under the force.

"That man murdered my sister." He shook his head slowly. "And I did nothing about it."

"How do you know he murdered her?"

"She used to tell me about the beatings. I think she told me because she hoped I would step in and help her."

"Did you?"

"No. I let her down. I let my baby sister down," he whispered. "I was a coward. I was scared of the guy's money and what he could do to me. If I laid a hand on him, he would've had me locked up for life. But that doesn't matter now, does it? He killed her."

"How sure are you that he killed her?"

"Sure enough. And I'm going to testify for you guys in a few months. You're with the prosecution, aren't you?"

Hennessy didn't correct him. He didn't need that level of trouble.

"And I'll say whatever I need to say to take him down," Dillion continued, stopping only to take another swig of his Budweiser. "And if I can't take him down in court, then I'll take him down any way I can. He won't get away with it." He turned to Hennessy. "But I've heard that he'll plead guilty before then. Is that why you're here? To tell me he's taken the deal?"

"No," Hennessy replied carefully, not wishing to aggravate the situation into a bar fight. "I'm here to tell you that he's been offered a deal, but he's rejected it."

"You came all this way to tell me that?"

"I did." Hennessy stood. "Thank you, Mr. Dillion. We'll talk again soon."

Hennessy patted the man on the shoulder and quietly left the bar. He didn't need Dillion to work out that he was working for McGovern.

As he headed back to his pickup truck, he was satisfied that the meeting had told him everything he needed to know—Paul Dillion was the worst sort of witness. He was a man willing to lie through his teeth to ensure McGovern was convicted.

CHAPTER 29

ELLIOT MCGOVERN walked through the front door of his home after a night out at the club.

Seeing Stephen Clements was one thing and drinking with him had started as the high point of an otherwise boring night. Clements had been something of a reprieve for him, and he enjoyed sharing old war stories from back in the day. But when the former NFL quarterback questioned McGovern about the murder, things turned south.

Clements questioned him like a seasoned detective, interrogating the man with rapid-fire precision. When McGovern stumbled, Clements accused him of murder. McGovern exploded, his ranting and raving becoming so loud and animated that every single set of eyes in the club turned to watch the spectacle.

Clements sat bug-eyed, watching Elliot as he threw one accusation after another at him. Not wanting negative press from other patrons, management soon showed up with their security in tow and escorted the two men from the premises. The problem was that Elliot had no intention of leaving, turning his attention to the newcomers and unloading a fresh round of ranting that could compete with broadside cannons.

Things were never going to end well when he began pointing his finger at the club manager. Harvey

Lewis wasn't the kind of man who took criticism on the chin, and when Elliot questioned the man's integrity accompanied by a finger prodding into his shoulder, security finally stepped in.

There was no hesitation as they walked him out of the club. They told him not to come back.

At that point, he found his mind running wild with crazy and outlandish thoughts. For one, he was positive Dillion had followed him home, maybe to retaliate for the whole restraining order mess. As he closed the front door behind him and faced the empty home lying before him, he tried to fine-tune his senses to detect where the intruder might be hiding.

But fine-tuning one's senses while still processing a few too many cognacs was something that never ended well. Elliot heard things he was sure confirmed Dillion's presence in the home, from random creaks upstairs to distinctive clicking coming from the kitchen. It was as if the entire house had come alive, calling to him in a jumble of different forms of communication.

During daylight hours and when not under the influence of a few pints of alcohol, he would have recognized the noises for what they were, like the fridge, freezer, ducted cooling, and more. But standing in the hallway with the last traces of whiskey still on his tongue, courtesy of the final few shots he'd had, the very ambiance of the home seemed to have turned against him.

"Who's hiding?" He called out the question louder than he expected and almost jumped as his echo bounced back at him. Not wanting to appear scared in case someone really was watching him, he called out again, louder than the previous time. "Where are you?"

He grinned as the echoes bounced around the huge foyer. With the ceiling a full two stories above, it made his voice sound as if he was standing inside a concert hall.

When something loud clicked in the kitchen, he froze.

"Who's there?" he called out, his chest tightening as he took a couple of steps back.

When his cellphone rang, he jumped back even further, hit the door with his back, and screamed again.

He fumbled the phone from his pocket and stared at the screen, but in his haste, he accidentally thumbed the accept call button. He held his breath as the silence from the phone reached out to him, mingled with the silence of the home that enveloped him like a veil of horror.

"What do you want?" he snapped.

"You know what you have to do," a voice snarled at him. He didn't recognize it but it sounded as if the voice itself had been manipulated. His alcohol-affected brain tried to make sense of it, but he found the fog hanging over him was too thick to push through.

"Do what?" It was all he could manage, his eyes searching for the source of the voice, as if it was in the room with him. He looked at the screen again, saw the number was private, and listened for clues. "Who is this?"

"You know who this is," the voice clarified. "Plead guilty to the charge, or else you die. Do you hear me? Plead guilty or die."

The phone clicked loudly in his ear, the call ending before he could fully comprehend the message. He looked at the screen to see if the person had hung up, then held it back to his ear and screamed, "I'm not pleading guilty!"

He stumbled forward a few steps, looked at the phone again, and tossed it aside. It hit the edge of the staircase, the screen shattering on impact. He stumbled toward the living room and the couch he'd been using as his bed and wondered how things had gone bad so quickly. As he dropped onto the cushions and closed his eyes, his father was already invading his thoughts, about to take him on a wild ride through his dreams.

And before the night was through, there were screams, lots of screams, as his worst fears came to harass him in his sleep.

CHAPTER 30

WITH ONLY a week until the start of Miller's trial, Hennessy struggled to juggle both major cases.

He woke with a start, sitting bolt upright as drops of sweat shot from his brow. What he could remember was the look of horror on Wendy's face as he told her about Luca, the original scene twisted into something like a horror movie.

He rubbed his eyes, a thumping headache already in the works as he felt the familiar pain behind his right eye. Thankfully, with the headache pushing forward, it nudged the remnants of the dream back into the shadows, where Hennessy hoped it would remain.

Knowing time was of the essence if he wanted a chance at suppressing the headache before it really took hold, he went to the bathroom and prioritized painkillers. He poured three caplets from the bottle, looked at them questioningly, then added a fourth, popped them in his mouth, and swallowed with the help of a glass of water.

He slowly walked into the kitchen and checked his cellphone for the latest updates and was surprised to see a message from John Kirkland waiting for him. He'd messaged at 5am.

Kirkland wanted to meet with him that morning. From the tone of the message, Hennessy got the feeling it was something urgent and, despite his apprehension about the man, sent a reply confirming his attendance. He sent Jacinta an email to let her know he was detouring to Kirkland's office that morning.

It took him a little longer to prepare than normal, thanks to the headache which continued to build, despite the painkillers he'd taken. While initially just a thumb pressing the back of his eyeball, by the time he was straightening his tie, the pain had increased to level three, with the tip of an icepick reaching somewhere in the vicinity of his cerebral cortex.

The drive through the morning rush hour traffic didn't provide any reprieve from the storm churning up his head, with bumper-to-bumper traffic courtesy of construction and flooding. He arrived at Kirkland's office at five minutes after eight, with Kirkland and McGovern already waiting for him.

"Geez, Hennessy, you look terrible," Kirkland said when he saw him, and it occurred to Hennessy that the man thrived on pointing out other people's flaws. "I would've stayed home if I looked like that."

"Didn't sleep well. It's the humidity," he said. "What's so urgent this morning?"

"I can't keep doing this." McGovern paced the floor behind the boardroom table, rubbing his brow. "This is killing me inside. I can't keep having this case hanging over my head."

"Elliot wanted to go over the prosecutor's offer again," Kirkland said, pointing at McGovern as if Hennessy needed reminding of who he was talking about. "He couldn't sleep, and he called me early this morning."

"The offer? You mean the thirty years?" Hennessy

placed his briefcase on the floor and sat on the opposite side of the boardroom table. "Well, as long as you're considering it, sure. Let's talk."

"We can do better than that, can't we?" McGovern said. "Y'all can get them down to manslaughter, right? I'd even take ten years. I'll say whatever you need me to say and sign whatever you need me to sign."

But Kirkland brushed him aside. "Elliot, think. There's no way we'll get them down to ten years. A manslaughter charge will still mean twenty-plus years if the judge hits you with the maximum. They've made it clear that they want you behind bars. The only way we can beat this is to take it to a jury."

"And if I don't take the deal and lose, it could mean a life sentence," McGovern said, dropping into the seat beside Hennessy. "I can't do life behind bars. I'm not that sort of man. I can't live like that. What about vacations? What about traveling? What about my freedom? I can't spend the rest of my life behind bars."

Hennessy looked at him and saw a man who appeared to have aged overnight. Lines that had been only partially visible a few days before now looked as if they had sunk into permanent fixtures. Deep chasms ran out from each eye, and his eyes looked distant, caught somewhere in the space between the real world and his imagination.

He didn't think this was a point that needed debating and found himself with an urge to shut Kirkland down. But the man did hold the leading chair position, which meant he held the greater power. Ignoring that fact, Hennessy leaned forward.

"Elliot, listen to me," Hennessy said. "If this goes bad, and you know as well as I do how quickly that can happen, this could turn into a potentially life-ending result. The prosecution has mentioned the death penalty. With a manslaughter charge, we can negotiate it down to twenty years. Given the prosecutor's position on this case, that's achievable."

"Would you shut up," Kirkland said. "Don't take it, Elliot. We can win this at trial."

"Do you really think so?"

"No," Hennessy shook his head.

"Yes, we can. We can win this with a good jury. That's all we need," Kirkland stated firmly. "We can tell the jury a good story about your drug-addicted wife, how she was cheating on you with a drug dealer, about how you tried to take her to rehab but she refused."

"They're all lies."

"As if that matters," Kirkland said. "We just have to get the right jury, and then tell a great story in court. Even with the evidence they have, we can still win it."

"This is killing me." Elliot continued to pace the room. "All this stress is making me want to jump off a bridge. I can't handle it anymore."

"Elliot, you're paying me the big bucks to give you the right advice," Kirkland said. "Don't plead out. We've got enough doubt to win over the jurors. We can do this. There are people sitting in prison right now who thought a manslaughter charge would be their savior, and, believe me when I tell you, they regret it every day of their lives."

"Maybe you're right," McGovern whispered.

"I am right, Elliot," Kirkland stated firmly. "Trust me on this."

By the time Hennessy left the office an hour later,

McGovern had been talked down from signing a confession.

But while McGovern had been convinced, Hennessy knew they had no chance to win a trial.

CHAPTER 31

HENNESSY WAS feeling the pressure. His headaches were building. He felt his shoulders getting tighter. His jaw seemed constantly clenched. There was always more than one case, always more than one place to focus his attention.

He walked through the streets of Downtown Charleston, lost in a daze, lost in a mountain of thoughts. He'd spent the hour over lunch walking the streets, trying to clear his head of the constant stream of thoughts that continued to rumble through. It didn't work. He couldn't switch off the mountain of information that just kept coming into his head.

A few drops of rain fell, and he looked up at the sky. It would only be a passing shower, but he decided to take the shortcut back to the office. He crossed into an alleyway, a block from the office. Just as he neared the mouth to the side street again, his feet tangled, and he went skidding onto the concrete.

At first, he thought it had been his own clumsiness, his feet catching each other as he moved a little too fast. But as he pushed himself back up onto his knees, pain exploded in his right side as someone stepped out from the shadows.

There were two of them. Hennessy was quick enough to duck beneath the second swing. He rolled back and managed to get to his feet. He stood tall, towering over the two solid men.

"Balter don't need no looking after from the likes of you," one of his attackers mocked, launching himself at Hennessy a second time. With his brain back in the game after a brief hiatus, Hennessy easily sidestepped the attack and swung himself. He caught the first guy flush on the chin, but another fist slammed into the side of his abdomen. It almost knocked him back off his feet, but he managed to grab the arm of the first one for balance, then spun and jabbed at the man's face.

The fight lasted for barely a few seconds, and both sides managed to get a few punches in, but not wanting to risk an upright defeat, the attackers soon backed away.

"Drop the investigation into Balter," one of the men sneered at Hennessy.

"Or we come back," the second one added before both turned and ran down the side street.

Hennessy took a moment, feeling his face before pausing as he tried to assess any injuries.

After making sure he was ok, he made a beeline back to the office. He breathed a sigh of relief as he walked through the door.

"What happened to you?" Jacinta asked the second she saw him.

"What hasn't happened to me?" he returned, not pausing as he headed into his office, grabbed a towel, and headed to the bathroom at the end of their hallway. "Give me a minute," he called over his shoulder before disappearing behind closed doors.

He emerged again, looking like he'd reawakened in an entirely different movie. After splashing his face with water and washing away the stress of the morning, Hennessy donned the spare suit he kept in his office for just such emergencies. Apart from a slight bruise on the side of his chin and a small nick on his ear, all evidence of the assault had been wiped away.

Jacinta had a cup of coffee waiting for him, and after thanking her, he gave her a brief explanation of his morning.

"Shall I call the police?"

"No, it's ok," Hennessy said. "I'll walk down there this afternoon and make an official report."

"Why do you think they attacked you?"

"James Balter has received the subpoena," Hennessy said. "Now it's time for us to exploit his anger."

CHAPTER 32

HENNESSY SPENT the morning in court, arguing for a motion in limine in the Miller case.

A motion in limine was a request for the judge to refuse to admit evidence that was irrelevant, immaterial, unreliable, or unduly prejudicial. Hennessy argued that including the client's financial records was irrelevant, including witnesses who testified about his mental health was prejudicial, and including evidence about his personal relationships was unreliable. Hennessy won on several fronts, dismissing minor evidence from the prosecution's case. Any reference to the dismissed evidence in front of the jury was grounds for a mistrial. It was a small win in court, but it made Hennessy a happy man.

He was sitting at his desk with a smile on his face when Jacinta knocked on the office door.

"John Kirkland just phoned. Said you weren't answering your cell." When he didn't respond quickly enough, her voice firmed. "Joe. He says it's urgent."

"I'm trying to prepare for Miller's case. We go to trial next week. I can't keep jumping every time McGovern has a tantrum." He searched for his cellphone and saw it sitting on his desk. "As the first chair, Kirkland has to handle that."

"He's at Elliot McGovern's house," Jacinta continued. "He needs you to meet him there as soon as possible."

"Did he say why?"

"No, but he said it was urgent."

He checked the screen of his cell. Five missed calls, and five notifications. The language Kirkland used didn't mince words. Hennessy fired off a reply to say he was on his way and grabbed his things.

Out in the truck, he paused as he held the keys in the ignition. Something felt off, but he couldn't put his finger on what. Aside from the injuries he'd sustained in the attack the previous day, there was something that bugged him.

He pushed the thoughts aside, cranked the truck up, pulled out into traffic, and headed toward Seabrook Island. As he merged with traffic, his mind worked its way back to McGovern and the blank stare he saw, the way the man's soul appeared fatigued and… and what? He tried to find the right word.

"Defeated," he whispered to himself.

What angered him about the situation was how Kirkland had been the one to steer the ship for the defense team. When Hennessy had first agreed to jump aboard with them, Hennessy had imagined that this would be a team effort, a team made up of more than just Kirkland and himself. But none of that had transpired.

As he turned onto Bohicket Road, he reconsidered the whole Dillion situation and how incessant the brother-in-law had been about getting justice for his sister. A sadness ran through him as he wondered whether Paul Dillion had finally followed through on his threats. Maybe this was the reason Kirkland had phoned him first.

"Not yet," he muttered, dismissing the thought as

nothing more than his vivid imagination. He understood the grief Dillion was going through, but despite the threats, he didn't think the man would actually go through with it.

As he reached the front of McGovern's home and pulled into the driveway, he saw Kirkland's Mercedes SUV with five police cars behind it. There was no Maserati.

Before he even got out of the truck, Kirkland was already waving to Hennessy from the door.

"Get in here," he called the second Hennessy stepped out. He disappeared back inside the house. Hennessy ran up the steps and through the front door. He found Kirkland standing by McGovern's couch.

"Care to tell me what's going on?"

Kirkland didn't answer. He reached out to the table, picked up a slip of paper, and held it out to him. Hennessy took it and read the brief note scrawled on it. The further he read, the more his eyes widened until he reached the end and stared back at Kirkland.

"Yeah, my thoughts exactly," Kirkland said. "Can you believe the nerve of this guy? A day after we convince him we can win this case, he writes a suicide note."

"So, you think it's legitimate?"

Kirkland turned on him. "You don't think it's legitimate? I mean, come on, after everything he's been through?"

"Is there a body?"

"The cops found his Maserati in the ocean. It looks like he drove it onto the beach and then into the water. Who in their right mind drives a Maserati into the ocean? They said the car was driven up to window height and that he jumped into the ocean. They say he must've drowned out there. There are all these pills here, and they think he swam out to sea, passed out, and will never be seen again."

"Oh, come on," Hennessy groaned and looked over his shoulder. When he was sure that none of the cops were listening, he lowered his voice. "Really? You don't see what this is? He's faked his own death."

"I wish I could share your confidence, but did he ever strike you as a person who would make something like this up? There's no body, but they think the swell and tides from the recent storm were enough to wash him away. The car was empty when they recovered it, but the windows were down. That's what they've put in the report. They're saying he drove into the ocean last night, and now his body is out in the Atlantic somewhere."

Hennessy groaned. He dropped the suicide note back on the table. He didn't believe it, not for a second.

"He's run away, nothing more," Hennessy said. "And if my suspicions are right, he's skipped the country."

Not wanting to entertain the notion any longer, Hennessy left Kirkland standing in the middle of the living room.

"Where are you going?" Kirkland sounded more frightened than annoyed, but Hennessy wasn't biting.

Without looking back, he called over his shoulder, "I have a trial to prepare for."

He didn't pause again until he was back in his office.

CHAPTER 33

TWO DAYS after the suicide note was found, and only days before the Miller trial, a body still hadn't been located.

With Zach Miller's case due to hit the courtroom the following Monday, Hennessy took off early on Friday to return home to the vineyard and make the most of a weekend with the family.

Hearing the news that Ellie had also returned home for the weekend from New York gave him more of a reason to hurry home, and by the time he arrived, the rest of his family sat on the front steps of the home, awaiting his arrival.

There was so much to work on, with not one but two weddings booked over the two days on the vineyard, and given the way the cellar had been selling wine, Hennessy knew it was an all-hands-on-deck kind of weekend. He made it a point to leave his briefcase in the truck as he turned off the engine, promising himself that he wouldn't look at it until at least Sunday. By then, he would have had enough time to lend a hand with things around the vineyard.

Once inside, he followed Wendy into the kitchen, where she was prepping their dinner. A true southern girl with generations of South Carolina DNA running through her blood, it was her incredible talent in the kitchen, which often reminded him of who she really was.

During one of their first overseas vacations, they had stayed in a bed-and-breakfast in the highlands of Scotland, and during the first night there, she'd convinced the resident chef to let her cook dinner for them, which she did. The surprise for Hennessy hadn't been her convincing the chef to let her cook; not even that she actually did. What surprised him was when she pulled out a genuine packet of grits from her luggage, having brought it all the way to Scotland.

"Mmmm," he said, taking a whiff as he looked over the simmering pot. "Shrimp and Grits."

Shrimp and Grits weren't just about her taking over a foreign kitchen in another part of the world. It was also a reminder of what happened during that particular vacation. It was a couple of weeks after their return from Scotland that they found out they were pregnant with their first child, a child who would be born and named Luca just a few months later.

"I know it's your favorite," Wendy said.

Coming home was one of the best feelings in the world for him. While the work he did in Charleston paid to help keep the banks from repossessing the vineyard, it was the work he did with his family which he loved.

Just as it normally did, the weekend went by in a flash. The weddings went off without a hitch, and Hennessy even managed to catch up with a woman named Joan Williams, who worked as a stenographer back in Charleston. She recognized him almost immediately, although it took Hennessy a moment to be sure he knew who she was. They didn't talk for long as she was prepping for the reception, and being one of the bridesmaids kept her busy.

The hardest part came Sunday evening when he and Ellie had to say their goodbyes and head off in different directions. He had to return to Charleston and do some final reading to prepare for the week's court appearances. Ellie, on the other hand, had to head back to New York, catching a flight from Greenville, although her plane wouldn't leave until later that evening.

Hennessy hugged and kissed his girls goodbye and left them just as he had found them a couple of days before, with each sitting on the steps as they waved to him. He drove off into the late afternoon sun slowly, taking a few final looks into the rearview mirror until he could no longer see them.

When he finally walked into his apartment a few hours later, he was beat, almost to the point of exhaustion, and instead of staying up to review more files, he hit the hay early and set his alarm. It was a plan that paid off because he felt rejuvenated when he awoke to the sounds of his alarm.

His usual morning routine felt like it was on rails, effortlessly moving him between the shower, the shaving, and breakfast without him sensing the slightest frustration. It was as if he had become a new man, courtesy of the fresh country air and the company of those he loved.

Kirkland sent him another update on McGovern just after eight.

The police had found some of his belongings, including a watch, his shoe, and his wallet, washed up further down the coast. Despite the lack of a body, the cops were about to officially declare him deceased. Hennessy shook his head but pushed the thoughts aside.

His focus had to be on Zach Miller and the trial that was due to start in a matter of hours.

CHAPTER 34

INDICTMENT

STATE OF SOUTH CAROLINA
COUNTY OF CHARLESTON
IN THE COURT OF GENERAL SESSIONS
NINTH JUDICIAL CIRCUIT
INDICTMENT NO.: 2022-AB-05-355

STATE OF SOUTH CAROLINA, V.
ZACHARY MATTHEW MILLER, DEFENDANT

At a Court of General Sessions, convened on 10th of September, the Grand Jurors of Charleston County present upon their oath: Possession, manufacture, and trafficking of methamphetamine and cocaine base and other controlled substances; penalties.

COUNT ONE
S.C. CODE SECTION 44-53-375.
POSSESSION, MANUFACTURE, AND
TRAFFICKING OF METHAMPHETAMINE
AND COCAINE BASE AND OTHER
CONTROLLED SUBSTANCES; PENALTIES.

That in Charleston County on or about 5th of September, the defendant, ZACHARY MATTHEW MILLER, did possess property represented by law enforcement as a controlled substance, in violation of Section 44-53-375 South Carolina Code of Laws (1976) as amended. To wit: ZACHARY MATTHEW MILLER did have possession of what he knew, or should have known, was a controlled substance and the said controlled substance was a value greater than twenty-eight grams per Section 44-53-375 (C)(2).

FINDINGS

We, the Grand Jury, find that ZACHARY MATTHEW MILLER is to be indicted under Section 44-53-375 South Carolina Code of Laws (1976) as amended.

*****

THE CHARLESTON County Judicial Center was in the beating heart of historic Downtown Charleston.

As Joe Hennessy walked toward the Judicial Center, he paused in front of City Hall, the second longest serving City Hall in the country, serving the city since 1818. He felt a sense of history as he gazed at the beautiful building that was originally used as one of the eight branches of The First Bank of the United States. Built in 1804 in the Adamesque style, it was designed by Charlestonian Gabriel Manigault, a gentleman architect credited with introducing the style to the city after studying in Europe. The semicircular projection on one side and the round basement windows were characteristic of his architectural style, and the white marble trim originated in Italy before it was cut in Philadelphia, adding to the sense of Adamesque style. There were tourists around, being led through the streets by charismatic tour guides, although the guides didn't mention that the modern story of crime and justice was happening only yards away.

After months of research, after months of investigation, Zach Miller had the chance to proclaim his innocence in front of a jury. The Circuit Solicitor's Office offered another deal in the week before the trial, but it still included fifteen months of prison time. Miller refused. He claimed he was innocent, he claimed he had no idea the drugs were in his dressing room, and he was not going to do a day of prison time. In his situation, with all the evidence against him, Miller was either brave, stupid, or a dangerous combination of both, but he was determined to fight it, determined to prove his innocence in a court of law.

Hennessy met Miller in the foyer of the Charleston County Judicial Center. They talked politely for a few moments about the humid weather before Hennessy led them into courtroom number five. Dressed respectfully in a fitted black suit, Miller entered the room and sat at the defense table, staring at the empty jury box where the people in charge of deciding his fate would sit.

The dominant colors in the room were a stark contrast—the walls were painted a light cream color, and the furniture was dark brown. The jury box was to the right of the room, next to the judge's seat, which was raised slightly. Behind the judge's seat was the Great Seal of the State of South Carolina, with the American Flag on one side of the seal, and the flag of South Carolina on the other. The ceiling was high, the hum of the air-conditioner through the vents was constant, and the smell was slightly musty.

The prosecution team, led by Jamal Lincoln, walked into the courtroom fifteen minutes later. Their confidence was clear. They weren't threatened by the case, the evidence, or the weight of media expectation. Jacinta arrived next, with a laptop and an arm full of files. The bailiff opened the doors to the public ten minutes after that.

As soon as the bailiff opened the doors of the courtroom to the public, the seats filled behind them. This was a celebrity trial, a newsworthy moment for the national media, and the crowd reflected that. Several reporters, some from as far away as the West Coast, lined the back of the room. Cell phones and electronic tablets weren't allowed in the courtroom, leaving the reporters to rely on the old-fashioned pen and notebook method to capture the news.

As the seats filled, the tension in the room rose. There was a buzz, a murmur of anticipation, an electric pulse. The crowd was excited to follow the twists and turns of the real-life drama.

"Five minutes," the bailiff called out, alerting everyone that Judge Andrew Fedder would soon enter the courtroom, and the show was about to begin.

Miller had several people there for support. His mother and sister were sitting close together, next to his ex-wife. A number of friends had also arrived, along with five former bandmates, wishing to support their friend in his hour of need.

"All rise. The court is now in session, the Honorable Judge Andrew Fedder presiding."

Judge Fedder walked into the courtroom from the far left corner, eyes forward, and focused on his seat. He sat down, moved several files on his desk, adjusted the microphone, and then raised his eyes to look out at the crowd. He then moved his thick-rimmed glasses, cleared his throat, and checked the files in front of him.

The bailiff confirmed the defendant's name before the lawyers introduced themselves to the court. Judge Fedder asked Miller if he understood the charges against him, and once satisfied, he called for jury selection to begin.

The morning was spent in *voir dire*, the jury selection process.

As groups of people were brought in, Hennessy and Lincoln fired off questions to the potential jurors. Question after question, statement after statement.

They looked for little clues from the answers, little expressions, little movements, anything that might show their bias in the trial. The lawyers asked the potential jurors about the television shows they watched. They asked them if they volunteered. They asked if they'd ever considered fighting in the army. Did they have children, what was their view on marriage, what was their outlook on the future? Were they politically minded, what sort of music did they listen to, what were their children's hobbies? Did they enjoy a glass of wine, beer, or spirits? Did they pride themselves on being Southern?

To effectively pick a jury, lawyers had to be certain of the case they wished to present. For Hennessy, the jurors needed to be smart enough to appreciate the legal standard of the case, and strong enough in their beliefs to apply it. He didn't want people who trusted their instinct, he didn't want spontaneous people, he didn't want people who took their personal biases into the case. He needed those who followed the rules, people who were driven by facts and figures, and who had an eye for the specifics.

And while the lawyers selected a jury, the jury selected an attorney. Mostly, jurors didn't want brilliance in the courtroom. They didn't want dazzling displays of intelligence from the lawyers. They didn't want fanciful stories of astounding genius.

They simply wanted the truth.

The jurors wanted to believe that the verdict they rendered was correct, and as such, they listened to the most credible story. Jury selection was the jurors' first impression of the lawyers and could make or break a lawyer's credibility.

After Judge Fedder let several jurors go for failing

to understand the legalities of the case, the prosecution dismissed five potential jurors, and the defense dismissed ten. Half the people that were left were exactly who Hennessy needed in the box. The other half, he wasn't so sure about.

Five jurors were under thirty, five middle-aged, and two were older. Some had families, some were divorced, and another was a widow. Seven men, five women. There was a manager of a drug store in his late twenties. Another was a junior accountant. One mathematician completing his Ph.D. There was a schoolteacher, a dance instructor, and a statistician who worked for the local government, as well as a computer programmer, a day trader, and a bus driver. A wide mix of professions, but one that Hennessy hoped would win the case.

The alternates were also selected. They would hear the evidence but, unless required by the court, they would take no part in the deliberations.

After the jury selection was completed at 2pm, Judge Fedder called a recess. Twenty-five minutes later, the crowd had resettled, as had the lawyers. The lull of the jury selection process was over, and the adrenalized excitement of a celebrity trial was back. There was electricity in the air, a pulsing heartbeat that threatened to explode.

Miller leaned forward in his seat, nodding to himself, running his hands up and down his thighs. He was working hard to contain the nerves that threatened to spill out. The crowd hushed when Judge Fedder returned to the room, but the tension remained.

When instructed, the bailiff walked to the door in the front corner of the room, guiding the members of the jury to their seats. Some appeared nervous, some appeared confident, and all appeared ready.

Judge Fedder turned to the jury and stated, "Madam Foreman, Ladies and Gentlemen of the Jury. Please stand and raise your right hand to be sworn: You shall well and truly try, and true deliverance make, between the State of South Carolina, and the defendant at bar, whom you shall have in charge, and a true verdict give, according to the law and evidence. So help you God."

The jurors confirmed their understanding, and Judge Fedder explained the process, including the function of the opening statements. "The opening statements are not an argument," he stated firmly. "The lawyers will not argue their case in their opening statements, and they will not set further the inferences which they think will arise from the evidence. They will simply tell you the actual evidence they will present and provide an overview of their cases."

He then invited prosecutor Jamal Lincoln to begin his argument.

*****

"Your Honor, ladies and gentlemen of the jury, my name is Jamal Lincoln, and this is my colleague, Michelle Saltmarsh. We represent the Ninth Judicial District Circuit Solicitor's Office, and we are here to present the charges against the defendant, Mr. Zachary Matthew Miller. As Judge Fedder has explained to you, Mr. Miller is charged with trafficking cocaine as defined by the State of South

Carolina Code of Laws.

This is the opening statement of this case, and it will provide a roadmap of what will be presented in this trial, as nothing I say now can be taken as evidence.

Mr. Miller is a musician by trade, a folk singer, and he has performed in concerts all over the country, and in fact, all over the world. He tours, on average, for five months at a time before returning home to Charleston County, where he resides. He owns a home on James Island, which he has owned for more than ten years. He has even built a recording studio in the backyard of that home.

There is no doubt that touring for his music career, which involves performing five nights a week, has taken a toll on Mr. Miller. In fact, Mr. Miller has described in numerous interviews details about the toll that touring takes on him. Five months on the road, five months of performing, five months of working himself to the bone. You will hear from witnesses who will testify that Mr. Miller has admitted to them that touring has taken a toll on him, both physically and mentally.

We all deal with the pressures of life in different ways. For some, it's a massage. For others, it's alcohol. For Mr. Miller, it was cocaine. You will hear from witnesses who will testify that they have seen Mr. Miller use cocaine. They will testify that they witnessed Mr. Miller snort lines of cocaine before, after, and even during a show. You will hear from witnesses who will testify that they saw Mr. Miller purchase cocaine on numerous occasions.

You will hear from the arresting police officer, Detective Belinda Ballentine, who will state to you that the police responded to an anonymous tip via the Crime Stoppers of the Lowcountry tip line. The tip stated that Mr. Miller had a sizable quantity of cocaine stored in his dressing room of the Charleston Music Hall, which he intended to use, and then sell the remaining amount after the show.

Detective Ballentine will explain that this tip included several specific details, and the decision was made to follow up on the tip. She will explain that they raided Mr. Miller's dressing room after he performed a show at the Charleston Music Hall.

You will hear from the Crime Stoppers of the Lowcountry tip line call center worker who took the call, and she will testify why they felt this was a legitimate tip worth pursuing by law enforcement. And that's important. The police can't just raid any person's property after an anonymous tip-off. No. The tip-off has to be legitimate, and it has to include specific knowledge of the situation, which this tip-off did.

You will hear from drug analysis experts, who will testify that the drugs were, in fact, cocaine.

You will hear from the South Carolina State Law Enforcement Division Forensic Services Laboratory, and they will tell you about the information they took from the crime scene, including a number of 'baggies' found in the backpack. These small, clear plastic bags are used by drug dealers to separate the drugs into smaller amounts for future sale.

You will hear from several security guards at the event, and they will testify that Mr. Miller was the only person with access to the dressing room that night. They will tell you that Mr. Miller stated he liked to be alone in the dressing room after a show, taking a few moments to 'come down from the high.'

And you will hear from Mr. Miller's former manager, Mr. Preston Wheeler, who will testify that Mr. Miller tried to sell him drugs on the night in question. Mr. Wheeler will testify that Mr. Miller stated he had cocaine to sell, and he wanted Mr. Wheeler to purchase a large amount of it.

While it's important to hear from these witnesses because their testimonies are important to understand the full picture, it's also important to remember the facts of this case—Mr. Miller was found in his dressing room, after a show, with a backpack that contained more than fifty grams of cocaine.

Now, let me make an important distinction of a legal term for you.

You will hear the term 'possession' used many times during this trial, and I need you to remember that this is a legal reference to the term. This refers to two things, physical possession and constructive possession. Physical possession is the act of actually having the item on you, while constructive possession describes a situation in which an individual has control over the item without actually having physical control of the item. Constructive possession is the ability and intent to exercise dominion and control over the item, while knowing the item was there. In the eyes of the court, a person with constructive possession stands in the same legal position as a person with actual possession.

Mr. Miller was the only person in the room when the detectives entered. The cocaine was in his dressing room, and he was in control of the drugs.

Do not let this clear violation of the law go unpunished.

Do not let the defense team stand up here and convince you that using these illicit drugs for personal use does not affect anyone else. It affects each and every one of us. The trickle-down effect of this behavior by the rich and famous encourages others to do it. Their use influences our children. This man is a role model, and if he is seen using drugs, then our children see that as appropriate.

Drug use creates more crime on our streets. It creates more violence. It creates more danger for our families, our friends, and our communities. We cannot allow the rich and famous to do whatever they like. We must punish those who choose to break the law, regardless of wealth or status.

Mr. Miller has shown a blatant disregard for the law, and he deserves to be found guilty. He cannot be above the law. Nobody can.

At the end of this trial, I will stand before you again and ask you to consider all the evidence we have presented and to conclude beyond a reasonable doubt that Mr. Zachary Miller is guilty.

Thank you for your time."

*****

Any trial was a story that unfolded through the narration of two storytellers, each spinning a different version of events to convince twelve people of their version of the truth. The jury was an important part of the storytelling process.

During the jury selection process, Hennessy identified two people who were likely to base their decision solely on aspects of the law. Juror five was a thirty-year-old mathematician—calculated, strategic, and focused—who was working on his Ph.D. at the College of Charleston. He was likely to consider every aspect of the event and how mathematically possible it was for the drugs to have been in the room before Miller arrived. Juror ten had a distrust for the police, having seen her brother arrested for a violent crime and later exonerated. Hennessy was surprised that the prosecution left her on the jury, but then, he could never be sure what the prosecution was thinking.

These were the two that he would direct his story at, these were the two jurors that he would focus his attention on during the trial. He would make eye contact with them, nod at them at the right times, and shake his head at others while also gauging their reaction. They were the ones that would most likely believe the story he was about to spin in the courtroom. And he only needed to convince one of them to have a reasonable doubt about Miller's guilt to have a hung jury.

As soon as Lincoln finished his opening statement, Hennessy stood and walked to the lectern near the jury box, placing a folder full of notes in front of him.

When invited by Judge Fedder, Hennessy looked at the jury, nodded, and began.

*****

"Ladies and gentlemen of the jury, Your Honor, my name is Mr. Joe Hennessy. I'm a criminal defense attorney, and I'm here to represent the defendant, Mr.

Zachary Matthew Miller.

Right now, Mr. Miller is presumed innocent. I need you to remember that as we go through this process—the starting point for this case is that Mr. Miller is innocent. Sitting there, looking at you now, Mr. Miller is an innocent man.

The onus is on the prosecution to present evidence that convinces you otherwise beyond a reasonable doubt. They won't be able to, of course, because there's no evidence to prove Mr. Miller had physical or constructive possession of those drugs. None. Not one piece of evidence presented to this court will prove Mr. Miller had possession of the controlled substance.

Justice does not seek to place an innocent man behind bars for a crime he did not commit. Justice does not mean that you convict a man because you feel he's guilty. Justice seeks to find the truth, and that is what you must do in this case.

The true meaning of justice is to be fair and unbiased in your assessment of the situation. You must listen to the facts. The facts. Not the story told by the prosecution, not the fanciful ideas that they want to present. No. You must listen to the facts. And if you do that, your decision will be simple— there's not enough evidence to convict Mr. Miller of any crime beyond a reasonable doubt.

There's no direct evidence in this case. The prosecution's case, and their fanciful evidence, doesn't even come close to the standard of reasonable doubt that we demand in this courtroom. The prosecution's case is based on circumstantial evidence alone. Circumstantial means the evidence relies on an inference to connect it to a conclusion. They wish to imply that the evidence proves his guilt because there is no direct evidence in this case. Just stories told by the prosecution, and stories told by their witnesses, that they wish to connect to an outcome.

Not one witness will tell you they saw Mr. Miller with that particular backpack. Not one witness will tell you they saw Mr. Miller handle the drugs. Not one witness will tell you they saw Mr. Miller sell the drugs.

We will present witnesses to you that will state Mr. Miller is not a drug user. He's been clean for over fifteen months. You will hear from his rehab team, and his closest friends, that he hasn't used drugs in more than a year.

We will present witnesses to you who will testify that many people had access to that dressing room. And we will present witnesses to you who will state that there were many things in that dressing room that did not belong to Mr. Miller.

Mr. Miller was not holding the bag when the police officers entered the room. Mr. Miller did not have physical possession of the backpack. Mr. Miller was not in physical contact with the drugs. In fact, the backpack was on the other side of the large dressing room. Even after testing it for fingerprints, none of Mr. Miller's fingerprints were found on the backpack.

You will hear that many people had access to the room before Mr. Miller arrived. You will also hear that many people had access to the room after Mr. Miller left. This was not a private room, and this room was not controlled by Mr. Miller.

In the great state of South Carolina, it's only a crime to knowingly possess a controlled substance. A person cannot be convicted if they were not aware of the illegal item being present on their person or within their control. The prosecution must prove, beyond a reasonable doubt, that Mr. Miller knew the controlled substance was in the room.

Now, the prosecution has told you the legal definition of the term 'constructive possession.' To reiterate, it's the ability and intent to exercise dominion and control over the item or the premises on which the item was found while knowing the items were there. That's a stretch in this case. Mr. Miller did not own the dressing room where the drugs were found. He was not the only person who could access that dressing room. He was not the only person who had the ability to exercise dominion and control over the items in the room.

In making your decision at the end of this trial, you must rely on the facts. You must be unbiased. You must be impartial. And above all else, you must be fair.

Remember, at this moment, Mr. Miller is innocent. That's our starting point, and the prosecution must prove beyond a reasonable doubt that Mr. Miller committed this act. They must present evidence that convinces you he's guilty beyond a reasonable doubt.

But there simply isn't enough evidence to do so.

When this case draws to a close, I'll stand before you again and point out how the prosecution has failed to present enough evidence. At that point, you'll use your common sense to make a decision. Your decision must be not guilty.

Thank you for your service to our great justice system."

CHAPTER 35

THE EXCITEMENT of the opening statements had created tension in the courtroom, two clear and dominant speakers telling different stories. At five minutes past 3pm, with the opening statements concluded, Judge Fedder instructed Jamal Lincoln to call the first witness for the trial. He wasted no time standing up and calling Detective Belinda Ballentine.

Detective Ballentine entered the courtroom from the doors at the rear of the room. She walked to the stand with a slight bounce in her step. Her gait was slightly uneven, but she walked tall with her shoulders pulled back, and her chin held high. She wore a black pantsuit, and the scent of her perfume wafted through as she passed. She presented an image of importance and competence, and more importantly for the jurors, dressed in a suit, she presented herself as a conveyor of the truth.

Presenting a strong first witness was essential to any case, and Ballentine was a tried-and-true performer. She'd testified many times over her years as a detective, sealing the deal on many drug cases.

As Ballentine swore her oath, Lincoln moved to the lectern near the jury, carrying a pile of folders with him. He took a moment to organize them, arranging them perfectly, and then began questioning the witness once she was settled in the witness box.

"Detective Ballentine, thank you for coming to the court today." Lincoln stood behind the lectern, looking toward the jury box. "Can you please tell the court your profession and your connection to this case?"

"My name is Detective Belinda Jane Ballentine. I've been a detective with the Charleston Police Department for more than ten years. I'm very proud to have the opportunity to serve my community." She looked at the jury, and they responded with polite nods. "I earned a promotion to Detective five years ago, and I work within the Special Investigations Unit, which is committed to the control and suppression of narcotics. We're part of the Central Investigative Division. My father had substance abuse issues, so I always knew that I wanted to save other children from the pain I grew up with."

"And how are you connected to this case?"

"I was the lead detective on the investigation into the tip-off of the drugs, and the subsequent raid on the dressing room in the Charleston Music Hall on the 5th of September."

"Have you previously led raids on premises to check for drugs?"

"I have. I've led many investigations in my long career. Perhaps as many as forty or fifty over the years that I've been a detective. When we're successful in taking drugs off the streets of Charleston, it fills me with pride. It's my honor to keep these streets clean."

"Did you bust straight through the door of the dressing room at the Charleston Music Hall?"

"No. My partner and I, Detective David Stenson, met with the event manager, and they told us which room Mr. Miller was in. We passed the security guard, identified ourselves, and proceeded to the door. We knocked first and then opened the door of the dressing room."

"And what time was this?"

"11:05pm. The show had finished at 10:40pm, and most of the crowd had left the building by this point."

"Can you please take us through what happened when you entered the room?"

"We identified ourselves as detectives with the Charleston Police Department and told the occupant that we had a tip-off that there was a large amount of cocaine in the room. We had a search warrant approved by Judge Eleanor Whitehall. With this level of reasonable suspicion, we searched the room."

"How many occupants were in the room?"

"Only one."

"Can you please identify that occupant?"

"It's the man sitting at the defense table—Mr. Zachary Miller."

"How did Mr. Miller react when you told him who you were?"

"He seemed confused."

"Were you the first person who found the backpack containing 50 grams of cocaine?"

"I was."

"Did you have your body-cam on?"

"I did."

"I'd like you to look at the screen and tell the court if this is the footage recorded from your body-cam at the time of the raid?"

Lincoln turned to the assistant prosecutor and nodded. The assistant typed several lines into her laptop, and then the screen at the side of the room came to life. After Detective Ballentine confirmed it was her body-cam footage, the court watched the screen for the next ten minutes, watching as the detective searched the room, before eventually turning to the backpack at the far corner. The backpack was hidden under a chair, tucked away in an attempt to hide it.

The footage stopped the moment Detective Ballentine removed the drugs from the backpack.

Lincoln turned back to his assistant, who then typed several more commands. The still pictures of the crime scene appeared on the monitor. First, it was the dressing room. Second, a photo of the backpack. Third, a photo of the inside of the backpack. Last, a photo of the drugs after they had been removed from the backpack.

"Do you know the approximate street value of this amount of cocaine?"

"Cocaine prices vary with supply and demand, but the average street value for this amount would be around $5000."

"And how did you determine this was cocaine?"

"A simple eye test told us it was possibly an illicit substance due to how it was packed. After the arrest, we sent the substance to the Forensic Services Division for further testing. This test confirmed it was indeed cocaine."

Lincoln looked at the jury and nodded. A few nodded in return. The footage was clear, it was precise, and it was incriminatory. Lincoln took a long pause, shuffling several papers on the lectern, allowing the vital information to sink into the minds of the jurors.

"Did you arrest Mr. Miller when you found the controlled substance?"

"I did. I read Mr. Miller his Miranda Warning and informed him that he was under arrest."

"Did you find anything else in the backpack?"

"Yes," she moved in her seat, nodding toward the evidence table at the side of the room. "We found a package of fifty 'baggies.' That's the term for small bags that are used to divide drugs up into smaller amounts for future sales. Because we found the baggies next to the drugs, it was clear to us that it established the intent to traffic this amount of cocaine. Also, the manner in which it was packed is not consistent with personal use."

"Objection," Hennessy called out. "Hearsay. Unless the detective claims to have seen the defendant use drugs previously, she cannot comment on whether or not the substance was for someone's personal use."

"Your Honor," Lincoln argued. "The detective is an expert in drug analysis."

"A 40-hour course from the DEA does not make an individual an expert, Your Honor." Hennessy rebutted.

"Sustained," Judge Fedder agreed. "Please only comment on what you saw, Detective Ballentine."

Lincoln paused and looked at the jury. When he saw several nods in the jury box, he continued. "After you sealed the scene, what was the next step in your police investigation?"

For the next two hours and fifteen minutes, Ballentine detailed the scene and the steps she took the day of the arrest. She followed procedure, she said, with all the i's dotted and all the t's crossed.

She took the court through the process, step by step, move by move. She kept her testimony factual, straight, never once straying into opinion. She talked about Miller's movements, what he said, and where he stood. She talked about where the backpack was located, how it was squashed under a chair, and how it looked like someone had tried to conceal it. She talked about the drugs and how she knew it was cocaine from the first glance.

Throughout it all, Ballentine kept focused, presenting herself as an authority on all that was right and proper. She was a detective, an expert on drug crimes, and the jury hung on her every word. They believed everything she said, and they believed Miller was guilty. Since it was late afternoon when her testimony finished, Judge Fedder called an end to the day's proceedings, leaving the jury with the detective's words ringing through their heads following the first day of the trial.

As the jurors left the jury box, Hennessy saw the jurors stare at Miller. It was clear what they were thinking—they had little doubt that Miller was guilty.

Hennessy would have to work hard to change that.

CHAPTER 36

THE FOLLOWING morning, when Hennessy was called to begin his cross, the tension in the courtroom was electric.

As he stood to move to the lectern, Hennessy looked over his shoulder. Media had filled the gallery. In the dark brown chairs behind him, there were reporters, podcasters, and note-takers. The bailiffs, armed for the occasion, stood at the side of the room, searching for any unusual movements in the crowd, ready to pounce on anything out of order. The air was stuffy, credited to the lack of air-conditioning overnight and the sun burning in the window to the far side of the room.

Hennessy drew a long breath and organized his notes on the lectern, before thanking the detective for her service to the community. The jury was awake and alert, paying attention to Hennessy's first questions of the case. The court was ready. The stage was set.

"Detective Ballentine, in your testimony, you stated you didn't break down the dressing room door. Is that correct?"

"That's correct."

"You simply knocked on the dressing room door and entered the room?"

"Yes, that's right."

"So, the door must've been unlocked?"

"Yes."

"Do you think that's unusual? To store that amount of cocaine in the room and not even lock the door?"

"Yes. I found that unusual."

"Unusual." Hennessy nodded and walked across to the defense table, flicking open a file on his desk. "Detective Ballentine, did Mr. Miller say anything to you when he was arrested?"

"He did."

"And what did he say?"

"He said that the backpack wasn't his, and he had no idea where the drugs came from."

"In fact, he insisted they weren't his, didn't he?"

"Most people do when they're arrested."

"Was there anyone else in the room at the time?"

"No, there wasn't."

"Was there anyone else outside the room?"

"No."

"No?" Hennessy raised his eyebrows. "Not even a security guard?"

"The security guard met us at the door to the Charleston Music Hall and guided us through the halls to the dressing room."

"Interesting." Hennessy raised his eyebrows. "Tell me, Detective Ballentine, did you find any money in the room while you searched it?"

"Nothing other than Mr. Miller's wallet. He had fifty dollars on him at the time."

"Did you find any weight scales?"

"Uh-uh."

"Is that a yes or a no?"

"It's a no."

"Did you find any ledgers or notes of drug sales and purchases?"

"No."

"And no amounts of rolled-up cash?"

"No."

Hennessy paused and sighed. One of the jury members nodded. "Would you expect to find these items in the room if Mr. Miller was dealing from there?"

"Not always. Sometimes drug dealers will weigh the drugs elsewhere. And not all drug dealers keep detailed notes of their transactions."

"But you found baggies in the room, yes?"

"That's correct."

"How would he measure the amount of drugs in the baggies if he didn't have weigh scales?"

"I'm not sure." Detective Ballentine shifted uncomfortably in her seat. "Maybe he was going to measure them somewhere else."

"Maybe he would do it somewhere else," Hennessy repeated. "Is it fair to say, Detective Ballentine, that you did not see Mr. Miller dealing the cocaine?"

"That's fair, yes."

"And Mr. Miller wasn't holding the backpack when you entered the room?"

"He wasn't holding the bag, no."

"Were there any other bags in the room?"

"From memory, yes."

Hennessy nodded and walked back to his desk. He typed several lines on his laptop, and a still photograph from the dressing room appeared on the monitor. "If you look at the still photograph taken after you arrested Mr. Miller, you can see five other bags in that room." Hennessy clicked another button, and the image highlighted the five other bags—two small bags under the dressing table, a shopping bag next to the cupboard, one by the door, and a guitar bag on top of a shelf. "Can you please tell the court if Mr. Miller owned those five bags?"

"I'm not aware of the answer to that question."

"Really?" Hennessy scoffed. "Did you search all those bags for drugs?"

"We did."

"And did you ask if they belonged to Mr. Miller?"

"He said that they didn't belong to him, but—"

"He said they didn't belong to him. Did you believe him when he said they didn't belong to him?"

She stared at Hennessy, her mouth closed, frustrated by the question.

"Detective Ballentine, please answer the question," Hennessy pressed her.

"Yes, I believed that he didn't own the other five bags in the room."

"You believed that he didn't own the other five bags in the room, but you didn't believe him when he stated he didn't own the black backpack?"

"That's correct."

"Why the distinction?"

"Because the other bags didn't hold anything of value."

"All those other bags in the room, and you determined he must be the only one who had possession of the bag." Hennessy shook his head, looking at the jury. "Did everything in the room belong to Mr. Miller?"

"I don't believe so, no."

"Looking at the photo of the room, there are

many items in the room. We can see a green couch, a mirror, a small refrigerator, and two red armchairs. Behind that is a guitar. Over in the corner is a make-up set. Do you think that make-up set belongs to Mr. Miller?"

"I have no idea."

"But it's in his constructive possession. He's the only one in the room at the time, so it must be his. Is that correct?"

"I can't comment on that because I don't know."

"I do," Hennessy moved back to the table. "The make-up set belongs to one of the building's owners. They store many things in the dressing room for their own future use, and for future use by the performers. Now, I'd like you to look at the picture of the crime scene again. Can you please tell me if Mr. Miller owns the couch?"

"Objection," Lincoln stood. "Relevance. Where is this line of questioning even going? We know that Mr. Miller does not own everything in that room."

"Mr. Hennessy?" Judge Fedder looked at him.

"Your Honor, we're trying to establish whether Mr. Miller owned anything in the dressing room, including the backpack in question."

Judge Fedder looked across to the witness. "Detective Ballentine, are you willing to concede that you don't know what was owned and not owned by Mr. Miller in the dressing room?"

"That's correct, Your Honor," Detective Ballentine confirmed.

"Then we have established that fact. The objection is sustained," Judge Fedder said. "Move on with your questioning, Mr. Hennessy."

"So it's fair to say that when you were searching

the dressing room, you were unaware of what belonged to Mr. Miller and what did not belong to Mr. Miller?"

Detective Ballentine sighed and looked at the judge. Judge Fedder indicated she should answer. She groaned, sighed again, and then leaned forward. "Alright. Sure. That's fair to say."

Hennessy tapped his finger on the edge of the lectern before concluding. "No further questions."

CHAPTER 37

"STATE CALLS Dr. Melanie Higgins."

The eyes of the court turned to the doors and followed the new arrival all the way to her seat.

Dr. Higgins was a short woman who had dressed in an expensive suit, which struggled to stretch across her sizable bust. Her hair had been pulled back into a tight bun, with thick, blue-rimmed glasses sitting on the end of her upturned nose. If Hennessy didn't know her to be a scientific expert, he would have guessed she was a librarian.

Lincoln waited patiently as the bailiff put the woman through her paces and, once she swore her oath, handed her over to the prosecutor. He began by thanking the witness for her time and asked her about her profession. Dr. Higgins explained that she worked for the South Carolina State Law Enforcement Division Forensic Services Laboratory, and her role was to test any substances that were to be presented in court.

Lincoln took her through the report, where she had documented details about the substance found in the backpack. She detailed the report, almost line by line, explaining the process and testing she went through to determine that the substance was, in fact, cocaine. Her testimony was deliberately bland, with no frills and no fireworks.

Although her testimony was dry and didn't convince the jury of Miller's guilt, it was an essential part of the legal process. The prosecution had to establish, without a reasonable doubt, that the substance was cocaine. In South Carolina courts, it had long been established that a simple taste or eye test from a detective was not enough to determine that the product was a controlled substance.

Once the fifteen-minute testimony was completed, Judge Fedder asked the defense if they had any questions.

"Thank you for taking the time to talk with us today, Dr. Higgins," Hennessy began, still sitting behind his desk, with a file open in front of him. "Does it strike you as odd that the cocaine found in the backpack was classified as almost pure cocaine, only cut with one other substance?"

"Objection," Lincoln chipped in. "Conjecture."

"She's an expert in her field, Your Honor. Dr. Higgins can comment on whether she found this odd."

He didn't need to explain any further as Judge Fedder waved for him to stop. "Overruled. You may answer the question, Dr. Higgins."

"Yes, it was surprising that it was almost pure cocaine. Usually, the cocaine that comes into my lab is cut with many different substances."

"How was this sample different?"

"Cocaine that was nearly pure, like the high-quality drugs we found in the backpack, would normally be reserved for high-ranking dealers, someone transporting the drugs into the state, not your average street-level seller with 50 grams. Usually, the cocaine has been cut many times by this point and may contain things such as powdered bleach or other cheap products."

"And how often, in your extensive career, would you say you've seen this level of high-quality cocaine on a street-level dealer?"

"In my experience, never."

Hennessy nodded. "Dr. Higgins, does cocaine have a signature?"

"Yes, cocaine has a signature depending on what it's been cut with and where it comes from. There are 19 coca-growing regions within South America identified by the Drug Enforcement Administration's Cocaine Signature Program. These 19 regions can be geo-identified by testing the cocaine using a combination of trace cocaine alkaloids, stable isotopes, and multivariate statistics. So to answer your question, yes, it can be identified as coming from a particular batch."

"And if you were to find another sample from that same batch of cocaine, you could identify it?"

"That's correct."

"Is there a database where these tests are stored and cross-referenced?"

"There is a database, but no, these tests are not cross-referenced."

"This test wasn't cross-referenced on the database?"

"That's correct."

"And what was found in the toxicology report on the cocaine? What else was it cut with?"

"Although it was almost pure cocaine, there were alarmingly high amounts of the drug ketamine found in this batch. It doesn't take much ketamine to profoundly impact the body."

"And how does ketamine affect the body?"

"Firstly, cocaine is a stimulant. It affects the body by releasing a flood of pleasurable neurochemicals, mostly dopamine. Ketamine, on the other hand, is a dissociative anesthetic. Ketamine may make the user feel detached from their body, which is known as falling into a 'k-hole.' It alters their perception of reality, and they can see, hear, and smell things that don't exist. While using ketamine, a user may have blurred vision, slurred speech, become physically uncoordinated, have a raised temperature and heart rate, feel nauseous and vomit, and sweat profusely."

"Have you viewed the body-cam footage of the arrest?"

"I did."

"And given what you've seen in Detective Ballentine's body-cam video, do you believe Mr. Miller used the cocaine cut with ketamine before this point?"

"Drugs affect everyone differently, but I don't believe so, no."

"So he had these drugs in a backpack that he didn't use before, during, or after the show?"

"I can't comment on whether he used it since he was not tested at the time, only how it may have affected him, and no, I didn't see any indication that he used it."

"Thank you, Dr. Higgins," Hennessy finished. "No further questions."

CHAPTER 38

THE SECOND detective, Detective David Stenson, testified to begin day three. It went as expected. Yes, he entered the room with Detective Ballentine. No, he didn't see anyone else enter the room. Yes, he saw the drugs in the backpack. They followed procedure, recorded everything, and saw nothing that indicated the drugs belonged to anyone else. It was all very accurate, all very reliable, but there was nothing in the testimony that pointed to the out-and-out guilt of Miller.

The testimony from the next witness, the manager of the Charleston Music Hall, was much the same. Yes, he let the detectives into the building when they showed him the search warrant. No, he didn't know that there were drugs in the dressing room. Yes, the dressing room was assigned to Mr. Miller. When the third witness of the day, Crime Scene Forensic Analyst Dr. Jim Hayes, walked to the stand after lunch, the jury was starting to lose focus.

For fifty-five minutes, Lincoln questioned Dr. Hayes about the analysis of the crime scene, painting a vivid description of the room. Dr. Hayes explained the photographs he took, where the bag was found, and the likelihood that the bag was deliberately forced under the chair to hide it. During the testimony, even Hennessy struggled to pay attention.

When Lincoln finished, Judge Fedder invited Hennessy to cross-examine the witness.

"Just a few questions, Your Honor," Hennessy stood. "Dr. Hayes, did you examine the backpack that was found?"

"Yes, we did."

"Did you find fingerprints on that backpack?"

"We couldn't establish any clear fingerprints from the item, but that's not unexpected. Finding a complete fingerprint match on an item such as a backpack can be quite hard. We found several partial fingerprints, but nothing that could be used in a report."

"Did any of those partial fingerprints match Mr. Miller's fingerprints?"

"We couldn't determine a match."

"Is that a yes or a no?"

"No."

"Did you find any DNA that matched Mr. Miller's DNA on the backpack?"

"We didn't test for DNA. DNA testing is an expensive process, and our department's funds are limited. We only test for DNA in situations where it's deemed essential."

"You didn't test for DNA?" Hennessy shook his head. "Dr. Hayes, can you confirm that, despite intensive testing, you found nothing on the backpack that indicated it belonged, or had been previously handled, by Mr. Miller?"

"That's correct."

Hennessy sighed, shook his head, and looked at the jury. "No further questions."

The fourth witness of the day, Charleston Music Hall employee Melanie Jones, was questioned next.

Yes, she assigned the key to the dressing room to Mr. Miller. Yes, he was the only one with the key. No, she didn't give the key to anyone else. Lincoln kept the questioning brief before the Judge turned the witness over to the defense for cross-examination.

Hennessy stood, walked to the lectern with a folder.

"Miss Jones," Hennessy began. "In your testimony, you stated you gave Mr. Miller the key to the dressing room at 5pm, when he arrived for the concert. Is that correct?"

"Yes. That's correct." Melanie Jones was a tall blonde, a former model in her thirties, and the events manager at the Charleston Music Hall. She wore a red dress with a yellow cardigan, complete with dangling red earrings.

"And what time was Mr. Miller due to appear on stage?"

"The show started at 6pm with a warm-up act, and then Mr. Miller was due on stage at 7pm."

"Is that the usual time someone arrives for a show that begins at 7pm?"

"Around then, yes. There was nothing unusual about it."

"And you gave him the key when he arrived?"

"Yes, that's correct. He was due to perform three shows that weekend—Friday, Saturday, and Sunday night—and then two more shows the following weekend. I told him to keep the key while the shows were going, but he only did one show as he had to cancel all the remaining shows because of his arrest."

"Did you enter the room before you gave the key to Mr. Miller?"

"Of course. He asked us to put a case of bottled

water, five apples, and some chocolate in his dressing room. I put those things in the room that afternoon, probably around 3ish, and ensured the air-conditioner was going. I put the water and the apples in the small bar fridge under the counter, and I put the chocolate on the countertop."

"Did you see the backpack at that time?"

"No, I didn't, but I also wasn't looking for it."

"Did you see any bags in the room at that time?"

"I do remember the red bag in the far-left corner. It'd been left there by the band who had performed the night before. I was going to move it, but it was out of the way, and I didn't think it would be a problem, so I left it there. We usually clean out the dressing rooms on Sundays."

"To confirm, there were bags in the room before Mr. Miller arrived?"

"That's right. There was also another black backpack that belonged to one of the lighting crew members that he'd left there from the week before."

"So it would be fair to say that many people have used that room in the past and have left items in there?"

"That's right."

"And any number of these people could've left items in the room that wouldn't have been removed?"

"If it's something big that's left behind, I'll remove it, but the small items are fine. It's a big room, and I like to think that the items left behind add to the ambiance of the place. It feels like a part of history."

"So abandoned items are often not removed," Hennessy repeated. "No further questions."

"Redirect, Mr. Lincoln?"

Lincoln stood quickly. "Tell me, Miss Jones, has

someone ever left something valuable in the dressing room?"

"It happens on occasion."

"And if they left something valuable in the room, say something worth around $5000, do they come back for it?"

"Sometimes, yes."

"And if they come back, do you inspect the items they've reclaimed?"

"No. I trust the performers."

"No further questions," Lincoln sat back down.

Before Miss Jones could be excused from the witness stand, a man from the back of the crowd rose to his feet and yelled, "We don't need drugs in Charleston! Lock him up!"

"Quiet!" Judge Fedder roared. "Bailiffs!"

"Take your drugs somewhere else!" The older man was pushed toward the courtroom doors by the bailiffs. "We don't want them here!"

As the bailiffs removed the man from the courtroom, holding onto his arms, he continued to yell. Judge Fedder turned to the jury and instructed them to disregard the interruption from the man.

The courtroom was sweltering, and Hennessy wasn't finished yet.

CHAPTER 39

THE ROOM was baking hot when the court was back in session the following morning.

The air-conditioner had malfunctioned overnight, the bailiff said, but it would work again soon, although it'd take at least an hour to fix it. Judge Fedder didn't want to wait, pushing ahead despite the oppressive conditions inside the courtroom. The seats were filled in the courtroom again, but this time, many in the crowd were using pieces of paper as small fans, creating a constant flapping noise. The musty smell was thick, and the air felt even thicker.

Lincoln wiped his brow and called the next witness.

Call Center Operator Mrs. Janine Walter came to the stand, flapping her shirt as she went. She was a larger woman in her fifties and didn't handle the heat well. Her face was red, and the sweat was visible on her brow. Lincoln offered her a glass of cold water, which she happily accepted, and said the AC would be working again shortly. Just as he did, something clunked above their heads, and the fans whirled into action. There was a small cheer from the crowd.

For twenty-five minutes, Mrs. Walter answered questions about the call she took on the Crime Stoppers tip line. They listened to the recording of the call, and then Mrs. Walter explained the organization's processes.

By the time Hennessy was offered the cross-examination, the room had cooled, and the redness was gone from Mrs. Walter's face.

"Mrs. Walter, I apologize about the heat in here this morning, and I thank you for sticking with us," Hennessy said, staying seated behind his desk. "Can you please tell the court how many drug-related tip-offs you receive a day?"

"A day? Not many." She shook her head. "Probably about one or two a week. We tend to get more tip-offs at the end of the week as it nears the weekend."

"And what do these calls usually involve?"

"Not much. Usually, the calls are not very descriptive. For instance, someone might call up and say that their neighbor is dealing weed, but they don't know who to, or how much, or where they do the deals. They just have a general idea."

"And do these calls usually get routed to the police?"

"Routed to the police? They're certainly reported, but these types of calls aren't followed up on by the police."

"Why not?"

"Because we must have a high standard of proof and credibility for an anonymous tip-off call to be investigated. We're trained to ask specific questions to draw out enough information for the tip to get the appropriate follow-up."

"And did you investigate who made the tip-off?"

"No, we did not."

"And do you have any idea where the tip-off came from?"

"No."

"Is it unusual to receive a specific tip-off with very detailed information?"

"It was unusual, and that's why we thought it was legitimate."

"And did you, in your professional opinion, consider this information to be credible?"

"It wasn't up to me to make that call."

"But in your professional opinion, as someone who has worked the tip line for over ten years, did you consider there to be enough information for this call to be credible?"

She looked to the prosecution table, and when she did, Lincoln sprang into action.

"Objection, Your Honor," Lincoln stood. "The question calls for speculation."

"Not at all, Your Honor," Hennessy argued. "We have an expert witness who has listened to thousands of similar tip-off calls, and she can testify whether this call was any different."

"I'm inclined to agree with the defense on this one," Judge Fedder stated. "The objection is overruled, and you may answer the question."

"Alright." Mrs. Walter wiped her brow with her index finger. "No, I didn't think there was enough evidence for this tip-off to be pursued, but again, it wasn't my call to make."

"And why do you think this call was forwarded to the police department?"

"Objection. The question directly calls for speculation."

"Sustained. I agree with the prosecution this time," Judge Fedder stated. "Watch your language there, Mr. Hennessy."

Hennessy nodded. "Let me rephrase. Was there anything to indicate that this call should've been followed up on over other tip-offs?"

"Not from what I heard, no."

"Interesting." Hennessy paused and looked at the jury. "No further questions."

CHAPTER 40

"THE STATE calls Mr. Cameron Tucker."

As the next witness walked through the courtroom doors, Hennessy could see why he might have been hired for the security job at the Charleston Music Hall. His frame was huge, almost scraping the sky at six-ten. And as for his weight, he must have tipped the scales at no less than three hundred, every single one of them rippling with muscle. His file said he was a former pro heavyweight boxer, a local legend who retired at thirty-five and was now working security at various venues.

It was almost comical watching him take the stand, the stairs leading up to the dock taken in a single step. He towered over the divider, and Hennessy imagined the chair protesting the way his own office chair did whenever he leaned into it.

Lincoln didn't waste time before jumping into questions for the witness, asking the guard to explain his role on the night in question. Tucker struggled to remember the answers to the questions that Lincoln had prepared him for, stumbling over several answers and correcting himself.

Through the guided questions asked by Lincoln, Tucker shared his role as backstage security that night, mentioning how Miller was one of the few performers who preferred to hide behind a closed door while he waited for his turn to take the stage. Yes, he thought it was unusual and assumed Miller was up to something he preferred to keep private. Hennessy promptly made an objection for speculation, but the damage was done.

Tucker insisted he saw nobody enter or exit the room while Miller was performing onstage. It was all Hennessy needed to hear.

When Lincoln finished, Hennessy began questioning him from behind the lectern.

"Mr. Tucker, you mentioned in your testimony that you were watching the doors of the dressing rooms all night. How long would you say you spent watching the doors?"

The guard's eyes remained fixed on Hennessy, and he could see why patrons would avoid arguing with the man. He had the kind of face movie producers would love, with a distinct shadow of threat sprawled across it. He kept his voice low. "My entire shift."

"For the duration of your shift, you stood by the door of the hallway that led to the five dressing rooms, and you kept guard?"

"Yes."

Hennessy nodded and slowly walked around the desk before he paused in the middle of the floor. "And the duration of an average shift for you?"

"Five hours."

"That's a long time to be on your feet."

"I have a stool."

Hennessy smiled and took another couple of steps forward before stopping again and making eye contact. "And does it get warm watching the door for five hours straight?"

Tucker shuffled in his seat. "It's not just one door

I watch. There are a few, but they're all in a row; all in the same corridor."

"Ok, and does it get warm? Does the club have AC?"

"It does."

"And during these five hours, I assume you get thirsty. Have anything to drink?"

Tucker's face briefly lit up, as if he sensed where the annoying lawyer was going. "Waitress normally brings me drinks, but nothing alcoholic when I'm on the job."

"Drinks? So, more than one?"

"Yes, more than one. Maybe a few during the night."

"And tell me, Mr. Tucker, after all these drinks the waitress brings you, does she also bring you the bathroom?"

A faint chuckle rose from the crowd, causing Tucker to shift uncomfortably in his seat again. "No, of course not. I go to the—"

He stopped short, as if catching himself saying something he shouldn't.

"Go on, Mr. Tucker. You were just going to tell us how you might go to the bathroom after all the drinks the waitress brings you."

"Yes, I might've gone to the bathroom."

"And did you go to the bathroom while Mr. Miller was performing?"

"Yes," he conceded. "Only for a minute."

"And while you were in the bathroom, do you think it might be possible for some unknown person to enter the room?"

"Objection, Your Honor, speculation."

"It's not speculation, Your Honor," Hennessy

replied. "The witness understands the layout of the building. I'm sure he can't possibly maintain eye contact with the door while taking a bathroom break, which means he can't confidently state whether a person has the time and the means to gain access to the room without being seen by the witness."

"Overruled," Fedder said and turned to Tucker. "You may answer the question."

"Mr. Tucker," Hennessy continued. "Was there a brief period during the night in question when you didn't have an eye on the dressing room?"

"I guess it's possible that during my two-minute bathroom break that someone could've snuck in there."

"Thank you, Mr. Tucker. No further questions."

CHAPTER 41

DURING A trial, the most challenging part was the nights.

That's when Joe Hennessy couldn't sleep. That's when the stress of losing the case came to the forefront of his mind, thundering through no matter how distracted he became. He never managed more than five hours of sleep during a trial. He couldn't. Every time he tried to drift off, another thought would spring back into his mind, sending him off on another rollercoaster of thoughts.

It was bad during every trial, but it was especially bad when he was losing.

He'd managed to cast doubt on some of the witnesses against Miller, he'd managed to throw doubt on their testimonies, but he still wasn't in a winning position.

Preston Wheeler's testimony would make or break the prosecution's case. He was the one that was going to testify that Miller had offered to sell him drugs, and he was the one that was going to put the nail into the coffin. Hennessy needed something, anything, to throw doubt over his testimony, but he had nothing.

After another night of very little sleep, Hennessy waited outside the courthouse, leaning against the wall with a large takeout coffee, staring at the fast-moving clouds in the sky. When Lockett pulled up to the curb, the threatening rain clouds had already moved on.

"Needed to tell you about Stefan Moore," Lockett said as he approached. "Got something for you."

"The character witness against Miller?" Hennessy said. "He's up today."

"I found the link that we've been looking for. Stefan Moore is dating Wheeler's niece. The two go way back, and it looks as if Wheeler uses him for odd favors here and there."

"Do we know if Moore uses?"

"Nothing official, but on the night of Miller's so-called possession charge? He spent most of the night upstairs in the private lounge at the Charleston Music Hall, and yes, the rumor is that there was enough white powder scattered around the joint to look like it was snowing."

"Any footage of this private lounge?"

"No chance. There are cameras, but they're not linked to the other ones in the club, and we'd have no chance of getting our hands on the footage." Lockett came in closer. "But I have something else for you."

Lockett spent the next five minutes explaining the details to Hennessy and then handed him a USB.

Hennessy smiled. "Barry, you're a lifesaver. You're worth more than gold."

"I'll hold you to that."

The two men parted company, and Hennessy walked through the security checkpoint with a smile on his face.

Inside the Charleston County Judicial Center, he found Miller in the foyer, rubbing his forehead repeatedly. The foyer was subdued, and the tension amongst the people waiting for their turn in court was obvious. Miller looked nervous, more wound up than he had ever seen him before. Hennessy had a bad feeling he'd be seen as the drug-addicted cokehead the prosecution hoped to prove he was. Unless he calmed down, he would make their job harder.

"Try to take some deep breaths," Hennessy said, leaning in close and lowering his voice as a member of the prosecution walked past them. "Think happy thoughts."

"Happy thoughts? How am I supposed to think happy thoughts in this place?"

Hennessy knew he was right but continued advising his client. "Try. You can't look agitated to the jury. They're watching you, and anything you do will be judged. They'll think you're still using if you're jumpy and nervous."

Miller took a few moments to calm himself and followed Hennessy through to courtroom number five. The bailiff let them into the empty room, and they settled at the defense table, preparing for the day ahead.

Soon, the court employees showed up, with the stenographer, bailiff, and several guards taking up their positions. Hennessy took it all in, remembering the first time he'd ever sat behind one of the tables with a case unfolding right in front of him.

"Just breathe," he repeated to Miller, who had begun to fidget again.

The man's eyes continued darting around the place, appearing as if he was wired directly into the building's power supply.

Hennessy's advice to his client seemed to work, and by the time the bailiff called the court to their feet, Miller had settled down considerably, his hands resting in his lap. All eyes turned to watch Judge Fedder enter, shuffle to the bench, and take his seat behind it. After a quick scan, his eyes focused on Hennessy, made eye contact with him for a moment, then turned his attention back to his paperwork. He called for the jury. The pressure was on.

The case was heating up, and it was all on the line.

CHAPTER 42

JAMAL LINCOLN had dressed in his best suit, which fitted perfectly to his broad frame.

He knew this was his week. This would be the week that he would finish the case. This would be the week his face would be broadcast on every media channel. This would be his week to show the city that he was the man to lead them in the fight against crime. Justice would be served in this case, and he'd make a name for himself. This would be his week to see his name in lights.

It was Hennessy's job to make sure none of that happened.

On Thursday morning of the first week of the trial, Lincoln called Mr. Stefan Moore to the stand. A well-dressed, lanky, twenty-five-year-old with dark circles under his eyes walked in. His shoes were expensive, as was his watch. His one diamond earring cost more than a small car.

Lincoln started his questioning, reading off a piece of paper, and Moore answered the questions factually. Yes, he knew the defendant. Yes, he'd partied with him before. Yes, he was at the Charleston Music Hall on the night of the 5th of September.

"Can you please describe what you saw on the night of the 5th of September?"

"One of the lighting crew members invited me

backstage. He was one of the guys I went to school with, and he did a lot of work at the Charleston Music Hall. He told me to come backstage after the gig, so I did."

"And did you see Mr. Miller backstage?"

"I did. Zach Miller just finished his set and was hanging out with a couple of the band members. I called out and said he'd done a great job, but he ignored me and turned away. I followed him and saw that he had walked down to the back corner of the main backstage room and was huddled over a table. I wanted to make sure that he heard me, so I called out again, and that's when I saw he was holding a rolled-up hundred-dollar bill, and he'd just snorted a line of white powder."

A gasp went through the courtroom. Miller shifted in his seat.

"Try to breathe," Hennessy whispered to Miller.

Lincoln didn't press on much further. The damage was already done. He asked several clarifying questions, and when satisfied that the testimony had the desired impact, he turned the witness over to the defense.

Lincoln looked at Hennessy and nodded. Turned away from the jurors, he offered Hennessy a smug smile. Hennessy shook his head.

When invited to begin his cross-examination, Hennessy rose to his feet, taking his time as he walked to the lectern. He let the tension build in the room, the jurors hanging on his every word.

"Wow, Mr. Moore, that was quite a story." He turned to the jury. "But it's not true, is it?"

"Objection," Lincoln called out. "Accusation."

"Withdrawn," Hennessy said quickly, but the

statement's impact remained. "Mr. Moore, can you please describe the room you and Mr. Miller found yourselves in?"

"It was backstage at the Charleston Music Hall. It was in the hallway, and there wasn't much space. Miller was heading into his dressing room when he stopped."

"And you saw Mr. Miller after his performance?"

"That's what I said."

"That's what you said, but is it what you meant?"

"What?" Moore looked confused. "Yeah. I saw him backstage. After the performance. On the 5th of September."

"And where were you during the performance?"

"Upstairs in a private area. I watched the show from the second level with my friends."

"Are you aware of what time the show finished?"

Moore shook his head. "I have no idea."

"It finished at 10:41pm. That's the time Mr. Miller stepped off stage according to the video presented by the Charleston Music Hall, who were recording the set." Hennessy walked back to his desk and typed several lines into his computer. A picture appeared on the monitor at the side of the room—Moore, with his arm around a female friend, was taking a selfie. "Can you please confirm that is you in the picture?"

"Yeah. That's me and my friend, Chloe. We went to the concert together, and that's a picture she took at the start."

"And where did you go after this concert?"

"Like I said, we went backstage, and then after that, we walked to the Cocktail Club on King St."

"Which, by calculation using Google Maps, is a five-minute walk."

"That would be about right."

"Can you please explain this next picture?" Hennessy tapped another key on his laptop, and the picture changed.

"That's another picture Chloe took as we entered the Cocktail Club," he leaned forward. "She loves to take selfies wherever we go, and she likes to post them as soon as we enter a place. It's her digital footprint."

"Her digital footprint, indeed," Hennessy said. "Mr. Moore, I'm sure you're aware that with social media posts, if you click on that particular post, it displays the time the photo was posted. So, knowing that, Mr. Moore, can you please look at the time this selfie was posted on Chloe's social media feed?"

Moore squinted, looked at the time, and then stopped. He sat back a little, mouth hanging open.

"Mr. Moore?" Hennessy pressed.

Moore stared at the picture, a blank look on his face.

"Mr. Moore," Hennessy raised his voice. "Can you please tell the court when that picture was posted?"

"10:39pm," he whispered.

"I'm sorry, Mr. Moore?" Hennessy's voice boomed across the courtroom. "What time was that photo posted?"

"10:39pm."

"And yet, Mr. Miller didn't step off the stage until 10:41pm." Hennessy's fist tapped the table. "Mr. Moore, you didn't see him after the concert, did you?"

He shook his head, blinking back tears from being embarrassed and overwhelmed. "I might've."

"You might've? You might've?!" Hennessy moved

back to the lectern, staring at the witness the entire time. "This is a court of law, Mr. Moore. This is not a place to guess. This is not a place for lies. So, tell me, did you see Mr. Miller backstage, after his performance, on the night of the 5th of September?"

"Listen, alright. I might've seen him, but I also might've gotten mixed up. It might've been someone else."

"Mixed up," Hennessy scoffed. "And you certainly didn't see Mr. Miller snort any cocaine, did you?"

"No," he whispered.

"So the question is—why are you lying to this court?"

"I… I must've got my nights mixed up. Maybe it was someone else I saw backstage. One of the crew, maybe."

"Mr. Moore, do you care to tell the court who Chloe is related to? Perhaps you'd like to share her last name with the court?"

He stared at the prosecution team, but they were all avoiding eye contact.

"Mr. Moore?"

"Her last name is Wheeler," he said.

"And is she related to Mr. Preston Wheeler, the disgruntled former manager of Mr. Miller?"

"Yes," Moore blinked back further tears, "Chloe is his niece."

"And did Mr. Wheeler ask you to lie to this court today?"

"No, no." Moore shook his head, but it was clearly a lie. "I just got mixed up. That's all. It must've been one of the crew I saw backstage."

Hennessy turned to Judge Fedder. "Your Honor. This witness has changed his statement in a matter of minutes. This is blatant perjury. I move to dismiss this witness and his entire testimony under Section 16-9-10 (A)(1), which states, 'that it is unlawful for a person to give false, misleading, or incomplete testimony under oath in any court of record, judicial, administrative, or regulatory proceeding in this State.'"

Judge Fedder turned to the prosecution. "Counsel? Any objections to the dismissal of this entire witness testimony?"

Lincoln shook his head. "No objections."

It was a big win for Hennessy, and he wasn't finished yet.

CHAPTER 43

JAMAL LINCOLN called for a recess.

The judge granted him the Friday to work on the case, allowing him to re-question his witnesses and return the following Monday.

At 7:05am on Friday morning, Lincoln called Hennessy. He needed to talk. And by the sounds of his croaky voice, he'd been working through the night. Hennessy notified Miller and then Jacinta and arrived at the Charleston County Judicial Center a little after 8am. Lincoln was waiting with his team.

The lawyers and their teams talked in the large conference room, spending thirty minutes arguing about a potential deal and negotiating on time served and fines.

Hennessy knew how it looked for the prosecution, and he knew what they were facing in the courtroom. There was shouting, fists slamming on desks, and lots of legal precedents thrown at each other.

When Zach Miller arrived at 8:55am, he joined Hennessy and Jacinta in the smaller conference room toward the end of the hallway. It was stuffy, the ducted air-conditioner whirling above their heads. The room was filled with the smell of coffee, thanks to the three freshly brewed lattes that Jacinta brought with her.

Miller couldn't sit down. He was too anxious, and

his nerves were getting to him as he stood at the side of the room. Hennessy leaned forward on the wooden table, his heavy arms causing it to wobble sideways, but not enough to spill the coffee.

"Lay it on me," Miller said. "And tell me it's good."

"The deal is an early guilty plea for possession of cocaine," Hennessy stated. "If you take the deal, they'll drop the trafficking charges. They won't even push for Possession with Intent to Distribute. They'll drop the charges right down to possession."

"Time?"

"One year in prison, one year suspended."

"Still a year in prison?"

"With time served on the GPS monitor, you're looking at eight months behind bars."

"Still eight months?" He threw his hands up in the air. "Didn't you hear them in there? Wheeler's niece's boyfriend lied through his teeth to try and convict me. The prosecution heard that, right? They've got to know how bad this looks for them. Why are they still chasing a conviction?"

"I know." Hennessy nodded. "I expected them to drop the charges altogether, but they didn't budge on the sentence. They said they have to save face and can't let you walk free. It would go against everything that the Circuit Solicitor has been preaching about, and this would play out very badly in the media. They don't want the rich and famous to get a free pass."

"But the drugs weren't mine!" He gripped his fists and tapped them lightly against the drywall. "Can't they see that? Preston Wheeler set me up."

"And that's what they're worried about. He's the only witness they have left to call, and he's going to make an appearance on Monday."

"Will they still call him?" Jacinta asked.

"They have to. He's the only witness that will testify that Miller tried to sell him the drugs. Without him, they don't have a case. His statement is what they've been building toward during this whole trial. But now, their star witness has turned into a major risk. If they put him on the stand right after Moore's testimony that was thrown out because he lied, it's going to look disastrous."

Miller paced the small floor space on his side of the room, mumbling inaudible words to himself before he stopped and looked back at Hennessy. "Do you think they'll change the plea?"

"They've got all weekend to consider it." Hennessy drew a breath and sighed. "But they've also publicly said that you won't get away from this without a penalty. If this was any other case, I'm certain they'd drop the charges before they called Wheeler to the stand. But in your case…" He shook his head. "Sorry, Zach, but I don't think they will. I think they'll take the risk and still call Wheeler."

Miller grunted and sat down at the table, staring at the grains in the wood. He thought for a moment and then looked up. "Do you think we can win? Do you think you'll tear Wheeler apart on the stand?"

"I can't guarantee it."

"But is it likely?"

Hennessy leaned back. "I wouldn't say likely. We know that Moore didn't go backstage after the gig, but if we can prove that Wheeler and Balter communicated somehow that night, and Balter planted the drugs, then it's signed, sealed, and delivered. But that's a big 'if.'"

"So, how do we prove Balter is the man?"

"We have to find out how they contact each other," Hennessy said. "My advice, as your lawyer, is to take the weekend to really think about this new deal. It's a good offer, and you'll only serve eight months behind bars. Take the weekend to consider it. The offer is on the table until court resumes on Monday morning."

Miller stood. "I'm not taking the deal. You can tell them to shove it. I've put my faith in you, Joe Hennessy. I know you can win this."

Miller held Hennessy's eye contact for a few moments before turning to the conference room door and exiting.

"He's got faith in you," Jacinta said. "He thinks you can win this."

Hennessy didn't respond, staring at the door.

He rubbed his temple as the strain of the week continued to make the same spot in his brain throb. With the weekend upon him, he wanted nothing more than to get home to the vineyard, hug his wife, and forget about life in the city.

But then Jacinta reminded him of something which would keep him in the city for the weekend.

"You ready for the memorial tomorrow?"

With no more signs of Elliot McGovern found in the week since his suicide note was discovered, the police had taken him off the missing persons list and officially registered him as deceased.

Hennessy was astonished at the rate they pushed the death through, but when he heard that Harold McGovern encouraged it, he wasn't surprised.

"I'll go to the memorial because Kirkland still owes me money for the work I did on that case," Hennessy grunted. "He won't escape me there."

CHAPTER 44

THE WEATHER was humid again, the thick and sticky air staying around for longer into the year than usual.

Hennessy didn't sleep well again that night, tossing and turning under the spluttering AC in his apartment. What were the jury members thinking? He didn't know. He wished he did. He wished each side was scored at the end of each day, and the result displayed on a scoreboard as they exited the room. Fourteen for the defense, seven points for the prosecution, is how he saw it. But did they see it the same? And was Wheeler's testimony going to turn it around for him? It was the great unknown, and the possibilities kept rolling through his head as the hours ticked past.

Wendy called early. There was another wedding at the vineyard that weekend. Hennessy had met the intended bride only once, and even that was once too many times for him. What he saw during the ten-minute chat convinced him she was an outright bridezilla. They had almost declined the wedding because of the woman's demands, but given the five thousand dollar fee the group had been willing to pay to use the venue for the day, both Wendy and Hennessy knew it wasn't one they could easily pass up.

"I wish I was there to help you," Hennessy whispered to her.

In true Wendy style, she acknowledged his comment but eased him gently aside. "I know you do, but we'll be ok. I have a pretty good team to help with this one, and let's face it, it's just a day, right?"

She was right, of course, right in every way. They did have a good team behind them, and their experience would ensure Luca's Vineyard provided the high-quality service it prided itself on.

"How about you? Ready to go to the memorial?"

"Yes, but I'm not sure why I'm even going."

"You still don't think he's dead, do you?"

"Not until they find a body. Meanwhile, Elliot McGovern will be hiding in some luxury villa in South America and..." He paused as the thought played out.

"Joe?"

He thought back to how McGovern had looked the last time he saw him, withdrawn, weighed down. He looked almost as defeated as Zach Miller had. "Or maybe he's walked out of his home and drowned himself in the ocean, and they just haven't found his body yet." He rubbed his temple again, trying to find the spot which would relieve him from all the stress and responsibilities, even just for a few hours. "I really don't know." He paused and smiled to himself. "What I do know is that I miss you."

"I miss you too. I wish you could have come home this weekend. But you'll be home after Miller's case is finished, right?"

"One hundred percent."

They had spoken for a few more minutes, and then once he hung up the call, he walked to the deck with a coffee, watching the daybreak cast its orange haze over the city.

As he sat sipping his coffee and listening to the city come alive around him, his cellphone beeped briefly. He still hadn't been paid by Kirkland's office, despite many emails and calls asking for the final payment. He'd have to corner him at the memorial, something he knew Kirkland would try his best to avoid.

Waiting until the last minute before he left, Hennessy drove through the Saturday morning streets. With traffic almost non-existent, he arrived at the memorial with nearly ten minutes to spare, something he had wholeheartedly tried to avoid.

He'd considered staying in his truck until just a couple of minutes before the scheduled start time, but people were looking at him. Reluctantly, he exited the truck and walked up to the hall at Lowndes Grove. The Grove was a two-story waterfront plantation estate built in 1786 on the Ashley River, located in the Wagener Terrace neighborhood. It usually hosted weddings but also had a long history of hosting memorials and funerals.

There were nearly fifty people inside the venue who mingled like old friends, laughing and smiling in subdued voices. Nobody seemed heartbroken. Nobody seemed sad. Hennessy walked to the table where the coffee was being served and asked for a large mug.

"I'm surprised you had the balls to show your face here," a voice said from behind him. He knew the voice, and then, turning to meet the man's eyes, recognition sank in.

Harold McGovern stood behind him with a glass

in one hand and an attitude in the other. He always walked with one hand tucked between the buttons on his jacket as if trying to emulate some sort of Napoleonic wisdom.

"Excuse me?" Hennessy wasn't in the mood for a scene and kept his voice low.

But McGovern Senior highly valued any opportunity to get a little attention from the masses over the need for privacy, even at a somber moment such as his son's memorial. "If you were such a hotshot lawyer, Hennessy, why didn't you get him off? You should've been able to clear his name. The case against him was weak. You should've had it thrown out. Any good lawyer would have. And I can tell you one thing for sure, you're not getting a cent from the estate. You failed, and you don't deserve to get paid."

As he stood staring at the man, two choices ran through his mind, and neither was appealing. He could either defend his honor, which would undoubtedly give Harold McGovern reason to continue arguing, or he could turn and walk out, leave the venue completely and avoid the confrontation altogether.

Ultimately, he went with neither, knowing either choice would come back to bite him. Instead, he held his hand out to McGovern, held his gaze, and said, "I'm sorry for your loss, Harold."

The moment he held his hand out, he knew what the man would do. Others were watching, and the McGovern patriarch knew he was on display. It was something Hennessy had banked on.

The man didn't even look at the hand held out to him. He simply huffed once and turned away. Within seconds, the crowd swallowed him up, well-wishers offering their condolences.

As the crowd mingled, Hennessy caught Kirkland's eye.

Kirkland turned away, but Hennessy made a direct line for him. Kirkland couldn't avoid him. As Hennessy stood next to Kirkland, he leaned down and whispered in the man's ear. "I still haven't been paid."

Kirkland paused for a moment, excused himself from the people he was with, and then nodded for Hennessy to follow him outside. Hennessy nodded his response.

There weren't many people outdoors in the garden space, just a couple of older gentlemen murmuring and puffing on cigarettes. Kirkland and Hennessy moved to the side of the yard, next to the tall hedges, away from prying ears.

"You don't look very sad," Kirkland began.

"Are you?"

Kirkland shook his head, then checked around to ensure nobody was listening. "I wanted him to go to trial so we could make lots of money. Did I think we could win?" He grinned. "Maybe we could've won in a trial, but it was unlikely. All I know is that it would've cost him a lot of money to take it that far."

"How honorable."

"It's not about honor, it's about money." Kirkland checked over his shoulder again and then lowered his voice. "The rumor is that Harold McGovern used his connections in the police force to officially list Elliot as deceased. The way I see it, if he is alive, if he's faked his own death, his father has covered for him."

"I thought the same thing all along."

"Not much we can do about it, though. He's officially dead."

"Even without a body? That's ridiculous. There's no way he's dead." Hennessy shook his head. "Who signed the death certificate?"

"Captain Callaghan. Old guy, just about on retirement, and he's been in the pocket of the McGoverns for years. With the death certificate signed off, the murder case against him gets filed away, the estate gets transferred to Harold, and Elliot is not on any missing persons list. Nobody is looking for him." He looked around again. "Sorry, Joe, but there's nothing we can do about it. We should dust our hands off and forget about it."

"I worked this case, and I deserved to get paid for my time."

"You'll have to take it up with the estate, I'm afraid." Kirkland's voice was firm. "Any retainer paid by McGovern has been eaten up in costs for my law firm, and that means we can't pay you. It's in the contract, Joe. You should know that. If you want your money, you'll have to file a claim against the estate."

Hennessy groaned before looking back to the memorial service venue.

"And a word of warning," Kirkland continued. "Harold isn't going to part with a cent of the money. He'll fight you every step of the way. That miserly old man won't want to part with his son's money. You'll spend more time chasing the money than it's worth." Kirkland patted Hennessy on the arm. "Sorry, Joe. You lost out on this one. Write it off and forget about it."

Kirkland smirked slightly and walked back into the service. As he walked in, Helen McGovern walked out.

"Mrs. McGovern," Hennessy greeted her. "I'm sorry for your loss."

"Don't be," she said. She wore a floral dress, flowing past her knees, and dark sunglasses. She appeared as if she was readying herself for a day out at a picnic. "Walk with me."

She began slowly stepping around the edge of the hedge, following the concrete path, head tilted forward. "You seem like a wise man, Mr. Hennessy."

"As Hemingway once put it, old men with wisdom is one of life's great fallacies. Men don't grow wise as they get older, they just grow more careful."

She smiled slightly. "I didn't want this memorial, but Harold insisted on it. It's all a show. It's just for his friends and the media."

"You don't think he's dead?"

She stopped and looked up at him, lifting her large sunglasses off and raising her eyebrows. "You do?"

Hennessy shook his head.

She nodded and began walking again. "We both know my son was more than likely guilty of his wife's murder. Even if he didn't kill her himself, I'm sure he had a hand in it somewhere along the way. And I think he knew his days of freedom were numbered, which is why he ran." She stopped walking. They were far enough from others to ensure their privacy. The smokers had returned indoors, leaving them alone in the yard. "I know Elliot hid a hundred-thousand dollars in cash in a safe at his vacation property in Florida. But I'll tell you something funny—his wife moved the money. She knew it was his stash fund, so she took it out before the divorce proceedings. There was no way she would let him hide that money from her."

"Why are you telling me this?"

"Because as soon as he realizes the money isn't there," she looked up at Hennessy and nodded, "he's going to come back here and demand cash from his father."

CHAPTER 45

ELLIOT MCGOVERN didn't like Miami.

Too many crowds, too much traffic, and too many people trying to be someone they're not. But as he sat on a bench at a bus stop considering his future, he wondered whether he could actually remain in town. It hadn't been his first choice, of course, but spur-of-the-moment decisions never ended with a person finding themselves in a place they had dreamed about.

With the mood he was in, he was ready to scream. Nothing made sense anymore. His head continued to itch from the hair dye he'd used to disguise himself as a blonde, and the face mask made breathing so much harder. He pulled it back from his face for the fiftieth time, took a huge gulp of unfiltered air, then readjusted it.

"What are you wearing a mask for, dude?" a voice called from the other side of the street. McGovern looked in the person's direction and considered ripping the mask down and telling them to take a hike, but he knew why he wore it, and revealing his face wasn't an option. "Dumb sheep," the person muttered as they walked into the bathroom, leaving Elliot to continue with his plans.

A bus pulled in, but it wasn't the one he was waiting for.

The motel he'd been staying at felt a world away

from the life he'd been raised in. This wasn't how things were supposed to end up. The motel stunk, and the people staying there made up the lower end of the town's social class. Loud arguments filled most nights from dusk to dawn, and several times, he'd almost been mugged by a couple of homeless guys.

He shuddered at the thought of returning there, wishing he could jump on a bus and return to Charleston. That was where his life was; that was where his money waited for him. Money. His body tingled at the thought of getting his hands on a decent chunk of change. Of course, he'd already prepared a stash of cash, and it was right there waiting for him to come and get it.

It was in his vacation apartment on Miami Beach. Katherine loved Miami Beach. She would've moved there if he'd allowed her to, and every chance she got, she traveled down and fluttered about the beach, flapping about like some celebrity. He hated it but put up with it for her sake.

There was a hundred grand in cash in the safe at the vacation apartment. He'd put it there many years ago, an escape plan if anything ever went wrong.

His father had told him to lie low until after his death certificate was signed off, and then go to the apartment, take the money, and begin a new life in Costa Rica. His father had a contact that could get him there on a boat, and then his father would transfer a million dollars to set him up once he landed. It was all arranged. It was all done within a day of deciding to run, but he needed the hundred grand in cash to pay the man on the boat.

They couldn't risk going to the bank and withdrawing a large sum of cash before he disappeared, it would've been too obvious, but Elliot knew he had enough cash stashed away.

He checked the internet—it was a good turnout for his memorial, and the media was nice to him. They didn't mention Katherine's name once in the media report. That would've been Harold's work, protecting the family name, keeping their drama out of the spotlight even after his fake death.

He looked around, saw the man who'd called him a sheep, and waited for another dose of insults to be shouted at him. But the man ignored him this time, distracted by a woman carrying a small child. The man tried to speak with the child and the woman, but she was clearly annoyed and picked up her pace to escape the pest.

McGovern turned back to the bus parked at one of the stations, watching as the people began to board it. He could see inside, the passengers walking down the aisle between the seats, then dropping down into them. He boarded the bus, ready to go to the vacation apartment and get the money.

The bus slowly rolled forward, the people looking out at the world they were leaving behind. McGovern readjusted the mask on his face and quietly whispered a goodbye to them, knowing that for him, there was just a single way out of this mess.

He just needed the money.

CHAPTER 46

SUNDAY MORNINGS in Charleston were one of Hennessy's secret loves.

It was nearly impossible to travel more than one block without encountering an elaborately beautiful church ringing its bells. With that, it was definitely impossible to live for more than fifteen minutes without hearing a church bell. The bells chimed everywhere, all Sunday long on the Peninsula.

He walked the streets, watching people in their Sunday best greet each other and then proceed to the many churches. Passing the churches brought a smile to his face, although he hadn't been inside a church since he carried the casket of his ten-year-old son out of one. Most of South Carolina's communities were built around churches, but he just couldn't step inside one again. He tried to once, but he couldn't bring himself to step over the threshold. How could he, when so much was taken from him? How could any higher power let that happen to his son? He appreciated that people needed faith, he appreciated the community it created, but he couldn't face the church again.

"Maybe one day," he whispered to himself as he stood outside the tall steeple of a Baptist church. "Maybe one day I'll find my faith again."

The sun was shining, and the weather had cooled,

bringing a calmness that descended over Charleston. Children were laughing, adults were gossiping, and smiles were abounding. Wendy still attended church every Sunday in Greenville and always invited Joe to come along, but he just couldn't do it.

As he wandered the streets, taking in the sights and sounds, Barry Lockett called.

"I've got it." He was direct and to the point. "I'll meet you in the office in an hour."

Hennessy checked his watch and agreed.

An hour later, Hennessy was in his office, a freshly brewed coffee on his desk. The building on Church St., one of the main thoroughfares of activity in Downtown, felt empty without the usual activity of a weekday. During any normal weekday, a buzz hung over each floor of the building, with people constantly coming and going from several businesses that called the place home. The sounds of life seemed to traverse each floor, with the stairs, the extraction fans, the beeps and bumps filling the air with energy. But not on a Sunday.

On a Sunday, the building struggled to raise its activity level above a slight murmur. The parking lot at the back of the building sat empty. The faint hum of the building itself seemed dulled by the air of the weekend, something Hennessy compared to the atmosphere of a resort. It was as if the building itself, the raw essence of it, understood that Sunday was its day off, the one day of the week where it didn't need to function as an office building and instead, it could take time to re-energize for the upcoming work week.

Hennessy sat at his desk with the laptop open and was busy looking at new trucks when Barry Lockett walked through the door. Not feeling ready to discuss the possibility of buying a new truck with anybody, he closed the laptop's lid a little too fast, a fact not lost on the Australian.

"Don't tell me you were looking at naked women."

Hennessy grinned, then laughed. The PI's endless ability to pull one-liners out of thin air in a heartbeat always made him laugh. "No, not likely," he said. "What have you got?"

"I went through Balter's trash last night and found a laptop."

"A laptop?"

"He just threw it out. It was pretty old, but that didn't stop me from taking it."

"What's on it?"

"I have no idea yet. I know a hacker who lives in Myrtle Beach, and I'm on my way there now. He says that this sort of computer usually takes about twelve hours to break into, and if he can get into it, it'll take another twelve hours to pull out all the saved passwords."

"He can do that?"

"Not with newer laptops, no, but these older ones are easier to hack. The codes weren't as difficult back then. The hacker has a program that can bypass the security features on these older computers. If he can pull the passwords, then we can see how Balter and Wheeler communicate. We'll have his email addresses, his phone provider passwords, and his social media accounts. If they communicate online, we'll find it."

"I don't want you to break the law, Lockett. I'm not willing to break the law to get the information we need."

"Then we'll have to find a way to do it legally."

"How?"

"The hacker always said that if he can reprogram an old computer, he can resell it. All he's doing is wiping the drive. But of course, to wipe the drive, he has to bypass some information stored on the laptop. Officially, he's not breaking into the laptop, he's just wiping it. Now, if we can get a breadcrumb, just a small piece of information from this laptop, then we can search the dark web for any links. It's a long shot, but from what I've heard, Balter often uses the dark web to communicate about his deals."

"Preston Wheeler is due on the stand tomorrow morning." Hennessy looked at his watch. "That's just over twenty-four hours away."

"Then I better get out there." Lockett stood. "I'll call you the moment I know anything."

"If you can find out how they communicate, do it," Hennessy said. "But you have to get the information legally."

CHAPTER 47

NO BETTER offer came from the prosecution.

They wouldn't budge on the year in prison, and Miller wasn't interested in taking the offer. Preston Wheeler's testimony was the key—if the prosecution had prepared him well and the questioning went flawlessly, if everything went according to plan, then the jury could be swung in their favor. If they got it wrong, Miller walked out the door.

After the testimony of Stefan Moore, they all knew the case relied on how credibly Wheeler presented himself. The tension in the courthouse was unbearable.

As the crowd filed in, no one said a word. Miller sat quietly, biting his nails as he stared into the empty space in front of him. Hennessy stayed quiet as he read line after line of his notes, and the prosecution team didn't say a word to each other.

Hennessy's phone buzzed. It was Lockett. Looking at the bailiff, he nodded and then stepped out to the hallway to take the call.

"Tell me it's great news."

"Not quite," Lockett was apprehensive. "The hacker got into the computer but is still working on accessing the saved passwords. Fifty-five email addresses were found on Balter's computer, but one is of particular interest. One of the most regularly accessed email addresses on the computer has never sent or received an email."

"Go on."

"So this email address set alarm bells ringing for our tech-guy, so he looked into it further. The email address was opened many times at many different IP addresses."

"What does that mean?"

"It means that lots of people were accessing the account and communicating via their drafts in the emails."

"Why?"

"Because drafts don't show up as an outgoing message. The IP address wouldn't identify outgoing messages because none were sent," Lockett said. "It's a technique used by drug dealers to avoid having sent emails show up on IP tracking. Outgoing messages can be tracked by the FBI, but drafts can't."

"That's the account that we need access to. I need to know what that account has been used for, but I need your methods to be above board. Legally, remember?"

"I think we're in luck. I'm going to need at least fifty minutes. I'll contact you the second we've got anything."

Hennessy ended the call and stepped back into the courtroom. He could feel the nerves in the pit of his stomach.

The courtroom was filled, a hush remaining over the crowd, everyone aware that this was the final roll of the dice. Either way, whatever way the testimony went, this was going to be a story.

Hennessy looked at his watch and then checked his phone. Nothing further from Lockett. Nothing from the laptop and nothing from the hacker. If Wheeler's testimony was quick, he'd have to stall until Lockett could get the information to him. Hennessy had plans, but it was going to come down to the wire.

Judge Fedder entered the room, looked at the prosecution, and raised his eyebrows. Lincoln shook his head, indicating that no deal had been reached. Judge Fedder expressed his surprise and then asked the bailiff to bring the jury members in.

They sat, looking at Miller, wondering what was left to say.

When asked, Lincoln stood. He unbuttoned his jacket and called Preston Wheeler.

Wheeler entered the courtroom and walked past the defense without so much as a look, but once he sat on the stand, he made eye contact, his gaze cold enough to freeze gasoline. The second he'd been placed under oath, his eyes returned to Hennessy and held his gaze.

Wheeler had dressed in a dark blue suit, complete with a white shirt and a dark blue tie. His black hair was slicked back, and his long, tan face was clean-shaven. He was doing his best to appear credible to the jury, but all Hennessy could sense was sleaziness.

Lincoln walked to the lectern. All eyes turned to him. The silence meant that everyone's full attention was on him.

"Thank you for talking with the court today, Mr. Wheeler," Lincoln began. "I understand how hard it must be for you to testify against your friend. Can you please begin by telling the court how you know Mr. Miller?"

"I first met Zach ten years ago, when he was a small-time performer playing small bars and venues.

He was singing at a wedding function that day. He was performing a few cover songs, and I couldn't help but notice the power he had in his voice. Once he finished his set, I went over and asked him if he had any original songs. He replied that he'd written a few, and I told him to come to my office the next day, and to bring his guitar. He did, and I was blown away by what I heard."

"And what was your occupation at the time?"

"I was, and still am, a music talent manager. When I met Zach, I was managing a few rock bands, a few cover bands, and a few folk singers. I think I had fifteen people on my books at the time, so I was pretty busy, but I knew I couldn't pass on the opportunity to manage Zach, so I made room for him in my schedule. We worked together for a few years, and I managed to book him all over the country. About five years into our contract, he released a great song, and I managed to get it played on radios all over the country, and then I managed to get it played by several social media stars. That's when his biggest song, 'Help Is On The Way,' went viral. It hit the Billboard charts. Top five for five straight weeks. That song had millions of downloads, streams, and sales, all because of what I was able to do with the management of it."

"And I assume this song made money?"

"It made a lot of money. In that year alone, Zach's earnings surpassed five million dollars."

"Wow. That's a lot of money." Lincoln faked his surprise. In truth, they'd spent most of the weekend rehearsing their lines. "Did you think that this money changed Mr. Miller?"

"Objection to the word 'think.'" Hennessy called

out. "It's hearsay."

"Sustained," Judge Fedder confirmed.

Lincoln nodded. "I'll rephrase. During the time of this very successful song, did you feel there was any change to Mr. Miller's behavior?"

"Objection to the use of the word 'feel.' Again, it's hearsay." Hennessy repeated.

"Sustained."

"Let me try again. When Mr. Miller's behavior changed—"

"Objection. Leading the witness."

"Sustained," Judge Fedder said. "Mr. Lincoln, you know better than that. He's your witness."

Lincoln took a moment to look over his notes, compose himself, and then continued. "Mr. Wheeler, did you personally witness any change in Mr. Miller's behavior in the year that his song hit the charts?"

"I did."

"And can you please describe the change you saw in Mr. Miller?"

"Zach was always a nervous soul. He was a superstar on stage, he had a real presence behind the microphone, but off-stage, he was nervous and fidgety and anxious. That year, five years ago, was the first time I witnessed Mr. Miller doing drugs."

"Where was this?"

"Backstage at a show in Chicago. I saw him snorting several lines of cocaine."

"And you're sure it was cocaine?"

"It was."

"And did you see him use drugs regularly over the following years?"

"I did. After a while, it was becoming a problem, and as his manager, I had to help him out. I tried to get him to go into rehab numerous times, but it wasn't until a year and a half ago that he admitted himself to a rehab clinic. From there, he got clean."

"And was that the last time you heard Mr. Miller mention drugs?"

"Unfortunately not, no." Wheeler shifted in his chair and drew a long breath. "He called me on the 4th of September and asked if I wanted to buy some cocaine."

One of the jury members gasped, and another shook their head. Lincoln paused for a few moments to let that statement sink in.

"And what else was said during this conversation?"

"Mr. Miller called me and said that he was using again, and that he'd just received a supply of good quality cocaine. He invited me backstage to his show at the Charleston Music Hall to do some lines, but I declined. I didn't want to see my friend go through that again." He shifted in his chair and avoided looking at Miller. "I tried to talk him out of it, but he said it was his right to do what he wanted."

"Did he say how much cocaine he had?"

"He said he had $5000 worth, and he asked if I could move some of it for him. He needed me to sell it. He then asked if I wanted to join him in snorting lines backstage the next night."

"And did you go?"

"No," he shook his head. "I wish I did, knowing what I know now, to try to stop him, but I chose not to see my friend go through that again. If I couldn't talk him out of it over the phone, then I wouldn't be able to do much good face-to-face."

"That must've been hard to hear," Lincoln

nodded. "Did Mr. Miller say where he got the drugs from?"

"No, he didn't."

"But he was trying to sell them?"

"Yes, he was."

Lincoln sighed and moved back to his desk. After a strong testimony from his star witness, he had to address the weakness in their case. "Now, following up on Thursday's testimony, I will ask if you know Mr. Moore?"

"I do. He's dating my niece."

"And did you ask Mr. Moore to lie to the court?"

"No."

"And why do you think Mr. Moore lied to the court?"

"Objection to the word 'think.' Hearsay."

"Sustained."

"Let me rephrase." Lincoln waved his hand in the air. "Had you ever complained about Mr. Miller to Mr. Moore?"

"I had. A few times, actually. Zach was getting harder to manage, and I told my niece how much it was getting to me."

"And is Mr. Moore the sort of person who would help you out, even if you didn't ask him?"

"He is."

"Thank you, Mr. Wheeler. No further questions."

Lincoln turned to Hennessy, facing away from the jurors, and smirked. He felt like he'd turned the case around. Lincoln felt he was back at the winner's table.

But now it was Hennessy's turn to discredit the star witness.

CHAPTER 48

"MR. HENNESSY, any questions for this witness?"

Hennessy looked at his computer, checked his emails, and then looked at his phone.

"Mr. Hennessy?" Judge Fedder pressed. "If you're not going to question this witness, I'll excuse him."

Hennessy's phone buzzed on the table. It was Lockett. He was ready.

"Your Honor," Hennessy stood. "May I request a fifteen-minute recess to talk to my investigator?"

"You've had plenty of time to prepare for this testimony, Mr. Hennessy."

"We have, Your Honor, but new information has come to light, and I would like to request a brief recess to discuss it with my investigator."

"You have five minutes." Judge Fedder was firm. "And don't be a second late."

Hennessy raced out of the courtroom. The call with Lockett was brief. Lockett then forwarded an email with the details he'd found, and Hennessy opened the attachment on his phone. He scanned the lines of data, nodding as he went.

After using the full five minutes, Hennessy stepped back into the courtroom, ready to begin his questioning of the star witness. Once back at the defense table, he placed the phone down and opened his email. He buttoned his jacket and moved to the area between the lectern and the jury box. He stood, one hand resting on the lectern, and stared at Wheeler.

"Mr. Wheeler, you stated that you and Mr. Miller are friends." Hennessy paused and looked at the jury. "Can you please tell the court the last time you saw or talked to Mr. Miller before the 4th of September?"

"I can't recall."

"You can't recall," Hennessy repeated and returned to his desk. "I have the date here, Mr. Wheeler, because your last interaction was, in fact, in a room with him along with contract and corporate lawyers on the 15th of July, was it not?"

"That's correct."

"And why did that meeting involve lawyers?"

"We were sorting out a contract dispute. It happens sometimes."

"And what was the dispute about?"

"Our contract," Wheeler replied. Lincoln had predicted this line of questioning and had prepared the witness well. "We were sorting out a dispute. Zach wanted to go in a different direction, but he was still under obligation to my firm, contractually. I didn't want to involve lawyers in the dispute and jeopardize our friendship, but this happens in business sometimes. It was nothing personal."

"You stated it was the day before the concert, on the 4th of September, that Mr. Miller called you?"

"That's correct."

Hennessy picked up a piece of paper. "But in fact, you called him, didn't you?"

"I don't recall."

"Now, you don't recall?" Hennessy waved a piece

of paper in the air. "These are Mr. Miller's phone records. They show an incoming call from you on the 4th of September. That call lasted only fifty-five seconds. Are you telling this court that Mr. Miller, someone you haven't talked to in a month and a half, someone you're having a contract dispute with, told you about the supply of drugs, then offered to sell you some, in a fifty-five-second call?"

"It was a brief call, but that's what he said."

"Were you angry that Mr. Miller didn't want to keep you as his manager?"

"It wasn't a question of anger. It was a question of contract law."

"But this question is about anger—were you angry that Mr. Miller didn't want to re-sign with you as his manager?"

"Not angry." Wheeler drew a long breath. "But disappointed."

Wheeler was very well prepared, but Hennessy expected him to be prepared for that line of questioning.

However, he knew Wheeler wouldn't be prepared for what was coming next.

"Mr. Wheeler, can you please confirm your residential address is 5 Logan St., Charleston?"

"That's correct."

"And can you please confirm that the email address, 'jbalt.quiet.78@gmail.com' belongs to you?"

Wheeler squinted and then looked at the prosecution. Lincoln shrugged his shoulders. "Ah. I'm sorry, I don't recognize it."

"Really?" Hennessy returned to his desk and opened the email from Lockett on his laptop. "The registration of the email account is geo-located to an

IP address. An IP address is an 'Internet Protocol Address.' It's a unique address that identifies a device on the internet. Now, it's important to note that these numbers aren't random. They are mathematically produced and allocated by a division of the Internet Corporation for Assigned Names and Numbers. ICANN is a non-profit organization established in 1998 to help maintain the security of the internet and allow it to be usable by everyone. Do you follow, Mr. Wheeler?"

"I do."

"So, in essence, IP addresses are the identifier that allows information to be sent between devices on a network: they contain location information and make devices accessible for communication. Now, the IP that registered the email account 'jbalt.quiet.78@gmail.com' is geo-located to your home address. So, I'll ask you again, did you create this email address?"

"Ok. Sure. I didn't create it, but I access it." He shrugged. "There's no crime in using an email address."

"Are you the only one with access to that email address?"

Wheeler sat back slightly, his mouth hanging open.

"Mr. Wheeler?" Hennessy pressed. "Are you the only one with access to that email account?"

"I don't recall."

"In fact, that email address was accessed numerous times from two IP addresses in the days before the 4th of September. One belonging to your home address, and another belonging to a laptop owned by a man named Mr. James Balter. Can you please confirm to the court that you know Mr. James

Balter?"

Wheeler kept his mouth shut. He sat up straighter.

"Mr. Wheeler, can you please answer the question?"

Wheeler shook his head slightly.

"The prosecution would like to call for a short recess," Lincoln stood when he saw the witness struggling.

"What on earth for?" Judge Fedder grunted.

"There appears to be new information coming to light, and we would like to discuss it with the witness."

"New information?" Judge Fedder sighed. "He's your witness, Mr. Lincoln, and I've yet to see any new information presented. No, the request for a recess is denied, and the witness may answer the question."

"I..." Wheeler shifted across his seat. "I want to withdraw my testimony."

"Pardon?" Judge Fedder gasped. "You can't withdraw your testimony. You're sitting in the witness stand, and unless it incriminates you personally, you will answer the questions put to you, or you will be held in contempt of this court. Is that clear, Mr. Wheeler?"

Wheeler didn't acknowledge the judge, turning away from him with a shocked look on his face.

"I'll ask again," Hennessy's voice rose. "Do you know Mr. James Balter?"

"I do." The sweat was becoming visible on Wheeler's brow.

"And can you confirm that Mr. Balter also has access to that email address?"

"If you say so."

"It's not up to me to say so, Mr. Wheeler. I'm

asking you the question—can you confirm that Mr. Balter also has access to that email address?"

"There's no crime in that."

"Then answer the question."

"Ok. Sure." Wheeler shrugged. "James Balter has access to that email address."

"And do you know if Mr. Balter has sent emails from that account?"

"Now, hang on." Wheeler held up his hands. "It sounds like you've accessed the email account. You can't do that. That's breaking a federal law."

"Are you aware of the dark web, Mr. Wheeler?"

Wheeler nodded. "I am."

"And are you aware of the private forum, 'Charleston Notes?'"

"I've heard of it."

"And are you aware that within this private forum, which is only open to invited members, the owner of the email address posted the address and the password, along with the words, 'you can access the email, as long as you don't send anything. You know what to do.'?"

"Your Honor, objection." Lincoln stood. "Can we please have some relevance here?"

"We're almost there, Your Honor," Hennessy stated. "Just a few more questions."

"Overruled, but get to the point, Mr. Hennessy."

"Now, Mr. Wheeler, is it true that you and Mr. Balter communicated via drafts in this email address?"

"Lots of people use the drafts folder for that email address. That's how Mr. Balter likes to be communicated with. You put your name in the draft subject line, and he answers it. He doesn't like things to be sent. He's paranoid. He thinks that if the email remains in the drafts and isn't sent, it can't be accessed. Once the communication is completed, the email is deleted, and there's no trace of it."

"But if the draft is typed on a laptop, the keystrokes can be identified as accessing each site. Anything written while on that internet site is coded into the computer's history. Were you aware of that?"

Wheeler stared at Hennessy, stunned.

"I guess not," Hennessy said. "Is it true that you communicated with Mr. Balter via the drafts folder for the email account so it wouldn't be detected by law enforcement?"

"Objection," Lincoln leaped to his feet. "Accusation."

"Sustained. Unless you have evidence of this, Mr. Hennessy?"

"Withdrawn. Mr. Wheeler," Hennessy continued, "is it true that you asked Mr. Balter to plant 50 grams of cocaine in the dressing room?"

"Objection! Your Honor!"

"Mr. Wheeler! Is it true that you paid Mr. Balter to set up Mr. Miller?!"

"The objection is sustained!" Judge Fedder boomed. "If you ask another question like that without evidence, Mr. Hennessy, I'll hold you in contempt! If you have evidence, now is the time to present it to the court."

Hennessy looked at the jury. They looked at him with great concern and confusion.

Juror number ten was looking at Wheeler with disgust.

Hennessy turned to Lincoln, who was also studying the jury. He could see the doubt spread across Lincoln's face.

Hennessy walked back to his desk, the damage almost done. "We have no further questions right now. However, we reserve the right to recall this witness as a defense witness."

CHAPTER 49

JOE HENNESSY and Jacinta Templeton sat on one side of the conference room table. Zach Miller sat on the other side of the table, incessantly tapping his leg. The stress on his face was showing, his brow furrowed together to confirm his worries.

The small conference room air conditioner pumped in cold air, rattling above their heads, providing at least some distraction from the stress. The small round wooden table that took up most of the space was scratched, with a few coffee mug stains on it. The windowless room smelled like fresh air hadn't been through the room in months, but no one noticed.

"Take me through the new deal again?" Miller said, biting one of his nails.

"A five-week sentence for a guilty plea to possession of cocaine. That time is already served, under the amendment to Section 24-13-40, of the South Carolina Code of Laws, because you've been wearing a GPS monitor. Effectively, you sign the deal, and you're free to go."

"But I still plead guilty?"

"The prosecution needs to save face. They know where this is headed. They know that we're going to call James Balter to the stand and tear him apart. We've reserved the right to recall Wheeler and continue that line of questioning. But there's also still a small chance that something goes wrong between now and the end of this case. Maybe the wrong witness says the wrong thing, or a juror interprets the law differently than it's applied, and we lose the case. As your lawyer, I must advise you it's still possible."

"But you heard them in there—Wheeler set me up."

"Maybe. The evidence we have might not have been obtained legally. There will be doubt about it. Did my investigator follow the law when he found the information? He tells me he did, but we may have a problem presenting it in court. The prosecution is going to object to any such evidence, and given the potential questions about how we found the evidence, there's a very strong chance that the judge won't allow it to be included in the trial." Hennessy leaned forward on the table, turning the file around to face Miller. "So the question has to be, do you want to risk it?"

"No." Miller stood and began pacing around the room. "But I'm also innocent."

"As this is your first offense, the prosecution has also agreed that you won't have a conviction recorded."

"No conviction recorded?"

"That's correct."

"So really, I'm free to go today? No time in jail?"

"That's right."

"And what will they say publicly?"

"They'll say drug cases are hard to process through the system. However, they consider this charge a win. They'll say that you 'served' time for your crime. And then they'll say it's a warning to all other rich and famous people that they're not above the law. They'll spin this story so they look like the winners."

"And I look like a drug user." Miller leaned against the back wall of the room, tapping his head against it. "And what about Wheeler and Balter? What happens to them?"

"I'd say that the evidence on the dark web is enough to keep the cops sniffing around their business."

Miller picked up the pen on the table. "This is ridiculous. I'm innocent, and I'm about to sign a form that says I'm guilty."

"Well," Jacinta said. "Think about all the times you used cocaine in the past and were never caught."

Miller raised his eyes to stare at Jacinta. "That doesn't help."

"Sorry." She smiled. "But it's true. You were never caught before, even though you broke the law many, many times. Maybe this is the universe just catching up with you."

Miller gripped the pen tightly, staring at the bottom of the page.

"Ok." He scribbled his signature and then slammed the pen down. "So that's it? I'm free? This nightmare is now all over?"

"We have to take it to the prosecution," Hennessy said. "But apart from that, you stand before the judge, take the guilty plea, and then walk away."

"It still doesn't seem fair," Miller groaned. "But given the circumstances, I'll take it."

The three of them stood. None of them had a smile to offer. Hennessy opened the door for them to leave.

The ordeal was almost over.

CHAPTER 50

THERE WAS a strange mood in the room at the Poogan's Porch restaurant, not full of celebration, but also not commiseration. It was like they'd just tied the Super Bowl, neither team a winner but neither team a loser.

Poogan's Porch was a Charleston institution, a place where Hennessy celebrated the end of each major case. Inside a Victorian townhouse, the enchanting establishment had been serving some of the best Southern-style food in the Palmetto State since the 70s. The beauty of locally sourced dishes mesmerized both locals and tourists. Filled with history, charm, and character, the grand old building showcased the majestic appeal of Southern life.

Zach Miller lifted his glass of red wine and clinked with Joe and Jacinta. "To a win, almost," he said.

They all clinked glasses and smiled. It was raining outside, the noise heavy through the rooms, creating a sense of comfort indoors.

"It's blowin' up again," Jacinta said. "They said this will be the last storm of the year, but they think it might even be a hurricane. Right now, it's a tropical storm, but I don't like the idea of it getting heavier."

"That wind is getting strong," Miller added. "I think it's almost time to batten down the hatches."

After he signed the deal, Miller spent the rest of

the day in the courthouse, filling in forms, having his ankle bracelet removed, and finalizing the case. After the deal was signed, sealed, and delivered, Hennessy took his team out to one of his favorites.

Despite the subdued mood, they laughed as they ate their food, reflecting on a tough two months of drama.

"Everyone thinks I'm guilty, you know? They think I snorted those lines of cocaine backstage," Miller said as he ate the famous Poogan's Bone-in Fried Chicken. "But on the plus side, all this attention has been good for my career. My music sales are through the roof. That must really hurt Wheeler now."

"Do you think you'll continue to tour?" Jacinta asked. "Now that sales are so great again?"

"I don't know." Miller shrugged. "I might wait a while for all this to blow over before I put myself back out there. It's a strange feeling—getting off the charges, not going to prison, but not really winning."

"It was the best we could do with the situation we had." Hennessy sipped his wine. "We had to be realistic, and although we might've won, there was always the chance that we wouldn't have. It was risk versus reward."

"I guess the legal system isn't infallible."

"Not even close," Hennessy replied. "There are many innocent people locked up all across the country. Blackstone's Ratio said, 'It is better ten guilty persons escape than that one innocent suffer,' and that's what I believe. We've got to protect the innocent people who come into the system, just as much as we have to chase the guilty ones."

"And I guess Balter and Wheeler are part of the

guilty ten that get to walk away free?"

"The past always catches up to men like James Balter and Preston Wheeler."

Hennessy's phone buzzed in his pocket, but he ignored it. He hated answering calls while eating a meal.

"How about your other case?" Miller pressed. "Do you think the McGovern guy got what he deserved?"

Hennessy shrugged, mostly because he didn't know the answer. He took a long sip of his Merlot, a fruity, punchy flavor, and then placed the glass back down. "Justice always finds a way."

For the next half an hour, they ate, laughed some more, and congratulated each other on making it to the end of the case. The food was delicious, the drinks delectable, and the atmosphere delightful. A member of a nearby group came past and told Miller just how much he loved his music, and he would continue to listen to it, no matter what happened in court. Miller smiled.

As they finished their meals, Hennessy felt his phone buzz again in his pocket. He took out his phone and looked at the number. It was Lockett. He had sent a message. It was just a single word, *Urgent.* Hennessy stood and made a call.

"Joe," Lockett said. "I've got something for you. And you're going to love it."

CHAPTER 51

THE TROPICAL storm was blowing hard as Hennessy arrived at the parking lot at the Battery just after 8pm. He pulled up next to Lockett's pickup truck and flashed his lights in the dark. Lockett gave him the thumbs up from inside the truck and smiled.

"He wants me to get out," Hennessy whispered to himself and looked at the storm through his windshield. It wasn't easing anytime soon.

Reluctantly, he stepped out of his truck, head tucked down to avoid the belting rain, and jumped into the passenger seat of Lockett's truck. The noise from the roaring wind and rain was almost deafening.

"It sure is a big one out there." Lockett smiled as Hennessy brushed some of the water off his hair. Lockett's newer truck dulled some of the noise, a comfortable cabin in the storm. "I've heard that the storm will hit just south of here after midnight. It's not a hurricane, but I'd hate to be out in it. It'd blow us away."

"Interesting place to meet," Hennessy said, looking out to the view in front of them as Lockett's windshield wipers worked overtime. A wave crashed over the seawall, thumping into the concrete and splashing the water high.

"I love it out here. It reminds me of my youth and the storms we used to get in Australia. Wild, crazy madness. I mean, look at that." Lockett pointed out the window just after two claps of lightning filled the horizon. "Big storms like this get me excited. There's an electricity in the air."

"You know what gets me excited? When you give me some great information."

Lockett smiled and nodded. "Well, you know those emails that we had access to?"

"Legally had access to."

"Yes, legally had access to them because the email address owner posted the address and password on a private forum on the dark web. And because I'm a member of that forum, I had access to it. I didn't know it was James Balter on that dark web forum, but once we were able to link the email address to him, it all became clear." Lockett smiled, knowing that he stretched the legality of his actions. "Well, I kept an eye on the emails, just to see what was coming in. After the court case, I didn't think I'd find anything new, but guess what? One new entry."

"From whom?"

"The title of the draft has the initials 'E.MC.'"

"Elliot McGovern. He's alive," Hennessy said. "What does the draft say?"

"He's asking Balter for help. He's written to Balter and says that the money he expected to be at his vacation home was taken, and now he needs to get back to Kiawah Island and see his father. He needs Balter to help him get through South Carolina without being seen, and he's offered Balter $10K for a night's work."

"He hasn't watched the news?"

"It appears not. He must've been too preoccupied with trying to stay dead."

"Did Balter respond?"

"He did. He responded in the drafts and said he could help him get to his father's place tonight." Lockett tapped his finger on the steering wheel. "Balter is picking him up from a bus station in Savannah as we speak. What do you want to do?"

Hennessy looked out to the horizon as another flash of lightning filled the night sky. "Nobody gets away with not paying me. I need to find him, and I need to get paid."

CHAPTER 52

ELLIOT MCGOVERN waited at the bus stop in Savannah.

The rain was pouring down, echoing through the streets, creating a noise that only subtropical rain can. Sheets of water were blowing through with the powerful gusts of wind, splashing him even though he was waiting far away from the edge of the building. The terminal had closed up for the night, leaving him and a few others to stand around and wait for their rides out of there.

With a face mask on and dyed blonde hair, he had little chance of being recognized, but to get back into the gated community at Kiawah Island to see his father, he needed a ride. There was no one left he could trust. He couldn't trust his associates, he couldn't trust his friends, and he certainly couldn't trust his mother. The only person he had any genuine faith in was the person who would do anything for money—James Balter.

The lights of a patrol car lit up the street. His heart took the brunt of the initial shock, beating so hard and so fast, the sweat on his brow instantly multiplied as a myriad of options screamed into his brain. Run, stop and fight, ignore it and see what happens; it was all open to him.

The cop never slowed and passed the terminal

quickly. McGovern exhaled loudly. He knew he was playing with fire. He glanced to his left, catching his reflection in a window. Staring back at him was a man he didn't recognize. He felt his stomach tighten as he stared at himself. The blonde hair made him look younger, he thought, a lot younger than he thought possible.

"I need to get used to this," he mumbled as he ran his fingers through his hair.

A couple of vending machines sat near the end of the building. McGovern went to the first, saw what he needed, dropped a few coins into the slot, and pulled out a Coke.

He had thought about stealing a car, but that would attract too much attention. He couldn't handle that. He was officially deceased, thanks to his father's efforts. With their family name on the line, his father worked his hardest and pulled off the near impossible.

He should've been on a boat to Costa Rica already. He should've already started his new life. But his wife, that dear Katherine, had taken all the money from their safe in the vacation home, leaving a note in its place.

'*You can't hide money from me,*' it read. '*I've taken the money to spend on clothes.*'

It infuriated him, but he had to keep a level head. He needed cash to skip the country, and he couldn't risk walking into a bank. He could've called his father, but he was sure that his father would've refused to take the call. No, he needed to speak with him face to face, and demand the cash.

His entire estate, left behind in the will, had gone to the old man, mostly because he didn't know who else to give it to. He didn't want to donate it, he didn't want to give it to his friends, and he didn't want his mother to touch a cent of the money. At last count, he had fifteen million dollars' worth of assets and shares.

His mother crossed his mind again. He'd be surprised if she even shed a tear.

A BMW sedan pulled up further down the road. Even through the heavy torrential rain, McGovern could see it was a nice car, much too nice for the area they were in.

He approached it, trying to catch a glimpse of the driver. The car crept forward, and then the driver lowered the passenger window. McGovern peered in.

It was James Balter, his current savior.

McGovern opened the door and climbed in. Not a word was said between them until they were further away from the bus terminal. After he navigated through the streets, Balter turned to his new passenger.

"I thought you were dead."

"Yeah, well, I'm not."

"The news said you were dead. I thought I'd lost one of my biggest coke buyers, and I was quite disappointed. I thought, who's going to buy most of my supply of coke now?"

"How lovely."

"Hey man," Balter laughed. "I'm a businessman first. All those times I sold the gear to your wife and you, I was giving y'all the best stuff. Top of the range. And then you wanted to kill her, well, I thought I'd still have at least one buyer hanging around. But no, you took off as well."

"I'm not staying long."

"So we're going to see your father?"

"That's the best option I have left. He won't be too happy to see me, though."

"Then you'll probably need this." Balter reached across to the glove compartment, opened it, and pointed to a Glock 42.

McGovern took the handgun, checked it was loaded, and then placed the weapon by his side. "Thanks."

"So, where are you supposed to be?"

"Costa Rica."

"Why didn't you make it?"

McGovern watched as the lights drifted past in the heavy rain, watching as they left Savannah behind and hit the I-95. "Katherine took the stash from our vacation home. She must've known about it. I was supposed to take that money and contact a guy who could get me into Costa Rica without a problem, but she'd cleaned out the safe, leaving a note that she took the money."

"Well, you certainly got her back for that." Balter laughed heartily. "You showed her."

"Yeah." McGovern began to chuckle and then broke out into a loud laugh. "A bullet in the skull. That showed her who's boss."

CHAPTER 53

THE RAIN hadn't let up.

Since he knew the attendant at the Kiawah Island community's gates, Barry Lockett was able to drive his pickup truck through without a problem. When he pulled up to the small hut surrounded by palmetto trees, he slipped her a fifty, and she lifted the barrier arm, allowing him to breeze past.

As they drove toward Harold McGovern's house, his windshield wipers were on overdrive.

"Do you really think he'd risk coming back here?" Hennessy said as he sat in the passenger seat. "With everything that's happened, why come back to a man that hates you?"

"Because he's arrogant enough to think he can get away with it," Lockett stated. "And can you imagine that guy without money? He wouldn't last a week before turning himself in. Where do you think he was headed before he turned back?"

"Somewhere in South America, where it would've been easy to disappear. Maybe Central America. All I know is that he wouldn't have survived in South America without a cent to his name," Hennessy laughed. "He would've had a meltdown within the first day."

Lockett chuckled as well as they drove along the private roads. According to the satellite images that

Hennessy searched on his phone, there was a parking lot near Harold McGovern's mansion, which led to a walkway to the beach. Lockett turned into the sheltered area, killing the lights before he arrived, and turning into the far corner of the dirt lot. He parked under the shelter of a large oak, although the rain was still belting through.

"Nobody is coming out here in this rain," Lockett said as he looked around. "Nobody's going to give us any trouble until the morning, and we've got a clear view of the road. According to the map, there are only five more houses up this street, so given the time and the weather, it's a fair bet if someone passes us tonight, it's going to be Balter and McGovern."

"It's a good plan," Hennessy agreed.

"So, where do we wait? If they met at the bus terminal at 8pm in Savannah and came straight here, I think we're right on time. Fifteen minutes, maybe less. Do we wait inside or outside?"

"On the roof in a tropical storm," Hennessy joked. "Now that would be something. You can jump on him as he walks underneath."

"Ok, maybe not the roof," Lockett chuckled. "So we just sit and wait."

Lockett stayed silent for only a few moments before he turned to his companion. "Do you think he killed her?"

"The wife?" Hennessy nodded. "At the start, I wasn't so sure, but as the case went on, it became clear he was guilty."

"So he shot her because they were going through a divorce?"

"And it was a well-thought-out plan. He went to the restaurant, made sure he said hello to a few people to corroborate his alibi, and then left for a bathroom break."

"And that's when Balter picks him up."

"Balter is the go-to guy for many of the people around here. We know he was dealing coke to the family, so it makes sense that McGovern used his services."

"So Balter drives McGovern home, McGovern goes in, shoots his wife, plants the drugs to make it look like a drug deal gone wrong, and then goes back to the restaurant to confirm his alibi." Lockett tapped his hand on the steering wheel. "And then he leaves to return home and finds his wife dead on the floor. That's crazy, mate. The guy isn't exactly running with his full mob of kangaroos in the top paddock."

"Kangaroos, uh?"

"I'm just saying—crazy."

"He thought he owned her. He thought she was his possession. She came from nothing, and he had everything." Hennessy watched out the window. "There are lights in the distance."

Lockett leaned forward, checking down the road. The lights were approaching.

It was time.

CHAPTER 54

"THAT'S THEM."

Lockett checked his glove box, pulled his Glock out, and confirmed it was loaded. He pulled out a second handgun, a model 63 Smith and Wesson revolver, and handed it to Hennessy.

Hennessy checked it. It was loaded. "Are you sure we need these?"

"He's a killer, Joe. It's better to be over-prepared than under-prepared."

The lights of the car moved past.

Lockett cranked the truck, leaving the lights off, and crept forward through the heavy night rain. He followed the white line on the side of the road, barely visible, but was cautious not to alert Balter and McGovern of their arrival.

A hundred yards up the road, the car turned into the driveway of Harold McGovern's estate.

Lockett kept his pickup truck on the line on the side of the road, windshield wipers moving frantically, and then turned down the one-lane gravel driveway.

"I can't see anything," Lockett growled. "Tell me if I go too far on your side."

"You're on target," Hennessy confirmed. "They've stopped. Pull up behind that tree."

Lockett tossed the truck into neutral, rolling forward behind a large live oak tree. "I'll leave the keys in the ignition in case we need to get away quickly."

The rain eased as they exited the truck, but they could barely hear anything besides the wind. They watched the BMW sedan in the distance as it parked in front of the large estate home.

McGovern stepped out of the passenger seat, holding an umbrella, and Balter stepped out of the driver's side with a hooded raincoat.

"Elliot!" Hennessy called out over the wind and rain.

McGovern turned and squinted into the night.

"We need to talk." Hennessy stepped out of the shadows, twenty-five yards away. He kept his hands raised and visible, showing McGovern that he wasn't a threat.

McGovern took a couple of panicked steps back. "Joe Hennessy? What is this? How did you know I was here?"

"Your email to Balter." Hennessy came closer, squinting as the rain washed down his face.

Lockett circled the yard, keeping in the darkness, trying to get within striking distance.

"What do you want?" McGovern looked to Balter, who remained cautiously by the driver's side of the car.

"I need to get paid, Elliot, and dead men can't pay bills."

"Is that what this is?" McGovern laughed. "You want to get paid?"

"I need to take you in first."

"Take me in? Are you serious? You think you can take me in?"

A light went on in the foyer of the estate mansion.

Hennessy's attention went to the house. McGovern drew his weapon and pointed the handgun at Hennessy.

"Get back," he snarled through the light rain as Hennessy approached within twenty yards. "Get back, or I'll shoot."

Hennessy didn't doubt him. Even through the wind and rain, the look on his face screamed panic. He had a nervous finger on the trigger.

"I said get back," McGovern repeated. "The man I trusted my life with. Is this how you repay me?"

"This isn't the right way to do this, Elliot. Why don't we go into Charleston and work this out? I want to understand what's going on, that's all. Put the gun down, and we can talk."

"Talk?" His voice sounded amused as he considered the offer. "You think I want to talk?"

"I think you want to walk away from this with your life."

McGovern broke into laughter. "My life? My life ended the day I took you on for my defense." He spat on the ground. "You take that as your payment. You were supposed to be on my side, counselor. You remember your oath, don't you? You were my lawyer, and you've betrayed me."

"You didn't pay me, Elliot." Hennessy kept his hands up. Lockett crept his way forward in the darkness.

Hennessy took a step forward, but McGovern reacted, taking a step back and raising the pistol to eye level. Hennessy looked to his left. Lockett was in the shadows, ten yards away.

"I said stay back." McGovern eyed Hennessy as a malicious grin formed on his face. "Think you're such a great investigator, finding me here? Is that how you caught your kid's killer?" Hennessy felt a flash of pain but resisted. McGovern saw the reaction and pounced. "Yeah, there you go. Not so clever, after all. How long has it been, huh? Twenty years? And still no clue about who took your kid's life."

"Don't mention my son," Hennessy snarled, feeling his self-control coming undone.

McGovern laughed in the rain.

Lockett crept closer. Ten yards. Almost striking distance.

"You know that's not how this works," Hennessy shouted over the wind. "There's an active investigation into your wife's murder and—"

"Screw the investigation. We all know I killed her. Do you have any idea what she was going to do to me?" It was the first time he heard genuine emotion fill the man's voice. "She threatened to take my money. My money, man. All of it." He swallowed hard, grinned, and nodded. "We both knew I couldn't do anything about it."

Balter moved back to the car.

As if signaling his intention to end the conversation between them, McGovern stared at Hennessy, and aimed for his face. "And since I've already killed before, you'll believe me when I say that unless you get out of my way, I'll kill you as well."

"Elliot, we can—" was as far as Hennessy got before Lockett turned the interaction on its head.

Lockett charged out of the shadows. McGovern twisted around quickly to face him. For his size, Lockett moved with incredible speed. Lockett lunged forward, swung an arm at the handgun, and slammed it into the shadows.

Lockett swung again. His fist caught the fugitive in the cheek. McGovern fell.

Hennessy drew his weapon.

A shot was fired through the night.

Hennessy dove to the ground, as did Lockett. Hennessy raised his head to see Harold McGovern at the door of his home, rifle in hand. Balter was at the driver's door of the BMW, twenty yards away. Balter shouted something at McGovern, but they weren't able to hear it over the wind.

"Get off my property!" Harold shouted. "Get out of here!"

"Dad!" Elliot yelled, standing up and raising his hands. "It's me!"

"You're dead!" Harold raised his rifle again and aimed at Elliot.

"Don't shoot!" Elliot yelled. "It's your son!"

"My son is dead! But if he's alive and stupid enough to show up on my doorstep, he'll soon be dead!"

Balter had heard enough. He dove into the BMW and roared it around the end of the driveway. He spun the car around until the passenger door faced Elliot. "Get in!"

Elliot paused briefly, staring at his father on the mansion's steps.

"Get in!" Balter repeated.

Elliot took one last look at his father and then lunged into the passenger seat.

Within a moment, McGovern and Balter were gone.

CHAPTER 55

"GET IN the truck," Lockett screamed. "Let's go!"

Hennessy looked toward the man standing at the front door of his mansion. Harold lowered the rifle to his waist.

Hennessy leaped to his feet, moving fast and reaching the truck well in front of Lockett. He jumped into the driver's seat and fired up the vehicle. The engine roared to life, and Hennessy wasted no time slamming it into gear, hitting the gas, and spinning it around. Lockett jumped into the passenger seat.

"They might make a mistake on the wet roads." Hennessy tore down the gravel driveway as the rain increased again. "But we have to catch them before the exit to the island."

With just a single road leading off the island, Hennessy knew he would eventually catch them. All he needed was speed.

Hennessy roared the pickup onto the street, flying down the road, racing through the rain.

Balter was barely a few hundred yards away from them. His BMW weaved around the tight corners. Hennessy followed, determined to catch him.

"I can't let them make the main road," Hennessy grunted. "They'll get away on the open road."

Hennessy dropped the truck back a gear, roaring through the gears with aggression, fueled by his need to deliver justice.

The BMW turned sharply around the next corner. Hennessy gripped the handbrake, yanked the steering wheel, and followed. The truck slid across the road, almost out of control, until the tires gripped and raced them forward.

The following speed bump did little to slow him down.

"Hit him, Joe!" Lockett yelled, gripping the door tightly.

Hennessy floored the truck, thundering around the next bend. He got close, and clipped the back corner of the BMW. Balter's vehicle slid and weaved on the wet road until he regained control. Balter wasn't stopping, and nor was Hennessy.

"Joe!" Lockett yelled as they narrowly missed a tree.

He ignored Lockett. The BMW was his target. They raced down the street, corner after corner disappearing behind them. Hennessy hit the accelerator with anger. Pushed it as hard as it would go. The BMW was slowing around the corners. Hennessy closed the gap again. He pushed the truck harder. Dropped it back another gear. Forced the engine to roar.

There was a pool of water on the road. The BMW hit it at speed. It began to lose control. The back end of the sedan was fishtailing down the road.

"Joe!" Lockett screamed. "Watch out!"

The tires of the BMW slipped.

The back of Balter's car moved sideways on the wet road. He had lost it.

The BMW clipped a tree, launching them into a spin. They spun off the road. Hit a ditch. Then came the impact.

The BMW flipped. Landed on its roof. Sprung back into the air. Rolled. The sound of crunching metal was thunderous. The BMW hit another tree, wrapping around it.

Hennessy slammed on the brakes. The truck slid to a halt.

He leaped out of the truck, searching the smashed wreck. He could see blood. A lot of it.

The BMW was squashed, not in the same shape it was only moments before. The roof was pushed down. The windows were blown out. It was missing a door.

Lockett stood next to Hennessy. He pulled out his phone and dialed 911.

When he saw the car was safe, Hennessy scrambled into the wreck. He tried to help McGovern and Balter, but the roof had collapsed. They were out cold.

Another car stopped. Next, the police arrived. Then the ambulance. Soon, under the heavy rain of a tropical storm, the area was covered with swirling lights.

Elliot McGovern and James Balter were alive. But only just.

CHAPTER 56

IT TOOK the authorities almost a week to process everything that had happened.

Hennessy had spent much of the week in and out of the police station giving statements. There were several interested parties he needed to fill in. Hennessy explained that he didn't break any laws—all he wanted was to get paid.

James Balter had found out that the 'Accessory before the Fact' laws in South Carolina were particularly harsh. Section 16-1-40 of the South Carolina Code of Laws stated that 'A person who aids in the commission of a felony or is an accessory before the fact in the commission of a felony by counseling, hiring, or otherwise procuring the felony to be committed is guilty of a felony and, upon conviction, must be punished in the manner prescribed for the punishment of the principal felon.'

Facing thirty years behind bars for being an accessory to the murder of Katherine McGovern, James Balter began singing like a canary.

He claimed he didn't know what Elliot McGovern would do that night. He claimed all he did was drive a car. For a good deal from the Circuit Solicitor's Office, five years in prison for drug possession charges, he laid everything out on the table.

He told the prosecutors everything he knew—

from drug deals, to violent offenses, to unsolved murders. He sold out associates, he sold out networks, and he sold out friends. He sold out everyone he could think of. The list of people that fell under his confessions were long, and the arrests were numerous. The police could barely keep up with the number of people they had to arrest.

The papers ran headlines about Balter and his exploits. They loved the story of a lifelong criminal rolling over on everyone. The media attention ensured that whatever time he served in prison, it would not be an enjoyable experience. Hennessy would be surprised if he lasted the five years.

Among those he sold out to avoid the accessory charge was Preston Wheeler.

Balter admitted that Wheeler had paid him to plant the backpack in Zach Miller's dressing room. He admitted that Wheeler had paid him 50K to set up the singer. And he admitted that he made the call to the tip-off line, setting up Miller for drug charges.

Wheeler faced several charges, including drug trafficking, drug possession, and perjury. Hennessy sat in the back of the courtroom, at the seat nearest the door, and listened to Preston Wheeler plead guilty to the charges in exchange for a deal of fifteen months behind bars. A smile washed over Hennessy's face when Wheeler was led away by the bailiffs.

After he stepped out of the courtroom doors, he sent Zach Miller a message. The reply he received less than a minute later said it all. It was a photo Miller had taken of himself, grinning widely and flashing a thumbs-up. Hennessy then confirmed to Miller that he would take the case back to court to have any records of Miller's guilt reversed. Miller sent another smiling photo back, this time with a big cheesy grin and a peace sign.

Only days later, Hennessy was back in courtroom five of the Charleston Judicial Center. This time, he sat in the front-row. The seats behind him were full. Media had packed in, as had the Brady family. Helen McGovern sat near the exit, and Harold McGovern sat behind the prosecutor's desk, next to his younger mistress.

Hennessy caught Harold's eye as he took his seat. He could tell there was no love lost between them. Hennessy grinned when the senior McGovern mouthed something to him. He didn't care, not about an angry man embarrassed by his son's actions, or a spoiled son who considered himself above the law. The McGovern family had reigned over the city long enough, and this was the first step in bringing their empire down.

John Kirkland stood by the defense table, a solemn look on his face. He turned around to face Hennessy, raised his eyebrows, and nodded to the seat at the defense table. Hennessy shook his head.

There was tension in the air when Elliot McGovern was brought in via the side exit, dressed in a bright orange jumpsuit with the words 'SCDC INMATE' emblazoned on the back.

The man looked more dejected than he ever did. He was skinnier. His head had been shaved, and he had a black eye.

When the murder charges were officially read out, Elliot McGovern began to cry.

His sobbing filled the gallery of the courtroom, his head bowed as he wept. And just when Hennessy didn't think things could get any worse for him, a dry, raspy voice yelled, "Face it like a man. Stop being pathetic and weak! You're no son of mine!"

Harold McGovern was escorted out of the courtroom, and five minutes later, Elliot McGovern entered his plea for the murder of Katherine McGovern.

"Guilty," he said.

Prosecutor Nadine Robinson confirmed the deal for thirty years, and it took all of fifteen minutes for McGovern's day in court to be finished.

As he left the courtroom, Hennessy smiled. Justice had been served.

CHAPTER 57

JOE HENNESSY rolled his sleeves up to his elbows, wiped his brow, and opened the file on his desk, trying to keep his focus on the next case. There was always another file to process, always another client to defend. He had yet another DUI on his desk, this time an elderly man who had never been charged with a driving offense, not even a parking ticket, despite driving for over five decades. The man had just tipped over the legal limit of 0.08, and was charged by an overzealous young cop. Hennessy would fight the misdemeanor charge on a technicality, noting that the young cop had missed some of the paperwork required.

"You look focused." Barry Lockett stood at the door to Hennessy's office. "Do you mind if I disturb you for a few moments?"

"Come right in." Hennessy waved him in and closed the file. He was happy to have his eyes taken off the paperwork for a few moments. "I was looking to take a break, anyway."

Lockett walked in, apprehensive in approach. He sat in the chair opposite Hennessy and looked around the room. Lockett wasn't one to avoid hard conversations, so Hennessy gave his investigator his full attention.

"I hear Balter rolled over on everyone," he

quipped.

"He did. He gave up all the people that he could. He'll still go behind bars for drug charges, but he's avoided the accessory charge for the murder of Katherine McGovern. He told the police he had no idea what Elliot was doing that night, but obviously, that wasn't true."

"And McGovern?"

"Admitted everything. Took the guilty plea and thirty years behind bars to avoid the death penalty."

"Wheeler?"

"Gone as well. Once Balter admitted he planted the drugs backstage before the show, he turned on Wheeler and said that Wheeler paid him to do it. Wheeler got fifteen months."

"Zach?"

"He's good." Hennessy paused and leaned forward on the table. "I'm sure you're interested in these things, but it seems like you're avoiding something."

Lockett grunted slightly and looked away.

"Barry? What is it?"

Lockett leaned forward, swallowed hard, and kept his eyes on the ground. "Remember how you asked me to look into Richard Longhouse and who else he's asking to sign the non-disclosure agreements with?"

Hennessy nodded.

"Did you sign the non-disclosure agreement?"

"No, and I don't think I will. Why?"

"Word is that he asked at least ten people to sign them. He's cleaning up shop before his run for Governor."

"We knew that."

Lockett drew a long breath. "He visited the Lee Correctional Institution."

"What for?"

"To visit someone."

"Who?"

Lockett didn't answer, looking away from Hennessy.

"Come on, Barry. Spit it out. Who did Longhouse visit at Lee Correctional?"

"John Cleveland."

The breath caught in Hennessy's throat. His world stopped spinning. "John Cleveland? Are you sure?"

Lockett nodded. "I'm sorry to be the one to tell you that, and I'm sorry that I have to bring up those memories for you again. But I thought you should know."

"John Cleveland was the number one suspect in Luca's death," Hennessy whispered to himself. "Why would he need Cleveland to sign the form?"

Lockett shrugged. He didn't know the words to say.

"When did they meet?"

"Yesterday. My contact inside the prison said that Cleveland was a pretty happy guy. He was boasting about making a thousand dollars just by signing an NDA for Longhouse."

With the emotions overwhelming him, Hennessy stood and walked out of the room.

CHAPTER 58

WALKING AROUND the vineyard always helped Joe Hennessy forget.

It helped him forget the stress, it helped him forget the pain of losing his son, and it helped him forget his failure to ever bring his son's murderer to justice. It had been that way for twenty years.

He spent his weekend on the land, checking on the grapes, fixing fences, and inspecting the netting. He spent time talking to Jack Allen, who owned some of the neighboring lands. The storms were bad, Jack said, but he'd seen worse. Most of the vines had survived the storms, Joe explained, but the amount of water that fell might hinder some of the growth in the lower sections. They shared a laugh over the fence, talking about long-forgotten memories before Joe left to drive the tractor around the vineyard.

At the far end of the property, on the crest of a hill, he stopped and looked out at the horizon. It stretched a hundred miles in the distance, the rolling hills appearing small under the enormous southern sky. Sitting there, gazing out to the best nature had to offer, he studied its beauty. At some point in his life, simply enjoying a magical moment had become enough. He didn't need to document it, he didn't need to photograph it, or paint it, or blog about it, or even remember it. That moment, washed under the natural beauty of the South, was enough.

When he returned to his homestead at a little after five, he could smell fried chicken cooking. Wendy greeted him as he stepped inside and she told him to clean up in time for dinner. Casey joined them for a meal, talking about the highs and lows of another week in her teenage life. There was so much drama that Joe struggled to keep up. After Casey thanked her mother for the perfect fried chicken, she returned upstairs to her bedroom, no doubt to talk to some boy via some social media app.

Joe and Wendy retired to the porch after dinner, a bottle of Merlot to share. They sat and watched the sunset, talking about the upcoming weddings that were scheduled. After a while, the conversation softened, and they sat in silence, watching as Mother Nature put on another calming display of colors. After the sun had set, disappearing behind the horizon, she turned to him and smiled, but Joe didn't return the smile, instead looking into his glass of wine.

"What is it, Joe?"

He hesitated before realizing he could hide nothing from her. "There's something you should know."

"Then you should tell me."

"It's about Richard Longhouse and the non-disclosure agreement."

"Did you sign it?"

"No chance. Although we need the money, it felt too dirty. I couldn't justify it, no matter how much money was involved. But..." he sighed. "I asked Barry Lockett to look into who else he's asked to sign an NDA."

"And?"

"He went to visit John Cleveland."

She stared at him for a long time, her own words caught somewhere between her mind and the mouth that refused to speak them.

"John Cleveland was uneducated," Joe said. "He didn't finish high school. He couldn't hold a job for more than a month. He never stood a chance to make a good life for himself. At the time, he had the means to do it, but he had no motive."

"But Longhouse?" Wendy whispered.

Joe looked out to the horizon and didn't speak for another minute. Wendy gave him all the time he needed.

"He had motive... me..." Joe drew a long breath. "But he didn't have the means. He wasn't a killer, but now, I don't know how true that is. It might be nothing, but I need to know why Richard Longhouse talked to John Cleveland."

Wendy didn't answer.

For twenty-five minutes, they sat in silence, staring out at the horizon as the day became night.

The night sky filled with stars, glittering in all their glory. With little light pollution around them, the stars looked like a blanket over the world, filling every available space with a sparkling wonder. A light blue painted the middle of the sky, and numerous shooting stars dashed across, leaving trails of stardust behind.

The universe was amazing, Joe thought. It was so vast, so untouched, so undiscovered, so distant, and yet so close and mesmerizing. There were thousands of galaxies up there, thousands upon thousands of planets and moons and worlds and suns. It was incomprehensible to him. He gazed at the night sky, with its countless possibilities, and he wondered about the universe and all that there was. How vast it must be, stretching on endlessly, an infinite emptiness that was forever there.

As he watched the stars, as he sat under the magnificence of the Southern night sky, he felt something grow inside him. It was no longer grief. It was no longer pain. His feelings were morphing into a need for justice.

"If there's a chance," Joe said, "then I have to know."

"Yes," Wendy whispered. "If there's a chance, then we have to know."

THE END

ALSO BY PETER O'MAHONEY

In the Joe Hennessy Legal Thriller series:

THE SOUTHERN LAWYER

In the Tex Hunter Legal Thriller series:

POWER AND JUSTICE
FAITH AND JUSTICE
CORRUPT JUSTICE
DEADLY JUSTICE
SAVING JUSTICE
NATURAL JUSTICE
FREEDOM AND JUSTICE
LOSING JUSTICE

*****

In the Jack Valentine Series:

GATES OF POWER
THE HOSTAGE
THE SHOOTER
THE THIEF
THE WITNESS

PETER O'MAHONEY

Printed in Great Britain
by Amazon